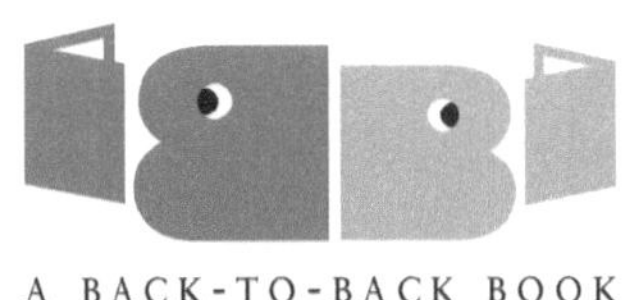

A BACK-TO-BACK BOOK

La Comtesse

Charlotte Rolfe

Back-to-Back Books
an imprint of Flying Corgi Media
Chelmsford, MA

Back-to-Back Books
An imprint of Flying Corgi Media
Chelmsford, MA
www.flyingcorgimedia.com

Text copyright © 2011 by Charlotte Rolfe
Illustrations © 2011 by Tim Robinson
Cover Photograph © 2011 by P.S. Stevens
Book Design by David Freedman

Flying Corgi Media and colophon and Back-to-Back Books and colophon are trademarks of Flying Corgi Media, Inc.

This book is a work of historical fiction. Apart from the well-known actual people and locales that figure into the narrative, all names, characters, places, incidents and dialogue are the product of the author's imagination and are not to be construed as real. Any resemblance to actual events or persons, living or dead, is entirely coincidental.

Cataloging Data
Rolfe, Charlotte
    La Comtesse / Charlotte Rolfe —1st ed.
    p. cm.
1. France —History —1789-1815 —Fiction.
2. Wine and wine making —France —Burgundy —Fiction.
3. France —History —Revolution, 1789-1799 —Fiction. I. Title

Form/Genre: Historical fiction.
                Love stories.
ISBN 978-0-9839460-1-4

Printed in the United States of America

For Rosa Mae

Acknowledgements

First, I wish to thank Flying Corgi Media for embracing this project, and giving me the opportunity to write the first pair of Back-to-Back Books. I particularly want to thank Susan Gates for her many years of help and support for my writing career, Priscilla Stevens for her insightful editorial suggestions and beautiful cover photos, and Madeleine Needles for coming up with this terrific idea to foster communication across the generations. Thank you to David Freedman for his outstanding book design. I am also grateful to Mary Kramer for the time she spent proofreading.

I owe an enormous debt to Susan Cushing who read the manuscripts in the early days. Her enthusiasm for the stories made us think this idea would really work, and her many years of experience teaching elementary students, along with her keen eye for detail, helped improve both books.

Our beautiful models, Kate Gretchell and Victoria Parlee, were so generous in giving their time on a very hot day to dress in period costume for the cover shoot. I thank them, as well as the beautiful Papillon, Dolce, and her owner, Jennifer Morris, for helping to create our wonderful covers. The pictures were taken in the beautiful garden of All Saints Episcopal Church in Chelmsford, MA, and I thank them for the use of their site. I also thank the Old Chelmsford Garrison House in Chelmsford, MA, for their costume help.

Everything is not on the Internet, and I want to thank the excellent staff of the Chelmsford Public Library for their willingness to borrow the many books that I needed to keep my feet firmly in the era of the French Revolution.

Last, but by no means least, I thank my incredible husband for the many hours of reading, editing, and driving. I had his loving support for this project from the very earliest days, and could not have done it without him.

La Comtesse

1

THE CHÂTEAU STOOD STILL AND SILENT in the oppressive August night, its windows brilliant with the light of a thousand candles. The sky was dark, the moon and stars covered by ominous black clouds of the approaching storm. The air was heavy with the dampness of rain that refused to fall. Even the night creatures were silent, as if listening for the sounds of the approaching tumult.

On the balcony, a young woman waited in the clammy heat, her eyes searching through the darkness. Perspiration trickled from her forehead down the side of her face, to the whiteness of her neck. Absently, she took a linen handkerchief from her waist and wiped away the moisture. She stared down the tree-lined avenue that led from the gates of the estate to the courtyard below. Peering into the blackness of the night, she listened and waited.

The sudden sound of boots striding across the tiles of the balcony caused her to whirl about in fright. With an exclamation of relief, she ran into the arms of her husband. The young comte held her close, softly comforting her.

"My baby? How is my baby?" cried Gabrielle as she looked up into his eyes.

"Shhh, my dearest. You must speak softly. Even the fireflies can be spies in troubled times like these." As he spoke, he guided her to the railing along the outer edge of the balcony.

"But, Phillipe, my arms ache – my whole body aches – to cradle my tiny infant in my arms. I want to hold the tiny hands...."

"You must stop this, Gabbi." Phillipe looked into the soft brown eyes, calling her the name that he only used in their most private moments. "We both must speak carefully if we are to make sure the child is safe."

"But do you really think they will come?" Her imploring voice begged for some hint that the confrontation could be avoided. "Maybe it will be like in Cluny. Rumors say that the townsfolk drove back the marauders trying to harm the monks. Can we not expect some protection?"

"We are not priests, Gabrielle. And," he added bitterly, "the life my father led was certainly not fit for a monastery. Five years will not erase the memory of his cruelty, of how merciless he could be. I am afraid that we may have to pay for sins that are not ours."

Phillipe, comte de St. Vivant, looked into the darkness and back through the last few years, wondering if he could have done more to keep this night from happening. His father had been a product of the old provincial nobility, haughty and ignorant, who looked with scorn upon the peasants. He also saw no need for education beyond the basic skills. It was Phillipe's mother, though frail in health, who demanded with her dying breath that her son be allowed to go to Paris for a formal education.

Phillipe's years away from the estate had made him part of a new generation. The change had begun during his last two years in Paris. Phillipe had come in contact with a group of nobles with enlightened ideas about equality and liberty. His attitude toward the workers on château lands had been profoundly affected as he read the works of the philosophers and talked late into the night with his new circle of friends. His father did not welcome the change in his son and threatened to bring him home. After that Phillipe kept his views to himself, but continued to study and learn.

During this time he had also met and fallen in love with Gabrielle. Not a member of the nobility herself, she was the daughter of a wealthy banker, whose loans to certain nobles had paved a way for her entrance to court life. Intelligent and loving, she welcomed the carriage rides in the long afternoons when Phillipe had shared his passion for an end to despotism and his desire for a new constitutional monarchy. His father had been pleased when their marriage was arranged, the same way so many other peers had welcomed the daughters of wealthy financiers with rich dowries to mingle with their rank.

His father's death from heart failure five years before had provided the young comte with the opportunity to put into practice the changes in which he so strongly believed. He no longer exacted the champart, a tithe on the peasants' produce. He had given up his monopoly over the bread ovens and flour mill, and had only kept it on the grape press in his effort to revive their foundering winery. Gabrielle had been his ardent partner, supporting him by day, renewing their love by night. If only there had been a little more time.

"But surely the household servants will protect us," Gabrielle's soft voice broke into his thoughts.

Phillipe pulled her close, and once again held her in his arms. "Do you see any servants guarding the doors, Gabbi? No, the anger of the mob makes even strong men frightened. I do not think that there will be anyone to protect us. I only wish that you had gone with the child."

She looked up into the eyes that she loved so dearly and softly replied. "No, my darling, my place is here with you." Gabrielle laid her head against his chest and held him close, comforting as well as seeking comfort.

The strong young comte looked into the night, searching for signs of the unrestrained populace that a fearful but still loyal servant had told him would come. He would remain here, in his home, and try to reason with them. He prayed for a miracle to keep the rabble back, but knew in his heart that the accumulated anger of many years would not be turned away with only words. Gently, he bent down to kiss the head of his precious Gabbi, to smell the soft hair where tendrils now frizzled in the heavy, damp heat of the night.

"Do you think that they will harm us?" questioned his young wife.

"I can only guess. I know that in other places they have been destroying what they call the symbols of tyranny. They will tear down the coat of arms, and will demand to burn the seigneurial title and papers dealing with land ownership. Since those papers are safely hidden elsewhere, we can only try to convince them to leave, and maybe by tomorrow the brigands will have gone on to another town. If that happens, I will ride as if on wings to bring our own precious child to your arms again. Until then, be assured that our baby is safe and well."

Gabrielle's voice choked as she whispered, "If only I could have gone with you tonight. I would feel so much better if only I had been able to go with you."

"But you are not strong enough yet, and I had to go carefully, making sure that no one suspected or followed. It is best this way."

The couple stood silently, clinging to one another. He thought of the night, only two days ago, when their baby had been born. Gabrielle was only allowed to hold the child for a moment, only allowed to caress the tiny form once to her breast; then she gave it away to safety. The screams of despair that were meant to fool the servants into believing that the infant was dead were, in reality, the cries of anguish of a mother forced to allow her child to be taken away mere moments after its birth.

Phillipe too grieved for their only child, spirited away for safety. At his wife's insistence he had cautiously gone to a secret meeting place to reassure her that the child was healthy. He grieved that he had been forced to take the infant from her arms just when they should both be rejoicing in the thrill of birth. And he despaired that the times had become so dangerous for them all. Events in the nation would overwhelm his small efforts toward change. There had been too many like his father, too many greedy for power and lust, to give him a real chance. A passion for freedom was sweeping across France. And he feared that others like him, quietly working toward change, would be swept away along with the despotic aristocracy that for too long had consumed the wealth and vigor of the nation.

A distant noise pulled him away from his thoughts. Slowly, but relentlessly, the noise was coming closer. Soon he was sure that he would see their torches. If only the threatening storm would break now, and throw its ferocity against them, driving the mob away to seek shelter. Then maybe in the new day's light, they would think again and turn their wrath toward another city, a different estate. But the oppressive air remained still, the rain refused to fall. And the mob came on.

"Gabbi, my sweet," Phillipe looked down into her lovely face, cupping her chin gently in his hand. "Before they come I must tell you one last time that you have been the center of my universe. Every moment together has been sweet and precious. And my joy at watching you grow with our child has been unbounded. If I could not have one more minute in your presence, I could still live a lifetime of happiness with my memories of you." Softly he kissed her, then more passionately. How he adored this wonderful wife of his!

Gabrielle returned his kiss, matching his ardor. Then she looked up into his strong, handsome face and murmured, "We have done well, my dear. We have tried to make life better for our workers, and we have produced a marvelous child. Some people will not have so much joy in even one day of their lives." She caressed his face with her hand and repeated, "We have done well."

"And if we must … leave? If it is finished?" he began questioningly, not wanting to say the words.

But the young comtesse finished his thought for him. "If we must leave, we will pray that our child will someday come to this place. Possibly the things you have hidden will be found, and our child or our grandchildren will know of our life, and something of the ones who went before us." She smiled at him; she had come at last to a place of peace in her heart.

"And if that happens, God will let us watch, and share in their joy." Phillipe returned her smile, and once again held her close.

The sound of the mob came closer now, and flames from their torches could be seen moving slowly up the avenue. A breeze began to stir the air, softly ruffling the skirt of the simple gown that she had chosen. The gentle current became ever stronger, blowing the drapes at the windows in the great hall behind them.

The couple kept their eyes on the wave of humanity moving forward, and so did not see the face that was revealed by the movement of the curtains.

It was a young boy, a child of the estate, who would never have dreamed of entering the hallways and rooms of the château before now. But he had been in town, heard speeches telling him that this land and its wealth were also his, and with the knowledge that those speakers would soon be here to claim that wealth, he had dared to come into the great house. He had wandered through its gilded rooms, looked at the magnificent furnishings, and, yes, even taken items that caught his fancy.

The boy had moved quietly, sneaking on to the upper level, and upon seeing the comte and his wife, had hidden behind the heavy brocade of the drapes and listened. He sneered at their love and at the comte's claims that he wanted to make life better for the peasants. The comte de St. Vivant had never tried to rectify the injustice done to him. Was not he a bastard brother to this man? Why, then, should the comte be allowed to live in such opulence while he lived in a simple cottage?

Quietly, the boy stood and listened. He heard bits of their secret, and dreamed of the treasure hidden for their child. He would find that treasure first. It was his right to have their prize if not their name.

Suddenly he heard the voices, the shouts of the men and women standing under the balcony demanding that the comte and his wife come down to them. He listened scornfully to the attempts of the man to reason with them.

"Are you one of the townspeople? I do not recognize you." Phillipe spoke evenly, with almost a hint of friendliness in his voice.

"I am Lazare, citizen of Paris. I bring word from the National Assembly to the citizens of Burgundy of the great reforms that have taken place, reforms that I am sure you have kept secret from your tenants."

Phillipe looked down at Lazare, choosing his next words carefully. The man looked more like a criminal than a representative of the Assembly. He wore the blue and red coat of an army uniform with the sleeves ripped out. Unbuttoned, it hung loosely around his body showing bare skin beneath. In the heat, his filthy hair was matted to his forehead, and a patch covered one eye. Looking over the crowd, Phillipe realized that these were not just the laborers from the estate or village, but also a crowd of the itinerant poor who wandered the roads and had followed Lazare in hopes of plundering châteaux and finding something of value. Even now he could see some of the people dressed in finery that he was sure they had stolen from other manors as they made their way from Paris. His people he could deal with, but this rabble frightened him.

"I have not told my people about the decisions of the National Assembly because I have not seen the complete documents. I am waiting for official couriers to bring the news."

Lazare leered up at him and grinned through his rotting teeth. "I am an official courier. I carry papers 'On the king's orders'." He drew a paper from his pocket and turned toward the cheering crowd, holding it high for all to see.

Phillipe had heard about these papers, documents that encouraged the peasants to burn the châteaux, and suggested that the owners would poison the wells and hoard grain to make their lives worse. He did not know where the documents came from, but he knew that they were dangerous.

Lazare turned toward the crowd and shouted, "Has he told you that you are no longer tied to the land, and you are free to work your own farms, keeping the profit for yourself? That you can cut the wood from the forests to keep your freezing families warm in the winter?"

Shouts of "No!" echoed through the crowd, almost timidly at first, then with gathering strength.

Encouraged by their response, the man from Paris turned to Phillipe and continued. "Have you told them that they can now catch the animals of the forest to feed their hungry bellies, and that the birds in the dovecotes are theirs as well?"

More loudly and more fiercely the crowd answered, "No!" some shaking their fists, others holding high pheasants and foxes that had been trapped that very day in the fields of the estate.

Phillipe held up his hand to silence the crowd and tried to answer the man. "Citizen Lazare, I know that there was great hunger in Paris last year; however, here I make certain that all of the tenants have plenty of fuel in the winter, and that none go hungry at any time. These people know that they have only to come here and tell me of their needs and I will see that their needs are met."

"But why should they have to come to you and beg?" the man demanded. "They are the ones who work the fields; it is their labor that makes you rich. Why do they not have the money to see to these things for themselves?" He turned to the crowd and roared, "I'll tell you why. Because he and the others like him have sucked the wealth from the mouths of your babes. They take the sweat of your brow and turn it into rich furnishings for their palaces, and gaudy jewelry for their whores."

The crowd was beginning to respond to the words of hate that

Lazare was spewing. Again Phillipe tried to calm the mob with soothing words. "But I have been working with your leaders to make life better for all of you. Ask Paul, or Gaspard. They will remind you of what I have done here. Think back to when my father was here and how hard times were. The future will be better for all of you."

The man looked around and said, "Yes, let Paul and Gaspard tell us about your plans. How you will make everyone's life grand." He paused and waited. "Well, where are they, your Gaspard and Paul?" Silence. Then, with a leer, he turned back to the couple and the balcony and said, "They do not appear to be here. Maybe they did not believe your lies. Maybe you never said those things. But I do have someone who will speak. An uncle of yours, and a brother, from the other side of the blanket, so to speak."

Phillipe groaned and looked with regret down at his wife. This was what he had feared most, that the sins of his father and grand-father would be resurrected. Now he knew that on this night the entire tragedy of the past would be dragged forth to whip the crowd into a frenzy.

A sudden streak of lightening blazed across the sky, and the first gust of the storm tugged at the flaming torches. Thunder rumbled in the distance quieting the shouts of the mob.

Phillipe seized the opportunity and spoke persuasively to the crowd. "The storm is near, and some of you have brought your children. Why not go to your homes now, until the storm passes? We will meet tomorrow in the town hall and discuss your needs. I will listen to anyone who wishes to speak. But now you should go before the storm breaks."

Some of the townspeople nodded at his words, but Lazare, knowing that he would lose the passion of the moment if they waited for the sober light of tomorrow shouted, "But why should we leave? Is this not your brother? Is this not your uncle? Surely you will give them shelter from the storm in your home." And Lazare, grabbing the two men by their arms, swept them forward and through the entrance of the château. The few firebrands from town and the rabble from Paris followed closely behind, streaming into the lower rooms and up the grand staircase. The townspeople, holding back at first, followed them into the brightly lit rooms, staring in awe at the richness of it all.

Lazare and his companions marched on, up the staircase and through the gallery, then out on to the balcony where the comte and his wife stood. Gabrielle could smell the wine on their breath, and odor from their unwashed bodies. She pulled closer to Phillipe, trying to gain strength from his touch.

The mob gathered around the couple, enclosing them in a circle of simmering hate. Again Lazare led the way. "We demand the land deeds and title to seigneurial rights."

"I can not give you those papers. They are not here," replied Phillipe, trying to keep his voice calm.

"Liar!" screamed Lazare. "But that is no problem; we will tear the château apart and find them."

"I cannot stop you from destroying anything, but you will not find any papers here. They were removed several days ago."

Lazare looked boldly into the young nobleman's eyes and then turned to the crowd. "Do not worry, citizens. The papers should be burned, but his word will be good enough. Surely the comte de St. Vivant can be held to his word." The crowd nodded in agreement, not sure what their leader meant.

The brigand from Paris turned back to the young comte and hissed, "Since we cannot have the papers, we will have your word, my lord. You will swear to renounce your title to the land and rights."

Phillipe threw back his shoulders and replied with intense emotion in his voice, "That I will not do, citizen. My family has held title to this land since the Treaty of Arras in 1435. It was presented to my ancestor by one of the dukes of Valois, Philip the Good. We have lived here and worked the land ever since. Some of the comtes were good lords, some were not. But it is mine now, and I intend to keep what is mine."

Lazare looked cunningly at the Phillipe, knowing that he had trapped him in his own pride. "But what right have you to keep it all to yourself? Should you not share it with your uncles and brothers, and sisters, too? I'm sure that there are many with St. Vivant blood who can make an equal claim." The voices of the people lifted in agreement as another flash of lightening crossed the sky.

The crowd gathered closer to the couple, pushing them hard against the railing. Suddenly a drunken woman leered into Gabrielle's face. "Well, if my man is the comte's brother, then I must be your sister-in-law." She reached out a hand to touch the soft material of Gabrielle's dress, then moved it up toward her neck. "And if I'm your sister-in-law, I should have some fine jewelry to go with my station, shouldn't I?"

The woman reached out to grab the necklace, and Gabrielle lurched backward in fear. Weakened from childbirth and the heat of the night, she fainted, falling backward over the balcony. Phillipe reached out a hand to grab her, but suddenly felt himself being lifted over the side. In a flash, he turned to see the grin on Lazare's face as he fell to the courtyard below with his precious wife. The final sensation that either of them had was the touch of the other's hand.

The crowd stood silent on the balcony for a moment. The townspeople who had joined Lazare stared down at the two broken forms on the pavement below. But before they could think of recrimination, Lazare lifted his fist and shouted, "Liberty and equality to the citizens of France! People of St. Vivant, you are free!" The crowd took up the cheer and as the thunder filled the air they turned back to the rooms of the château. The rabble from Paris led the way, looting and destroying. Curtains were ripped down. Furniture was broken and thrown through windows. The comte's own bedroom was ransacked, and the woman who claimed to be Gabrielle's sister-in-law was seen dancing around the room in her dressing gown, with a powdered wig on her head. No one noticed that here and there townsfolk left quietly, taking nothing but their guilt that a good man and his wife had been killed on that night.

Above the sound of the storm, no one heard the soft mourning call of an owl.

In the courtyard the bodies of Gabrielle and Phillipe lay in the rain that had finally come, their hands lying one inside the other.

2

J UNE , 1809

T HÉRÈSE SAT IN THE SHADY GLADE beneath the forest canopy and wiggled her toes. The cold water of the stream felt refreshing as it circled her feet and ran swiftly on through the valley. She placed her hands on the soft grass and leaned back, her loosened hair catching the whisper of a breeze. Above her, the birds trilled their songs to one another in joyful appreciation of this beautiful day. A shadow of guilt crossed her forehead as she thought about her mother waiting for the mosses she had gathered that morning. But she was able to easily shake it away, knowing that her mother would also find the quiet serenity of the forest too tempting to resist.

A basket sat on the cool ground beside her. At the bottom rested the plants that she had been sent to gather. They were covered, however, with sweet, warm black currants that she had found along the roadside. The first of the season, they had been more than she could resist. Now Thérèse took one from the basket, savoring the syrupy sweetness of its almost over-ripened taste.

'I must be careful,' she thought, 'or there will be none left to give Mama to appease her for my being so late.' She chose one more, an especially plump berry, and then covered the basket with a cloth to end the temptation.

A chattering squirrel caught her attention and she laughed and spoke out loud. "All right. All right. I know I've stayed too long, and you are ready to have the forest to yourselves. I'll leave you alone for now, but you cannot always have this peaceful place for your own. Another day, and I'll be back."

Thérèse carefully wiped the water from her feet on her brown cotton skirt. She pulled her stockings on, and then her shoes, her feet feeling tight in the restricting leather. As she stood, she straightened her skirt over her white petticoat, then retied the strings that closed the neck of her bodice. Reaching to the ground, she caught up the black ribbon and tied her soft red hair at the nape of her neck, smoothing back the tendrils that curled around her face. Last, she picked up the basket and made her way back to the road, stepping carefully so as not to destroy the ferns and wild flowers that abounded in the shade.

Out on the road, her eyes adjusted quickly to the afternoon sunlight. It was early summer, and the air was mild and dry. A soft breeze stirred the trees that lined each side of the old dirt road. Here and there were open spaces where people had cut wood for cooking, and to use in their fireplaces in winter. But the saplings that were springing up would soon fill the gaps and close the woods once more.

As Thérèse rounded the curve in the road, she saw a horseman riding toward her. He was a handsome young man, obviously not one of the poor farmers who lived nearby. As he came closer she noticed his stylish clothes – the fawn-colored riding pants, a crisp white, ruffled shirt under his brown broadcloth coat, and fine riding boots. She wondered whatever was he doing in this poor district.

When he saw her, the young man cantered up quickly, then reined his horse to a stop and dismounted. He greeted her with a cheerful, "Ah, Mademoiselle, I am glad to find someone on this deserted road."

"Are you lost?" Thérèse smiled at her rather obvious question.

"It seems that I must be, although I followed the directions from town very carefully. I am looking for the Château St. Vivant."

"You are not lost then, just gone too far. You passed the entrance a little way back."

"But that is impossible." His blue eyes looked at her with surprise. "I have gone very carefully."

"It is very hard to find, especially with the fresh summer growth springing up everywhere. Since I'm going that way, I will be glad to show you where it is."

"I would be most grateful if you would." Leading his horse by the reins, he fell in beside her as they walked down the road. "I thought that I would have to ride back into town and try to find someone who could show me the way. And since it is so late in the afternoon, I was afraid that I would then have to wait until tomorrow to find it. My trip has not gone well. I planned to arrive this morning, but some storms outside of Paris delayed me."

Thérèse smiled at the talkative young man. The local farm boys rarely said much of anything, much less talked so freely to a girl. "Are you from Paris, then?"

"No, I'm from Bordeaux. I have been in Paris for the last month with my Aunt Catherine at an apartment in Faubourg St. Honoré."

"Bordeaux! That must have been quite a trip."

"Yes, it was really quite awful. Our carriage broke a wheel outside of Tours. Luckily, it could be repaired. But Aunt Catherine was in an awful state by the time we reached Paris and went to bed for two days."

Inwardly Thérèse grinned again to herself and wondered if the young man had also chattered this much in the carriage. That could well have added to his aunt's "state."

They had come to a path leading into the forest to which Thérèse pointed, saying, "That is the way to the château, sir."

The young man looked down the path, then at her, asking incredulously, "This is the entrance to the Château St. Vivant?"

"Yes, I'm afraid that it is. It's not very grand, is it? Which, I'm sure, is why you missed it. Didn't the people in town warn you?"

"Well, they said that it was hard to find, but I expected more than this." He took a few steps up the path, looking to either side for some sign of something more.

"I have been told that there were once wrought iron gates, but they were carried away long ago. There are some fallen stone corner posts under the brambles, and the line of the fence could still be found if you cleared away the nettles. But I'm afraid that very few people come this way, and the forest reclaims its own after awhile."

"You are sure that if I follow this path I will find the château?" He looked carefully at her, trying to decide if she were telling him the truth.

Thérèse's bubbling laughter filled the quiet summer air and she replied, "Yes, I am sure that you will find it. Look, I will walk with you to make sure that you don't go wrong. Then I can cut through the fields and will still get home before it's too late." Leading the way, she headed into the woods, with the young man and his horse following her.

When the path became a little wider, she slowed to walk beside him. "My mother tells me that this was once a great graveled avenue, where the carriages rolled smoothly up to the courtyard. There was a line of poplars on each side that blazed golden in the autumn light. There are still some left, but most were cut at some time or other for firewood. If you look carefully, you can still see some of the shrubs with their purple blooms that also lined the road." Thérèse sighed, then added, "It must have been very grand."

Silent for the first time, the young man walked beside her, looking carefully to each side, trying to see the things that she pointed out. Soon the wood became less dense, then opened up as Thérèse said softly, "Well, there it is, what's left."

The Château St. Vivant stood before him, shabby with the wear of weather and time. It was a square stone building with two main floors and a line of dormers in the steep slate roof. To each side was a single story wing with the same slate roof. At a few of the great windows he could see weathered bits of tattered brocade hanging on the sills and the vacant wood where glass panes had once reflected the summer light. The great balcony had leaves piled up in one corner, and a tree branch hung precariously from the rail. The white limestone façade, once polished to look like marble, was now chipped and beaten. And in the courtyard, weeds grew up between the paving stones where gallant horses had once waited for their masters to ride to the hunt.

Thérèse looked carefully at the young man as he took it all in. He studied the scene before him silently, then she saw him smile as he looked at the tangled growth of the once formal garden, now blooming a mingled chaos of pinks, reds, and yellows. And waving above them, lilacs had grown tall in the years of neglect.

"I love the flowers that grow here," she said. "These strong ones have multiplied in spite of the inattention and bloom every year. In the Spring I take great bunches to decorate the house for my mother's birthday, so that I don't have to pick the ones at home."

"I was thinking that my Aunt Catherine will have a wonderful time putting those gardens to rights, and pitying the poor gardener who will have to help."

"What do you mean? You aren't proposing to try to live here?" Thérèse looked at him with astonishment.

"And why not?" The young man returned her stare with complete assurance.

"But no one has lived here for years, and you can see for yourself that it's in shambles." Thérèse paused, then added, "Besides, it's haunted."

The young man laughed, then smiled as he gazed with pleasure at the château. "There is a lot of work to do, but I'm sure that the foundation is sound. And I'm not afraid of hard work. As for ghosts, they had better move out, because Henri Phillipe, comte de St. Vivant, is here to stay."

Thérèse stared at him in disbelief, then threw back her head and laughed out loud.

Bewildered and insulted, Henri stood tall and asked haughtily, "And why is that so amusing?"

Realizing how she had offended the nice young man, she placed her hand over her mouth to hide her smile, then tried to answer him as kindly as possible. "Oh, you are not the first, though it has been a long time since anyone has come. Mama said that the first few years were the worst, with many coming, claiming to be a cousin, or a child. One man even claimed to be comte Phillipe himself, raised from the dead, as it were. Most were looking for some kind of fortune that was rumored to be hidden here. A few came out of curiosity. But no one stayed for more than a few nights. They left hastily, claiming that it was haunted. No one returned."

Henri listened, then replied softly, "But I am different. I am the only son of the last comte, and I intend to stay."

Trying to be kind, Thérèse replied, "But that is impossible. One of the servants told my mother of the cries of anguish from the rooms on the night the child was born. It was born dead and taken to Paris to be buried the next day. And they had no other children."

"Ah, but that is where you are mistaken. The child was spirited away and into my uncle's care. He kept it a secret until two years ago. Then he told me who I am. And now I am here to make this a proper estate again."

"I wish you good luck, then. You have a great deal of work ahead of you." Thérèse looked at the sun getting low in the afternoon sky and realized that she must be heading home. At least now she would have a good excuse for her mother.

Henri sensed that she was about to go and spoke quickly, "Before you leave, can you not take a moment to show me through the château? I am sure that you have been in there many times, and could have some useful information to help me through these first few days, until my workers arrive."

Thérèse looked at him guardedly – not sure what to do. Mama would be angry that she had accompanied a stranger this far. But Mama also said to trust her instincts and, for some reason, Thérèse did not feel any cause to fear this enthusiastic young man. She also guessed correctly that he was a little lonely and wanted some company, and so agreed to show him the château. "But it must be a quick tour. Mama will be wondering where I am."

The two walked across the courtyard to the granite stairs. As they stepped into the entrance, Henri stared with awe at the grand staircase that led up from the central hall. Halfway up was a large landing against the wall, and here the staircase split into two sections which gracefully continued to climb along each side to the upper floor. At one time it must have been marvelous, he thought. But now, everywhere he looked he could see signs of the destruction that had taken place over the years. The few doors that were left had been torn from their hinges and lay broken on the floor. On the walls were holes where candle sconces had been pulled away. Bits of furniture littered the room and dirt was everywhere. In one corner, he could see a pile of straw where some vagrant had apparently made a bed. And above it all he could see the remnants of the once great chandelier that had glittered in the candlelight.

Thérèse saw him looking up and remarked, "I have heard it said that when they entertained, the chandelier held two hundred candles that lit up the night as if it were the sun." She smiled at Henri, then continued. "I warned you that the inside was very bad. It will take a great deal of money to make it habitable again."

But Henri was not interested in warnings. His curiosity had been piqued, and now he wanted to see it all. The château was not large in the style of the hôtels closer to Paris, but it had been carefully and beautifully built. Even though its furnishings had been stripped, Henri could tell, as he wandered from room to room, that the planner had spared no expense where quality was concerned. The grand salon and petit salon, the great dining room, the library, and the marvelous ballroom at the back that ran the length of the main building, all were there waiting to be refurbished to their former glory.

The biggest surprise for Henri was the little chapel. He had not seen it from the front, and so was astonished when Thérèse led him in through an archway at the end of a small hallway near the library. He wandered into its stillness, gazing at its softness. Then, remembering where he was, he stopped to genuflect and cross himself.

Thérèse was startled at his behavior, and asked hesitatingly, "Are you religious?"

Henri smiled comfortably at her and replied, "My Aunt Catherine is a woman of great faith. Not pious, mind you, but her religion has always been her strength. Even when there was great hostility toward the clergy, she held her faith and hid a priest on the estate at Bordeaux until Napoleon signed the Concordat in 1801. My aunt was relieved that once again she was allowed to be Catholic, even if there is no longer a state religion." Looking again at the little chapel, and realizing that the grime that was so pervasive everywhere else was absent here, he added, "Apparently there is another believer here, as well."

Relieved, Thérèse explained how her mother had been horrified that even the chapel had been plundered by looters, and when all seemed safe had carefully cleaned the pink granite floor and wiped down the white limestone walls. She showed him the black marble tomb of some earlier comte and the ancient altar where the gilding had been chipped away. The wall was blank where a painted altarpiece had been removed, and the hands on the statue of St. Vincent, patron of the vigneron, or winemaker, had broken away when it had been knocked down.

"At least the statue of the virgin was not harmed. Mama said that, in old times, grapes were placed in her outstretched hand on the Feast of the Assumption as a petition for a good harvest. Up until now, Mama has used this as a private chapel. There is no permanent priest yet in the church of St. Vivant in the town."

Henri looked around at the little chapel once again, at the soft pink glow that the floor gave off, and felt the peace of a greater presence which resided there. "Your mother is still welcome to come whenever she wishes, and I know that Aunt Catherine will want her here at those times when a priest can be found to say mass."

Thérèse returned his reassuring smile, and for the first time seemed to really look at him. He had soft, brown hair, and a square, fair-skinned face. He was a head taller than she, and strongly built. But the kind blue eyes seemed to say the most.

Realizing that she had been staring, Thérèse blushed, then said, "We must go quickly if you wish me to show you the rest."

They picked their way carefully up the staircase, avoiding broken tiles and missing railings. On the upper level, she showed him through the suite of rooms running along one side that had belonged to the comte and comtesse, then the guest rooms on the other side. In the great gallery that ran the length of the front, he could see where mirrors had once been placed in an attempt to copy the grand style of Versailles. Then she led him out onto the balcony.

Because many of the tiles had come loose, and were littered about, they stepped cautiously toward the railing. "From here they could watch for their company as the carriages rolled up the avenue," explained Thérèse. "And it was from this balcony that they watched the mob as it came that August night."

Henri looked out to the courtyard and at the invading forest, trying to imagine how it had been. "They must have been very frightened. I know my uncle told me how the people were whipped into frenzies of hate. I would not want to face them."

"The comte had been very kind to his people, and I am sure he hoped that tragedy could be averted. But the rabble from Paris came and swept the townspeople along. He and his wife were pushed over the railing, and died down there on the courtyard." Thérèse pointed to a spot in the weeds below, then drew in her breath.

Surprised by her action, Henri looked down to the place where she was pointing. There, amid the weeds, was a small bouquet of flowers beginning to wilt in the afternoon heat. He looked at Thérèse, still staring down, and asked, "Do you know who left the flowers?"

Thérèse silently shook her head, then turned to him and replied, "No one knows where they come from. Sometimes my mother finds them in the chapel, at other times in the bedrooms they used, but most often the flowers are there, on the spot where they died. People say that their ghosts leave them for one another. You see, the next morning their bodies had disappeared, and all that could be found were a bouquet of flowers and two feathers, one gray and one white. Then began reports of the hauntings. There were lights at the windows in the night, voices heard by people trying to live here. Someone said that they were chased by two great birds as they walked on the lawn. People quit coming."

"And your mother, was she not frightened?" he asked.

"Like your aunt, she has a great faith. But even she feels a special presence in the air when she comes here." Thérèse looked down at the courtyard, reflecting on the tragedy for a moment. Then she looked into the trees where the avenue led. Seeing the sun hanging low in the sky, she turned abruptly to Henri. "And now I must leave. Mama will begin to worry as nighttime falls, and I do not like to find my way through the woods in the dark."

Thérèse had walked only a short space across the balcony when she turned back to Henri with a bright look on her face. "I tell you what, why don't you come home with me? Mama will have dinner ready soon, and there is always more than enough. You will be my excuse for being so late, and she will be relieved that I had someone to protect me from the night."

"Are you sure that she would not mind?" he asked eagerly.

"Not at all. Mama would love to talk to someone who can bring her fresh news from Paris. And she will be able to answer your questions about the château. You must come."

Thérèse held out her hand, and without a moment's hesitation Henri accepted the invitation.

3

VOICES COULD BE HEARD UNTIL LATE IN THE EVENING at the cottage where Thérèse lived with her mother. Henri had been surprised when they arrived at a rather large stone dwelling with several rooms and a small second floor. Additionally, through the darkening summer light, he could see a well-built barn with a cow slowly eating hay in the fenced yard, and a large garden beyond.

More surprising still was Thérèse's mother, Alix Condé. Totally unlike her daughter, she was small with black hair and a narrow face. Her eyes, however, held the same open, friendly expression that her daughter's had, and she welcomed their guest without a moment's hesitation.

As Thérèse had said, dinner was nearly ready, and while Henri fed his horse in the barn, a place was added for their guest at the roomy table. The inside of the cottage held more unexpected comforts. There were curtains at the windows, real plates instead of the trenchers most farmers used, and sufficient chairs for more guests had they been needed. Henri also noticed that a generous number of candles had been lit to brighten the meal, showing other unusually fine pieces of furniture scattered throughout the room.

After a simple grace, Henri eagerly filled his plate with the chicken cooked in wine, vegetables and soft, warm bread. Alix smiled as she watched him hungrily eat while her daughter explained how she had shown him through the château and had found another mysterious bouquet of flowers left in the courtyard. Alix encouraged him to have a second serving of food, and then brought out a bowl of early berries and a tray of cheese for dessert. It was then that she asked him how he came to the Château St. Vivant.

"I knew nothing about it until recently. Before that I thought that I was just a poor cousin, raised through my uncle's charity. My uncle is Georges-Louis Girond, close friend to one of Napoleon's ministers. He was a merchant in Bordeaux and feared the turmoil that was coming toward the end of Louis XVI's reign. Through his business, he had several friends in England, and so he took large sums of money to a bank in London. In the following years, he carefully used that money to increase his business. It was a good time for a shrewd investor, and the growth of his fortune has been spectacular.

"When I was little, he bought an estate in Bordeaux that had been confiscated by the National Assembly, and that is where I was reared by his sister, my Aunt Catherine. He became a contractor for military supplies when Napoleon was First Consul, and through excellent service and well-placed loans, was able to become an important asset to the military by the time Napoleon became Emperor."

Alix smiled at his talkative nature, and gently prodded, "But tell me more about yourself."

"When he was a young man, Uncle Georges was a close friend of the comtesse's brother and had met her in Paris before she married. During those frightful days of 1789 my uncle received a note from him frantically asking for help. The comtesse's brother had been waiting in the woods the night that I was born. He spirited me away to a secret place for safekeeping until the mobs passed on to another region. After the comte and his wife were killed, he took me to Paris for safety. He was desperate, not having a wife of his own, and knew nothing about babies. My uncle found a nurse for me and sent me to his sister in Bordeaux, where I grew up. Aunt Catherine never married and was like a mother to me. Of course, she and Uncle Georges are not really my relatives, but that is how I have always known them. She taught me to read and spell, and hired a tutor when I was older." At this point he smiled a wry grin. "I confess that I was a poor student. I preferred to follow Bernard, the vigneron, around and learn about the making of the wines, for that was the business of the estate."

Alix cast a quick glance at Thérèse, smiling and raising her eyebrows, but this time did not try to prompt the young man. He would tell the story all in his own good time.

"As I said, Uncle Georges supplies the army with various things, and came through this region to get a wagonload of Napoleon's favorite Chambertin wine, which the Emperor required during his Austrian campaign in 1805. While here, Uncle Georges decided to find the estate and see how badly it had been destroyed. He did not want to say anything to me until he knew the extent of the damage. Then he checked in Paris to see if there had been any claims against the land. Of course all of the small holdings are gone to the farmers who lived on them, and some of the fields have been claimed, but there are still about 120 hectares left – nearly 300 acres – some of it forest, and all of the main vineyard. I guess that its remote location kept it from being bought by men like my uncle."

"Only after carefully checking all the records did my uncle approach his friend, the minister. Uncle Georges knew that Napoleon was giving official recognition to certain aristocrats as they returned to France, trying to balance the new nobility he created with the old establishment. And so the minister petitioned the Emperor and received an assurance that my rights to the title and what is left of the estate will be secure. Of course, Napoleon's wars keep him short of money, so my uncle's wealth has helped, along with the fact that my parents did not flee the country but were killed trying to protect their home."

"And so, then, you are officially the new comte de St. Vivant?" asked Alix carefully.

"Almost, Madame, almost. I have only to find some record of my birth or some other proof. Almost anything will do. And then it will be made official."

Alix frowned thoughtfully at his innocent reply. "But where do you expect to find the proof?"

Henri looked at her confidently and replied. "Of that I am not sure, but my Uncle Georges said that there will be proof somewhere and not to worry about it. He suggested that I look in the church records, or try to find if an old official is still alive and ask him. He also suggested that there might be something hidden on the estate.

Whatever happens, he is certain enough to advance me the money needed to get the winery back into production, and to once again make the château a place where people can live."

There was a heavy silence after his last statement. Thérèse looked at her mother, trying to guess what was going through her mind. He seemed so sure of himself, and yet....

Alix offered him a fresh glass of wine, poured some for herself, then spoke. "You may discover that finding old records is harder that your uncle imagines. The church of St. Vivant was ransacked the day after the château was attacked, and a large bonfire built on the courtyard in front of the church. Even the relics of St. Vivant, which centuries earlier the comte's family had sworn to defend, were destroyed." She paused to cross herself before continuing. "The priest was found dead that night, murdered, and his body left crumpled before the altar. Many of the offices of the town hall were also looted. And so you see, there will be very few places for you to look for the proof you need."

A knowing smile came to Henri's face, and his next words showed Alix that his youthful exuberance was not the least bit affected by her words. "It may make my search a little harder, but Uncle Georges has every confidence that my claim will be proven. He is confident enough to send his own man, Bernard, to assess the state of the equipment and decide what must be replaced. Bernard will be here in a day or so, and then we will begin."

The older woman said nothing, but nodded her head and raised her glass of wine to her guest. Then she rose to clear the table and reminded Thérèse that the cow was still waiting to be put in the barn.

Realizing how late it was, Henri thanked her for the marvelous dinner, adding that he should be on his way.

Thinking back to how she had found him earlier in the day, Thérèse spoke up. "Mama, do you not think it a better idea if Henri remains here? There is no moon tonight and the path can be hard to follow at times."

Alix readily agreed. "Of course, if you do not mind sleeping in the barn. There is plenty of clean hay, and I'm sure that it would be warmer than the château."

"If you are sure it would be no trouble." There was almost a relieved note in Henri's voice.

Alix assured him that it was not, and found a blanket for him to use. Thérèse led the way, showing him where to sleep. Henri helped her put the cow inside, then thanked her again for bringing him to meet her mother and inviting him to dinner. After bidding him goodnight, Thérèse walked quickly back to the cottage.

Her mother was standing in the kitchen, washing up the last few dishes, when Thérèse returned. Walking thoughtfully to her mother's side, the daughter picked up a cloth to dry and asked, "Well, Mama, what do you think?"

"I don't know, Thérèse. He is not like the others. He is certainly a charming, confident young man. And he must be very close to his aunt to speak so easily of his plans to women." Alix paused for a moment, looking carefully at her daughter. "We must wait and see. Time will prove whether or not he will stay."

In the barn, where he was already comfortably resting on a pile of sweet hay, Henri heard an owl's call in the distance, then the soft answer of its mate. He smiled to himself, then went quickly to sleep.

The next morning, when Thérèse went to collect the eggs, she found his horse already gone and the blanket that he had used carefully folded on a bench. As she went through her morning chores, she replayed the scenes of the previous afternoon and evening in her mind.

Henri was certainly a handsome man, energetic, and full of plans. The few boys and men that she knew were nothing like him at all. None had any hope for a better future. Several had been conscripted and gone to fight the Emperor's wars. There had been one, Gilbert, who seemed different, but he had been killed in battle. Only one of the conscripts returned, an arm and leg missing. Now he spent his days drinking and cursing the fact that he had lived at all. Everyone seemed to crawl through life, one day to the next. The Révolution had promised them freedom, but instead only brought hard years of hunger and fear. Henri had an air of fresh enthusiasm that she had never experienced.

Alix watched her daughter, knowing that the young man was on her mind. Toward midday she asked Thérèse to take a basket with lunch to the château. "I meant to send it with him this morning, but now you will have to go."

The excitement in the young woman was obvious. Thérèse quickly ran up to her room to comb her hair and look into the little bit of mirror on her bureau. As she put on a rust-colored bodice, she smiled at the little embroidered flowers she had sewn around the neckline of the muslin sheath. Her skirt was deep maroon, and flattering to her small round hips. "Not a beautiful lady of Paris," thought Thérèse, "but not an old farmer's hag either." Thérèse ran back down the stairs, grabbed the handle of the basket and headed for the door.

"I expect you home sooner than last night," Alix warned. "And there is a note in the basket inviting him to dinner again tonight."

"Of course, Mama. And I love you, Mama." Thérèse kissed her on the cheek, then flew out of the house into the bright summer sunshine.

The sky was a magnificent shade of cornflower blue, the clouds puffs of whitest white, and the air soft and sweet in the summer morning. Thérèse hurried down the forest path that she knew by heart, ignoring the woodland sights that she usually loved so much. Before long she came to the fields, and soon could see the château nestled on a plateau above the river. As she came closer, she saw the young man standing in the vineyard, looking down the long, sloping hill covered with overgrown plants.

Thérèse walked onto the back lawn above the vineyard and waved, calling, "Henri, hello!"

Hearing his name, Henri turned and when he saw her standing there, a bright smile lit up his face. He moved quickly, though carefully, through the plants and up the hill to greet her.

"Isn't it a wonderful sight? I've spent the morning looking in the vat house, and checking on the plants. I was so awed with the château yesterday that I missed the best part." He stood on the lawn, and spread his hand out at the fields below. "This is what I love, Thérèse. The land, and what it gives us."

Thinking once again how different he was from the other men she knew, Thérèse smiled at his energy. She held the basket toward him as she said, "Mama thought that you might be hungry by now, so she packed a lunch and something cool to drink."

"How wonderful! And yes, I'm famished. I could barely sleep last night, and so at early light I saddled my horse and found my way back through the forest. I felt certain that your mother would understand my desire to get back." As he spoke, Henri had moved up the lawn toward the château. He found a small bit of short grass where they could both sit, and invited her to join him. "Do you know anything about that garden?" He pointed to a fenced area at the crest of the yard where plants were neatly blooming."

"It is one of Mama's herb gardens. When the young comtesse became interested in herbs, my grandfather brought a wagon full of medicinal herbs just for her. My mother has kept the garden up all these years, because it is only here in the sun and soil of the château that some of them will grow." Thérèse suddenly looked at Henri. "You won't tear it down, will you?"

"Of course not," he exclaimed. "I was just thinking it is at least one part of the estate that does not need to be restored." He grinned his boyish smile at Thérèse, then turned to open the basket.

"There's a note from Mama for you as well. She wants you to come to dinner again tonight."

Henri stopped and looked strangely at Thérèse. "Your mother can write?"

Insulted, she quickly answered, "Well of course she can write! She can read as well, and so can I."

"I didn't mean to offend you," he looked at her a bit shame-faced as he spoke. "It's just that one doesn't expect a farmer's wife to be able to read and write."

"Well, she's not just a farmer's wife. My grandfather was a respected doctor in Dijon." There was a definite note of pride in her voice.

"Ahh. Then that would explain everything."

"Explain what?" she demanded.

"Well, your home and the furnishings. I just took for granted...."

"Took what for granted?" A fire was beginning to burn in her eyes that he somehow missed.

"It would have been only natural after the château was empty for someone to...."

Thérèse jumped up instantly and looked down at him with fury in her eyes. "How dare you even suggest such a thing! There is nothing in my home that was taken from the château. My mother's family, though not rich, was certainly capable of providing her with a sufficient dowry when they married. And my father's family, though not noble, has been here every bit as long as the St. Vivants, if not longer. And it is an insult for you to think that it would be 'only natural' for us to steal whatever we want. If my father were alive, he would deal with you, sir!" With that, she twirled about and headed for her home.

"Thérèse, wait." Henri raced after her and grabbed her arm. "Please, I'm sorry for what I said. I just thought...."

"Indeed you did not think, sir, or you never would have even hinted such a..." suddenly she stopped, and demanded, "What is that sound?"

She heard it again, a soft little mewing. Henri shrugged his shoulders and from the pocket of his coat he took a tiny kitten. Sheepishly he looked at her and explained. "I found the mother and three other kittens in the barn behind the vat house. This one wanted to play, so I thought that I would take it with me for a bit of company. When she grew tired I put her in my pocket."

Thérèse took the tiny kitten, holding its softness close to her cheek. She nuzzled its tiny nose, and then, holding it against her shoulder looked back at Henri. Her anger was disappearing as quickly as it had come, but she was not going to let him know that.

"I really am sorry, Thérèse. I hope you will forget what I said."

"You cannot come here and become the Lord of the Manor, insulting the peasants!" she said pointedly. "You will not get very far with that attitude."

"I never meant that!" he exclaimed. "You must believe me." There was such a look of sincerity in his eyes that she could do nothing else.

Nodding her head, she said, "We will let it be done. But do not think that we are simple peasants who can be taken for granted."

She turned to walk back to where the basket had been left on the ground, and he followed silently. While Henri began to eat, Thérèse played with the spirited little kitten.

As he took the contents from the basket he looked at her and commented, "You did not tell me last night that your father was dead."

"It is not something that one usually tells a stranger. He died five years ago in an accident when he was trying to help a poor farmer whose barn was falling down. It collapsed on him, and he was crushed." She looked out over the fields for a moment. "We miss him a great deal, but we have learned to live without him." The last statement was accompanied by a sigh.

For once at a loss for words, Henri resumed looking through the basket. He carefully took out the blackcurrant tart made from the berries that had been gathered the day before, the rest of the chicken from dinner last night, bread, and a wedge of soft yellow Epoisses cheese. "What a wonderful meal your mother has packed, and so much more than I can eat. Are you going to have some as well?"

"Maybe just a bite of cheese. Mama and I usually have just a small meal in the daytime, especially with a guest coming for dinner. And I must not stay too long or she will be cross with me after yesterday."

Thérèse pulled a long stem of grass and continued playing with the kitten while Henri hungrily ate. From time to time he stopped to tell her about some discovery that he had made, or about his plans. There was a comfortable air to their companionship, neither feeling as though they had to work to make conversation. The time passed easily.

"The barn will need to be pulled down and built anew. It is hardly safe for even one horse."

"My papa could have built you a wonderful barn." Thérèse paused and thought for a moment. "But there are men in town who worked with him. They will be glad of a little extra work."

"How did your mother come to meet a man who lived so far from Dijon?"

"Ah, that you will have to ask Mama this evening over supper. You must come if you want to hear their wonderful story." Thérèse stood as she spoke, and picked up the kitten for one last cuddle.

"Well, then, be assured that I will come. I think I can manage the path quite well by now."

"You know, there is another way. If you go down the avenue, then turn right on the road, you will soon come to our land. The way is not grand, but large enough for a wagon, and easy to find."

"I think that I will be content to follow the path through the forest until the 'avenue,' as you very kindly call it, is more than a footpath. I must start clearing it this afternoon or Bernard will not be able to bring the supplies when he arrives." Henri began to pack the leftover food in the basket as he spoke.

The kitten had fallen asleep again, and Thérèse handed it back. "You must make sure that she gets back to her mother soon. Poor little thing will be very hungry. And keep the basket." she added, "You can bring it with you when you come for dinner."

Henri walked over to a fountain that stood in the middle of what had been the terrace and set the basket on the outer edge where it would stay cool in the shade. As he gently laid the kitten on the cloth on top, his boot accidentally knocked the side of the fountain. The motion caused a piece of stone to fall away and he commented, "I suppose that this will have to be torn down."

"You cannot!" Thérèse exclaimed. "It is such a wonderful little fountain. I have never seen it work, but as a child I loved to come and sit on the edge, pretending what it must have been like." She hurried over to his side to show him its wonders. "There are twelve frogs with wide mouths positioned around the outer edge, just like the numbers on a clock. The column in the center used to have a large bunch of grapes on top which have been broken away, but you can see the grapevines and leaves running down the sides, and the little lizards and snails climbing through them. Mama said that there used to be a large cistern to catch rainwater on the top of the hill behind the barn, and when it was full the water would flow from the frogs' mouths and onto the grapes."

"But it probably cannot be fixed. I imagine that the pipes were crushed long ago, or filled with dirt."

Thérèse looked into his eyes and insisted, "But you could fill it with water and let little fish swim there. You must not just tear it down. I'm sure that the sight of the little frogs made someone very happy long ago."

It was obvious that the fountain was very dear to Thérèse, and so Henri promised, "I will let it stay for now and have a workman look at it. I suppose if nothing else, Aunt Catherine could plant some flowers in it."

Relieved, Thérèse assured him that some use could be made of it, and then turned once again to leave. Henri walked with her to the edge of the lawn, then stood watching as her slender form with the shining red hair moved toward the edge of the forest. Taking one final moment to look and wave at him, she disappeared into the cool wood.

4

ONCE AGAIN VOICES WERE RAISED in animated conversation throughout the evening at the Condé cottage. Dinner had been a lively affair. Henri, now quite comfortable with Alix and Thérèse, entertained them in his talkative manner with tales of trying to clear the growth from the avenue. Even though he had found a rusted old chopping knife in the barn and a piece of whetstone, he was not very successful at sharpening it, and even less able to fell any of the small trees that blocked the drive. Alix promised that she would send an ax home with him that very night.

After thoroughly exhausting himself, Henri had decided to explore more of the château. He planned to start in the basement, but a well-entrenched colony of rats had forced him to leave the kitchen quickly in favor of the upper floors. On the top floor under the steep slate roof, he had found several surprises. In the large open area that might have been a sitting room for the staff, he discovered some usable chairs among a pile of broken furniture which had been thrown in a corner. In another small room, there was a painted iron bed frame of the type that would have been used by house servants. And searching still further, he had discovered a small storage room where he found a little table and even a thin mattress, which, though torn, was usable. He spent the remainder of the afternoon bringing his treasures down and establishing a bedroom for himself in one of the rooms on the second floor.

"Aunt Catherine has promised to send a few pieces of furniture on the wagons with Bernard, and I'm sure that she will send a proper bed that I will put in the master's room. Still, this will serve me well for now. And I feel that I am beginning to make a little bit of progress at bringing order to the château. There is so much to be done that I admit to being overwhelmed at times."

"And you are so impatient to get it all accomplished," laughed Alix.

A quick grin appeared on Henri's face. "Well, maybe a little impatient as well. Still, I don't want Bernard to think that I have just been waiting for the two workmen that he is bringing. If I am to be master of the estate, then I must be willing to begin the work myself."

Thérèse could see the look of approval in her mother's eyes. Even though he had been reared on a wealthy estate, he did not seem to be afraid of hard work. Alix liked his pragmatic view of life and of the work that was required to fulfill his dream. "I just wish my Nicholas had lived to see the château alive with people again. He hated watching a building fall into disrepair, and especially one so beautiful as the Château St. Vivant."

Henri looked for a moment at Thérèse. When she nodded her head ever so slightly, he turned back to Alix saying, "Thérèse told me that he was dead, but very little more. How did a doctor's daughter from Dijon come to marry a man from so far away?"

A gentle smile came to Alix's face, and she answered softly, "It was just meant to be." She gazed into the flames burning brightly in the huge stone fireplace, and began to remember.

"As Thérèse told you, my father was a well respected doctor in Dijon. Our home was a happy, bustling kind of place, filled with friends and laughter. My mother did her best to teach me to behave as a proper young lady should, but I was a very curious young girl and always fascinated by my father's office. And since my two brothers were not interested in medicine at that time, Papa allowed me to follow him around and watch him at his work. I suppose I was a surrogate for the son who should have wanted to become a doctor.

"Anyway, when my mother died of a lung disease one very bitter winter, there was a huge hole in my life. Trying to fill her absence, I began to see it as a chance to learn more than she would ever allow.

Since the housekeeper was perfectly able to run the house, I began to appear with more regularity in my father's surgery next door to our home. I was always willing to wash up instruments, or clear off the counters. And I always had a thousand questions about everything that I touched. My father's friends warned him that I was learning more than a young lady should know – that I would become an old maid. But by that time I had become a very reliable assistant, and so my father closed his ears to their protests.

"One day I was filling some bottles with fresh herbs, when a young carpenter came to the office with an injury. A piece of wood he was working with had split and the jagged end had torn open his forearm. It was something that needed immediate care, and since my father had been called away to attend a sick friend in the country and would not return until after dark, I decided to deal with it myself. We talked as I worked, and I learned that he was from St. Vivant. He said that there was no work there for builders, and after a very bad year on his family's farm, he had come to Dijon to earn some extra money and send it home. In Dijon there was always a need for workmen to build the elegant town homes that the wealthy merchants and lawyers wanted. You could tell by the sadness in his voice as he spoke of home that he missed it very much. I cleaned the wound and bandaged it carefully, but I told him that he would need to return first thing the next morning to let my father examine it more closely for any splinters.

"I can assure you that I was in the office early next day, so as to be there when the carpenter arrived. I stayed in the background as my father spoke with him and checked over his arm. I pretended to be interested in finding out how well I had cared for his wound, but watched and listened to everything Nicholas said, for that was his name, Nicholas Condé. I was especially drawn to his gentle eyes. And I was disappointed when I heard him say that he planned to return to his farm as soon as possible. He was a very handsome young man, and in my silliness I had lain awake the night before imagining a romance.

"I saw him the few other times he came to have my father change the bandages, and once in the town when I passed a house where he was working on a roof. Then came that rainy afternoon when I was at home alone. Nicholas knocked on the door and asked to speak to my father. When I explained that Papa was not home, he told me that he was there to ask for permission to visit me. I cannot tell you how thrilled I felt. I insisted that he stay right then and wait until my father returned. While we waited, I learned a great deal about him, but most especially that I could listen to his strong, low voice forever."

Oblivious to her listeners, Alix thought back to that rainy afternoon when she first felt the fires of passion stir. And for a moment she experienced again the thrill that she had known just being close to him. A soft sigh filled the quiet night.

"Well, my courtship did not go as planned. Nicholas arrived early in the morning one week later to say that he had received word that his family was very ill. A sickness was sweeping through the region, and he planned to leave as soon as possible. He wanted me to go with him. It did not take long for me to answer. I was twenty, and knew that this would probably be my only chance for marriage. I am sure that if my mother had been alive, she would never have allowed me to go. It took every argument I could muster, but I was finally able to persuade Papa that for me this was right."

Alix smiled at the next thought, and continued, "And somehow my Papa was able to convince the priest to marry us that very evening. I never asked what he said or had to promise the shrewd old Father, but I am sure that it was very expensive. We left the next morning and I have lived here ever since."

"But, Madame, did you never go back to visit your father or brothers?" asked Henri.

"Only once. You see, when we arrived here a few days later, Nicholas learned that most of his family was dead. Only a married sister who lived in another town survived. Nicholas and I suddenly had all of the responsibilities of the farm, and I had never even milked a cow or cooked a meal. Those first few months were very hard, and I could not have adjusted if not for Nicholas' love and support.

"But that is not to say that I never saw my family again. My father came here that first summer with a wagon full of furniture that he felt should be mine." At this, Thérèse gave a superior sort of look at Henri that said, "just as I told you," then she turned her attention back toward her mother. "He also brought barrels filled with dishes and linens that the housekeeper said I would need.

More importantly, he brought me starts of the herbs that he had taught me to use during those years when I helped him. And he returned when he could, sometimes bringing one of my brothers, often stopping on his trips to Paris."

A sorrowful tone came into her voice. "That was where he was going the last time I saw him, on his way to see an old friend who was dying. Papa was killed trying to help the wounded in the Faubourg St. Antoine during the popular insurrection of 1795."

Alix paused for a moment, then realizing that her wonderful love story was ending on a sad note, added brightly, "But that was in more difficult times." She smiled and reached over to put her hand on Thérèse's. "I did take Thérèse to Dijon once. After I came to St. Vivant, my brother Roland finally decided that he wanted to follow in my father's practice as a doctor. When pigs destroyed some rare herbs that I needed for medicines, I went to Dijon to get replacements from my brother and took Thérèse with me. Roland no longer had an herb garden, so we had to go on to Beaune to finally get everything we needed. It became quite an adventure. And Thérèse did get to see the house where I was brought up, and the little church where Nicholas and I were married."

Alix turned to smile at Henri, "It was nothing like the trip that you have taken to come to St. Vivant. You have traveled from so far away. And the times are different now. I think when the estate is working again it will be better for us all."

"That is what I hope. And even though your husband won't be there, I hope that you will come often to see how the work progresses." Henri sat back in his chair, a little frown playing at the corners of his mouth. "I confess that I am ready for it to all be finished now, but after working this morning and accomplishing so little, I realize that it is a tremendous task that will require months, even years."

Alix tapped her fingers thoughtfully on the table. "You know, Henri, there are men from the village who would welcome a chance to work at the château. We have many workers who are quite skilled, but because the area is so poor, they have no chance to ply their trades. Sadly, they would agree to work for even a pittance if the pay was in hard currency."

"Bernard has already planned to look for local workers. He feels that there will be more interest in making the winery successful again if the local people are profiting from it." Henri paused for a moment, then rushed into his next sentence, obviously hoping for Alix's help. "In fact, we will need someone right away to show Bernard the differences in vine cultivation in this region."

Alix sat quietly for a moment, narrowing her eyes as she thought. "There are many here who make small amounts of wine each year for their own use. Some even have the odd barrel left over to sell to a tavern if they are lucky enough to find a buyer. None are particularly noteworthy in their ability." Once again she paused, slowly intertwining her fingers before her. Then she continued carefully, "However, there was someone who was very good at one time. He worked at the château for the young comte who was killed." She paused again, "Still, I don't know if he would agree...."

"Mama!" Thérèse jumped up and placed her hands on the table. "Mama, you can not mean old Gaspard! He's crazy!"

"Now just a moment, Thérèse. You have not heard me out. And he's not crazy."

"Everyone says he is!" Thérèse turned toward Henri and rushed on. "At times even I have seen him in the forest wandering near the château, his hair dirty and wild and a crazed look in his eyes. One time, when he saw me, he just stood there for a moment, staring as if he had seen a ghost. Then he started shaking his head and ran away shouting, 'No! No! Who are you?'" She walked around toward her mother's chair, and laid her hand on her mother's arm. "I told you about that day. Remember, Mama? I'm sure he is crazy. And all the people in the town agree. Why, Marie Patoit told me that...."

"Thérèse!" Alix's voice rang out sharply. "I will not have the stories that are told in the village repeated here." After looking sternly at her daughter, Alix turned to Henri. "Gaspard has had an unfortunate life. But at one time he was a master at making wine, and would have been the vigneron at the estate. I am sure that you could find no more knowledgeable person than he."

"But, Mama," Thérèse tried one more time, "He is so old! He has probably forgotten everything that he ever knew about the grapes. And anyway, they say he's just like a hermit these days and never leaves the forest."

"Once you learn something like growing grapes, Thérèse, you never forget it. It gets in your blood. And as for being too old, he is not much older than I am, and I dare you to say that I am too old to work." The look that Alix gave Thérèse made it quite clear that she would not tolerate any more interruptions. "And he's not a hermit, Henri. He just tries to avoid personal relationships these days. As I said, he has had an... unfortunate life."

Henri thought for a moment. Alix had been very helpful and he had no reason not to trust her word. Anyway, Bernard would know quickly enough if the man were not able to help. And if this Gaspard was as clever as she said, they would be able to learn a great deal from his experience. "If you say that he is the best, Madame Condé, then all I need are directions to his house, and I will ask him to come and meet Bernard."

The room was silent for a moment. "That will never do," Alix shook her head as she spoke. "He does not trust strangers and will not even speak to you. Thérèse and I have to go to St. Vivant tomorrow for market day, but after that I will go to his house and speak to him for you. I will let you know if he agrees."

"Then I will leave it to you." Henri rose to go then added, "Once again you have been an enormous help to me. I will not forget the kindness that you and your daughter have shown me."

"We have only done the same things that we should do for any neighbor, Henri. And I think that you will bring a great deal of excitement to a very dull summer. We should thank you." She put out her hand to the handsome young man with the delightful boyish grin.

Henri took her hand in his and honored her with a courtly bow. "Still, I shall remember, Madame."

Thérèse followed him into the night, holding a lantern high to light the way into the barn. She opened the door to the workroom, pointed to the wall where her father's tools were kept, and said, "Help yourself to whatever you need."

Remembering that Nicholas had been a builder, Henri looked at the wide range of implements carefully mounted on a wall. "If you are sure that I won't take something that you might need."

"We hardly ever use them now. When a neighbor is too proud to take her help for free, Mama trades her services for firewood or to have the garden plowed. But she does come out and keep them dusted and oiled. I think that she feels close to Papa when she touches the tools that he touched."

Henri was unusually quiet as he chose an ax and a few other items. In the quiet summer night there was an almost reverent air in the workroom. As Thérèse stood watching him, she remembered the times that her father had sat on the bench and repaired her toys, his large callused hands working as carefully as a surgeon's. Henri's hands, though large, were soft and fine, and looked out of place against the well-worn wooden handles. He took the tools and swung them over his shoulder, then turned back to Thérèse. "I'll use them carefully and return them as soon as Bernard brings new ones in the wagons."

Thérèse smiled at his concern. "Don't think that you have to be too careful with them. I am sure Papa would feel that tools are to be used." With a grin she added, "And I'm sure that you will wear out before they do." Then she turned to pick up a large basket from the workbench where she had laid it when they came in. She offered it to him, holding the handle with both hands. "Mama wanted you to take this. With market day tomorrow, and other work that needs to be done, we may not see you for a few days. So she filled it with food to tide you over until Bernard comes, or you come for a meal again."

Touched by their continuing kindness, Henri reached out to take the offered basket. As he did so, his hand brushed against Thérèse's for an instant, and in that moment a spark seemed to fly from her body to his. He looked into the soft green eyes, framed by white skin and warm red hair. Resisting the urge to reach out and touch the softness of her face, he stood for a moment spellbound by the feeling.

Thérèse felt the same current and for the first time looked past the affable, boyish nature to the strong, young man determined to put a broken-down estate back together. She blushed as she looked into his kind face, her eyes drawn to his. Carefully, she drew her hands away from the basket, clasping them behind her back. Then, biting her lip, she looked down quickly, her hair covering her face, unaware of the very sensuous picture that was revealed in the soft light of the lantern.

"Mama has put in some of her gingerbread." Thérèse struggled for something to say, fighting down the urge to draw closer to him. Reining in her emotions, she looked back at him and continued, "I hope that you will like it. She has become quite famous for her baking, and made a large batch especially for you."

"Gingerbread is a favorite of mine," he said, aware that he needed to leave as soon as possible, but equally aware of a desire that was persuading him to stay. He stood for a moment, not wanting to disturb the glow that he felt. Thérèse was looking up at him, not sure what to say next.

And then the feeling was shattered by the screeching sound of an owl, claiming the night. The noise startled them both, and they moved quickly apart as if in recoil. Thérèse lifted the lantern high again, and turned to lead the way into the warm night air. Henri followed close behind. After he latched the door, she bade him goodnight, then carefully picked her way back toward the cottage. Henri followed the path into the woods, unaware of the two large owls that watched him from a high branch on one of the trees that edged the forest, or of the girl who stood in the doorway of her house, watching until long after he could be seen disappearing into the darkened wood.

5

The following morning, Alix and Thérèse were up before dawn, hurrying to finish the chores that had to be completed before they could leave for the market. Alix milked the cow and goats, while Thérèse fed the animals and loaded the wagon with the plants and potions for which her mother was famous. The sun was rising high in the sky by the time they were on their way. The trip was not a long one, but the road they traveled was very bad. Many of the main roads in France were kept in good condition to allow Napoleon's armies to quickly move across the country. But this road only served the local farmers and was not considered vital to the nation. So they had to steer the wagon carefully, avoiding the many holes and especially watching out for the deep ruts created by the floods of spring and the early summer rains.

Finally, rounding a curve, they saw the town of St. Vivant nestled below. It was in a sheltered valley flanked by hills which rose steeply up from the river. Colorful tile roofs laid in geometric patterns gleamed up at them from the buildings. The streets straggled down the hillsides toward the center of town, which was lined with houses and shops made of stone. These narrow medieval thoroughfares clustered toward the open square, set neatly on a small plateau above the river's bank. The land between the square and the river had been left as a small common, the only relief from an otherwise crowded scene.

As the wagon made its way carefully toward the square, its occupants were surrounded by the sounds of voices raised in greeting mingled with the noises of the market. After settling the wagon and unhitching the horse, Thérèse and her mother began to shop from stall to stall. And as they shopped they took part in that ancient ritual of the day. For, in addition to being a time for business, market day was also a time for greeting old friends, learning news of ones who had not come, checking on the growth of children, and hearing tidbits of gossip. Today, of course, the gossip on everyone's lips was of the young man who had come to live in the Château St. Vivant.

Thérèse watched her mother as she spoke to one group of women. Alix was a master at revealing only facts and discouraging speculation. When one woman loudly complained that they might have to give back their land that had belonged to the old estate, Alix pointed out that there were laws to protect them from that. She listened as another woman declared that he could not be the heir because her sister had been there the night the child was born, and had seen the tiny coffin of the infant. Alix admitted that the story was hard to believe, but tried to point out that his coming might be a financial boon to them all. If he stayed, she added. The women snickered among themselves when she said that because everyone remembered the many who had come and gone before.

Knowing that the conversations could go on for quite a while, Thérèse left her mother and began strolling from one stall to another, greeting the vendors and admiring their wares. At one stop she noticed a stand of beautiful early berries and at another she commented on a particularly fine display of cheese. As she went, she made a few purchases using some of the small sum of money that Alix gave her each year on her birthday. Long ago, Thérèse had learned to choose her purchases carefully, guarding the precious coins. As usual, one of her first stops was to buy a bag of "anis," the tiny sugardrops with aniseed in the center that she dearly loved. The woman who made the candy had learned the secret of the recipe many years earlier from the Ursuline nuns of Flavigny. Her sweets had become a favorite of the townsfolk, and she was sorely missed on the days when she did not come to market.

Almost as soon as she had made her purchase, Thérèse found herself surrounded by a group of small children shouting their greetings to "Mademoiselle Thérèse." She put a drop into each chubby hand and suspected that they had been watching her and waiting until just that moment to stop her. However, she did not mind, because the children of the village were very special to her.

One of the failures of the Révolution had been the education of the children in remote villages. After the lands and wealth belonging to the church had been confiscated, there was no longer a source of teaching priests to educate local children. Many of the priests who did not lose their lives fled to safer lands. The towns were not able to take on the financial burden of education, and so the children were forgotten. One winter, Thérèse had begun to teach a few children who lived nearby the simple lessons that her mother had taught her. Soon others were asking to join her "winter school," as they called it. She had agreed, with the provision that girls must be allowed to attend as well as boys. The school had been extremely successful and she looked forward to the cold weather when they would begin again. To thank her, fathers brought things to the Condé cottage like firewood or game that they had trapped. Recently, there was even some talk in town of trying to find a way to pay her.

The little group thanked her for their sweets then, calling their good-byes, ran on to find another victim. Thérèse strolled on toward the square, browsing among the stalls and watching the people as they came and went. Stopping for a moment to greet a neighbor, she noticed how warm the woman looked wearing a quichenotte, a long, hood-like cloth bonnet that country women wore to shade their faces and necks. Continuing on, she shook her long red hair away from her own perspiring neck and was thankful that her mother did not force her to keep it covered when she came to the market.

Turning up a narrow side street, she walked toward a small shop that specialized in dry goods. As she opened the door, she paused for a moment to listen to the sound of the little bell mounted on the wall above, then stepped into the store. After her eyes adjusted to the dark, Thérèse began to walk past the cutting table when she noticed a bolt of wonderful cloth that the clerk was just unwrapping. Drawing closer, she saw a marvelous merino wool of deep green. Impulsively she reached out and gently felt the cloth, thinking how lovely she would look dressed in the fabric standing on the grand staircase at St. Vivant in the autumn light. The thought made her blush, and quickly looking up at the clerk she commented, "The cloth is very beautiful."

"It is truly exceptional, Mademoiselle. This is one of the very nicest bolts that I have had in many months. It came in a recent shipment from Chatillon."

"I suppose that it is very expensive."

Her suspicion was confirmed when he told her the price. She knew that she did not have enough for even a short cape, much less a dress length of the wonderful material. Sighing, she thanked him, and continued on toward the back of the store where she selected the embroidery floss that she needed. After paying the clerk, she left the store quickly, not allowing herself even to look toward the lovely green material as she passed by.

The sun was beginning to warm the summer air by the time she returned to the street. Heading back toward the square, she found that the heat and noise and smells of the market were becoming oppressive. She looked toward the river's edge, and thought to rest there when she noticed an old woman entering the church on the other side of the square. Impulsively, Thérèse followed.

Quickly, she crossed the square, covered her head, and opened the huge oak door with squeaking hinges. Immediately there was a breath of cool air and, stepping inside, she found the relief that she sought. She walked down the side aisle of the church carefully so as not to disturb the few bowed heads that were scattered here and there throughout the sanctuary. Then, finding a vacant bench in a stone alcove where she could sit, she placed her basket on the floor and looked around.

The church of St. Vivant had been built by an unimaginative architect many centuries before. The space was large and square, the effect balanced but heavy in its gothic appearance. Through the years, there had been attempts to improve it with paintings and gilded altars; however, most of those items had been destroyed when the church had been ransacked. Now it was a place for the old to come and remember their prayers in moments of need. It would take the assignment of a priest who came on a regular basis to restore it to prominence in the life of the village, especially the young people. Village officials had written to the archbishop in Paris requesting help, but there had been no progress. Maybe with Henri at the château, things would change.

Henri. Thérèse frowned. She knew that she would have to come to grips with herself on that subject. She had embarrassed herself in the shop by her thoughts. Lying in bed late last night the memory of his touch had stayed with her, driving her imagination with images of the two working together, grandly restoring the château. He was so different from the boys she had known, so handsome and so alive with ambition. It would be easy to become obsessed with him. Thérèse knew that she would have to get her emotions and her thoughts under control. Remembering the comments of the women earlier in the day, she reminded herself that there was some doubt even as to who he was.

Suddenly her concentration was broken by the sound of whispered voices in argument. She looked around for the source, and then realized that it was coming from the little chapel to St. Vincent. Curious, she leaned forward trying to discover to whom the voices belonged.

She was shocked to see her mother standing there and even more surprised when she realized that the person with whom she was arguing was old Gaspard. He was kneeling on the floor surrounded by tools and pieces of wood, and must have been working on a broken piece of altar when her mother found him. As Thérèse watched, she saw Gaspard shake his head vigorously; then, Alix reached down and placed her hand on his shoulder, looking into his face. She crept forward along the wall, and by listening carefully Thérèse was just able to make out the words that she spoke.

"But you are the only one who can do this, Gaspard. I have told him how good you are, and he is waiting for you to come and help. Please, do this for me." As she pleaded, Alix looked straight into his eyes.

Once again Gaspard shook his head. Then, Thérèse saw her mother stoop down to get closer. "You know why you must do this, don't you, Gaspard?" Seeing the stricken look on the old man's face, Thérèse realized that she must leave before she was found eavesdropping. Without making a sound, she reached down to take her basket and quickly left the church.

Out in the heat and noise of market day, she paused for a moment to think about what she had just seen. Why was it so important to her mother that Gaspard be the one to help at the château? He obviously did not want to go, and yet she had never seen her mother press someone so hard. Did her mother distrust Henri? And if that was so, should she also be wary? Thérèse shook her head and slowly wandered back to the place where their wagon was tethered.

After lunch came the busy time for Alix and Thérèse. Alix always left her wagon in a place where she would have afternoon shade. It was during this time that she was available to help anyone who needed attention to an ache or pain. St. Vivant had never had a doctor of its own, and so, through the years, Alix had become important to the community by using the lessons that she had learned in her father's office, although she had been very careful not to allow anyone to think that she possessed the knowledge of a doctor. It had taken a long time for her to be allowed to do more than attend births or nurse sick children. Finally the townsfolk had come to depend on her to cure all their ills, and Thérèse worked by her side to provide her mother with the right jar or herb when she needed it.

As various people came to Alix for advice or help, their wagon began to fill with fruits and vegetables left by those who insisted on paying for her herbs and potions with produce of some kind. Money was still very precious and rare for most of the people, not that Alix ever asked to be paid. Still, most insisted on payment of some sort if they could, knowing that there would probably be times when there was an emergency and they would have nothing to give her. When Thérèse saw several large baskets of berries loaded into the wagon she knew that tomorrow they would be in the kitchen for a long day of making jam.

During a lull in the flow of patients, Marie Patoit came by to see Thérèse. The daughter of a farmer who lived near the Condé cottage, Marie had been the closest thing to a girl friend that Thérèse had ever known. She was two years younger, and they had played together as children when their fathers had helped one another. As they had grown older and taken on more responsibilities in their homes, they found less time to spend together. So market day had become an excellent opportunity to catch up.

Marie had heard the talk about the handsome stranger, and wanted to know exactly what Thérèse knew. She stared with astonishment when she learned that the stranger had been at the Condé cottage and even stayed there one night. She asked Thérèse for every detail she could remember, shaking her head in wonder at all she learned.

Having finally exhausted the subject of Henri – Marie loved that his name was Henri – their talk turned to other things. While the two girls chatted, Alix worked on alone, knowing how seldom Thérèse was able to spend time with girls her age. She was near enough to hear some of their conversation, so she was able to laugh when she heard about the little gang who had surrounded her daughter for sweets. She also overheard Thérèse tell Marie about the beautiful green fabric, describing the feel and color in detail. The two could have talked on all afternoon if Marie's younger brother had not come to find her.

When the last wound had been re-bandaged, the last salve given for an aching muscle, Thérèse was left to tidy up the wagon and re-hitch the horse while her mother went to one final appointment. Alix always took a moment to visit a friend who was also a shop-keeper. Alix used the shop's address for any letters she might receive, and the shopkeeper would either hold them for market day or send a rider to deliver them to the cottage. Today she took a very long time, and Thérèse was beginning to be concerned that there had been bad news. Finally she saw her mother walking slowly back, carrying a package. Alix climbed into the wagon, then, with a smile, handed the bundle wrapped in brown paper to Thérèse. Even though she was excited, Thérèse untied the string carefully and opened the paper so as not to make a tear. Then she looked at her mother with shining eyes. On her lap lay a length of the wonderful green merino, long enough to sew a beautiful dress, and with it an illustration of a stylish dress straight from Paris.

Thérèse reached out impulsively to hug her mother as she exclaimed, "Are you very sure that we can afford it, Mama?"

"When I was your age I had many more fashionable dresses than you have ever had, because my papa loved to buy presents for me. I am sure that he would want a young woman as special as you to have something in which to feel beautiful."

"Oh, Mama! Thank you, thank you." Thérèse hugged her mother again, then with a glowing face looked at the gift once more.

Alix's face got an impish grin as she added, "Think about your Aunt Marguerite, Thérèse. She probably pays more than this for her petticoats."

Thérèse laughed as she nodded in agreement. Aunt Marguerite was married to Mama's brother Roland, and they lived an elegant life in Dijon. She was very beautiful, and always dressed in the latest fashions. Though it had been many years since Thérèse had seen her, darling Aunt Marguerite remembered how much Thérèse loved to read, and each year sent books not only for her, but also for her winter school. "If only Aunt Marguerite could see me in this wonderful new frock," thought Thérèse.

The long trip home that night passed unnoticed as mother and daughter spent the time talking about how they would begin to sew the handsome new dress.

AS THÉRÈSE HAD FEARED, her next few days were fully occupied with work. First, they had to deal with the vegetables and fruit that had filled their wagon from market day. Unhappily, the mild weather that had covered the province in the early part of summer was gone, replaced by hot and humid air. Therefore, they were both up early, sorting through the baskets, throwing out anything that had started to spoil on their bumpy ride home. As the day wore on and the temperature began to rise, Thérèse was left tending a bubbling pot of berries as her mother measured the sugar and pounded the fresh herbs that would be added. Thankfully, Alix took the job of skinning and salting down some game that one farmer had given her, leaving Thérèse to sweep out the barn and look after the animals.

The next day was even more oppressive, with a heavy dampness hanging in the hot air. In spite of this, Thérèse had to spend the morning weeding and hoeing the garden that had been neglected for days. Her mother insisted that she carefully cover her fair skin while she worked out in the hot summer sun, so today she wore a bonnet as well as a long sleeved dress. In no time at all she was damp with perspiration and had to stop often to wipe the trickles of sweat from her face. In the afternoon, Alix sent her to gather some mushrooms for a meat pie that she planned to make. Sadly, the mushrooms grew in a part of the forest in the opposite direction from the château and at such a distance that Thérèse was barely able to return before time to cook dinner.

The third day finally brought some relief from the heat when a pouring rain swept into the province before dawn. The two women spent the early part of the day dusting and sweeping out the cottage. Then, after a lunch of soup and cheese, they sat down with needlework to pass the rainy afternoon. As Thérèse finished the piece for which she had purchased the embroidery thread, their conversation naturally turned to the green cloth and to how the new dress would be made.

"I want it to look just like the picture, Mama." Thérèse had spent many hours dreaming about how she would look in the wonderful dress. She knew by heart the lines of the high-waisted gown with long sleeves, and she especially loved the short Spencer jacket with the military collar "à l'Emperor." In her mind she had placed herself in the picture, painted the dress the soft shade of green, and piled her hair high on her head with soft, red tendrils framing her face

"Yes, I think the pattern is perfect. But I thought that in addition you should have a little chemisette to wear under the dress; it would give it a different look when you didn't want to wear the jacket. I saw a lovely one in town once. It just covered the neck and tucked under the bodice, but gave the dress a softer look. And maybe with some écru lace at the neck? What do you think?"

Thérèse's eyes were shining. "I think that it would be perfect, but are you sure that we can make all of this?"

"Actually I have been worrying about just that. I have not done any sewing this fine for many years, and I would hate to ruin even a small piece of the cloth. That is why I am considering taking it all to Madame Gerricault and asking her to make it."

"Madame Gerricault? Are you sure that she would know how to make it any better than you?"

"Oh, yes, Thérèse. Even though it has been many years since she has been asked to do fine sewing, she is still the best seamstress that I know. You know that she learned to sew as a young girl at the château, and she had taken over all of the work on the young comtesse's clothes before the Révolution. I think that she would do a magnificent job, and would probably enjoy the challenge."

Thérèse thought for a moment, then said softly, "But wouldn't you have to pay her, Mama?"

"I think that I could work out something with her, and if we let her take her time, maybe she would be willing to do it for only a little. You cannot wear it until the weather turns cool again anyway. I think also that I could save some cost by writing down all of your measurements myself and taking them to her with the cloth. Then she would only need you at the very end for a fitting."

Though somewhat disappointed that she wouldn't be more involved in sewing the dress, Thérèse agreed to let her mother decide what was best. And that night she allowed herself to dream once more of the splendid appearance she would make dressed in the latest fashion and entering the château on Henri's arm.

Thus it was Saturday morning before there was a chance to visit the château again. The storm had left a freshness in the air and when Thérèse asked if she could go, Alix surprised her not only by agreeing, but also by accompanying her. Each woman carried a basket of food as they walked along the forest path, and Thérèse wondered out loud if the wagon had finally arrived.

The question was answered even before the château came into sight. The sound of axes on wood and men shouting to one another while they worked filled the air as the two women came to the edge of the woods. The sunlight shone brightly on the clearing that marked the border of the château grounds, and the progress that had been made was instantly visible. Two men were working on the avenue, cutting the largest of the trees that had grown there, and using the wagon horses to haul them to one side. Piles of smaller trees and brush could be seen everywhere, surely the result of Henri's work. The wagon, loaded high with furniture and barrels, had been moved along as they worked and would soon be able to drive right up to the entrance of the great house to be unpacked.

On the lawn there was a pile of broken furniture and other debris that had been discarded from the château. Looking up, Thérèse noticed immediately that the bits of tattered drapes were no longer to be seen hanging in the windows, and the branch that had lodged in the balcony railing had been removed as well as most of the leaves.

"Someone has been very busy," murmured Alix as she looked at the scene with approving eyes.

Thérèse was about to respond, but was cut off by a loud, "Hello! You've finally come!" The sound of Henri's friendly greeting was audible above the noise of the workmen. Alix and Thérèse turned to see him running toward them from the vat house, waving his arm. He slowed as he came closer, and continued, "I hoped you would be able to come for a visit today. Bernard and the men arrived yesterday evening, and you can see what they have been able to do. Isn't it wonderful?"

"But I can see that you have also been working," commented Alix.

Henri smiled and laughed as he spoke. "Yes, I became well acquainted with your ax. And please notice the blisters that I got in return." He held the reddened palms of his hands out to them. "But you must come now and meet Bernard. I have told him all about you and how kind you have been. And are those baskets full of more delicious food?"

Thérèse smiled as Alix replied, "We weren't sure if your supplies had come yet. Still, I think that there will be enough to share with the others for at least one meal."

"If there is as much as the other basket held, then there will be more than enough. However, since it tastes so good, I am not sure that I will want to share it," Henri added appreciatively. Then he continued, "Let me speak to the workmen for a moment; then I want to take you to Bernard."

They watched as another tree was felled, then Henri quickly strode over to one of the men. After speaking for a moment, gesturing with his arms all the while in his exuberant manner, he returned to where Alix and Thérèse were standing. "They've been working hard all morning and Bernard wanted to make sure that they take a little time to rest now that the sun is getting higher. They know that he wants to be able to unload the wagon by nightfall, but there is a lot of work for just two men. Bernard knows how to pick good workmen, then treats them kindly so that they are usually devoted to him." Watching as the men took a skin of water from the wagon and went to sit under a tree, Henri smiled. Then he said, "Come now, and meet Bernard."

After placing the baskets in the shade near the château's entrance, the two women followed Henri across the lawn to the short flight of stairs that led into the vat house. Stepping inside, they could smell the mustiness that came from years of disuse. Even though the large doors had been thrown open to let in the light and fresh morning air, the air still had not cleared. Inside, they saw an old wooden ladder leaning up against one of the vats, and the legs and back of a man leaning down into the huge wooden cylinder. Henri called to him and Bernard stood up; seeing the visitors, he immediately descended.

"These are the very kind people that I have been telling you about, Bernard. This is Madame Condé, and her daughter Mademoiselle Thérèse."

Bernard came striding forward to take the hand that Alix offered. "I am Bernard Montreaux, at your service." He bowed in a gentlemanly manner, then nodded to Thérèse. He was a very distinguished man, with a strong face and graying hair. His actions were those of someone used to being in control. Turning back to Alix, he said, "Monsieur Girond will hear of the great kindness that you have extended to Henri, Madame. On his uncle's behalf I thank you for befriending him."

Alix smiled at the gallant speech, and assured him, "It really has been our pleasure, Monsieur Montreaux. Henri is such lively company that we missed not seeing him these last few days and, as you see, have come on the first opportunity."

Bernard smiled fondly at Henri and replied, "So you have had a chance to hear how Henri can talk on and on. He is never one to let a conversation die."

Henri blushed at his words, and looked quickly over at Thérèse, who gave him a reassuring smile. She turned to Bernard, asking, "And are you pleased with what you have found, sir?"

"Some things are in worse shape than I had hoped. What is left of the barn and stables will have to be completely pulled down and rebuilt before winter. Another pair of horses will arrive with a carriage soon. Counting Henri's and mine, and the pair with the wagon, that will mean six horses with no shelter. And we had hoped to find more furniture in the house, but that was probably too much to ask."

"Yes," agreed Alix. "What was not destroyed by the mob was taken or ruined in later years."

"However," continued Bernard, "The château is sound, and this vat house is in much better condition than I expected. Even last night, as we tried to sleep here in the rain, we only found a few small leaks."

Confused, Thérèse broke in to ask, "But why would you sleep in here?" She turned toward Henri with a questioning look.

"I am afraid that it was my fault," admitted Henri. "After what Thérèse said about the mansion's being haunted, I had a problem sleeping because of all the sounds. I would lie awake and listen until late at night, and could not get enough rest. Yesterday, I decided that most of the sounds must be coming from the rats and other animals that had taken up residence. Since the air was so heavy from the rain, I decided to smoke all of the animals out. I built large smoky fires all over the château, especially in the basement, and retreated here to wait. I didn't mean to fall asleep, but I was so tired. And I did not expect that Bernard would travel in the bad weather."

Thérèse stared openmouthed at Henri as he spoke, and Alix turned her head away, covering her mouth so that he would not see her laughing.

"We thought that the château was on fire when we arrived," chuckled Bernard. "Smoke was billowing out of the small basement windows along the sides, and a lesser amount of smoke was coming from the windows on upper floors. I came riding up shouting Henri's name, fearing that he had been harmed. Imagine my surprise when I saw him standing in the door of the vat house, obviously half asleep."

Alix's shoulders were shaking from her attempt to hide her laughter, and finally she turned to Henri with a twinkle in her eyes and laughed out loud. Thérèse was appalled that her mother could find something so dangerous that funny, but Henri seemed relieved by her laughter, and added a bit proudly, "And it seemed to work, because the men went down there today and said that they did not see any animals. It will just take some time to air out, I guess."

"And meanwhile, we can sleep in here," added Bernard with a smile. Alix was pleased to see that he also seemed to find the humor in the young man's actions.

"So you think that you will still be able to use this building?" asked Alix.

"Without a doubt." Bernard nodded his head as he spoke, then raised his hand to point toward the vats. "I had not expected much to be usable, but these vats are a real work of art. They were made of a very fine oak, and carefully polished. They are a bit dried out, but with a good cleaning and some repairs, they will be ready for this season's grapes."

Thérèse looked at him in surprise. "Do you intend to make wine this year?"

"Only for our own use," Bernard replied. "And to begin to get a feel for the grapes and how they taste. The vines on the hillside have grown wild, but they are full of grapes. We must begin somewhere."

"And you will have enough of the rest of the equipment to be able to do this?" asked Alix.

"That is what Henri and I were beginning to decide," answered Bernard. "We had looked once quickly, and now were taking a more careful account. Those wooden hottes over there will all have to be replaced." He pointed at a stack of curved wooden containers that men wore on their back to bring the grapes in from the fields. "Mice and vermin have gnawed away at them until they are useless. We will add them to our bonfires – the outside ones," he added with a wink to Henri.

"Many of these other tools will also have to be replaced as well." Bernard was moving through the vat house as he spoke. "And Henri's uncle has already ordered a large shipment of the bottles with sloping sides that some of the wineries in Burgundy are using."

"And what of the wine cellars?" asked Thérèse. "Are they full of rats as well?"

"Surprisingly not," commented Bernard. "The old kitchen must have been a more desirable home. Come and see." And he led them down the stairs at the far end of the building.

The air was obviously cooler as they descended into the dark rooms below. Underneath the vat house was a maze of vaulted rooms, which were really more of a lower ground floor than a true underground cellar. The walls were finished in rough stone, and the timbers that supported the ceilings were huge, hand-hewn beams of solid wood, additionally supported by stone columns. A burning torch illuminated the area, allowing them to see the room that had once been filled with wine casks.

"I imagine most of the wine was carted away in the early days, and most of the empty barrels were probably taken away to be used by the local people," said Bernard. "It is probably just as well, because after looking at the few that are left, I doubt that they would still be usable. We will have to order more, but since we plan to try the new method where the wine is drawn off after the first year and stored in bottles until it is ready, we will not need as many as they used in the old days." He looked around the room at the old barrel racks, then added, "Those will probably need to be torn out and new ones built, and we will need a different type of rack to store the bottles by the end of next year."

Thérèse looked around as he spoke and imagined what it must have looked like in the old days. Now the floor was littered with bits of broken wood, and the few barrels were lying at odd angles all about the room. Still, she could almost detect the fragrance of the wine that had been stored here and wondered how it would be when the heavy smell of fermenting wine once again filled the air.

Bernard's words were interrupted by the sound of someone coming down the stairs, and, looking toward the door, he expected to see one of his workmen. He was surprised, therefore, to see a stranger standing there, waiting for a word.

Thérèse could not believe her eyes. The tall man standing in the dim light of the torch was Gaspard, but not as she had ever seen him. His hair had been neatly washed and was tied at the nape of his neck. His clothes were clean, and not rumpled. And he was freshly shaven. She had never seen him without his wild beard.

He looked uncertain, standing there, until Alix walked over to him and said softly, "Gaspard, you came." She pulled him by the arm over to where Henri and Bernard stood, and introduced him. "Henri, this is the man that I told you about. You will not find anyone in this region who knows more about growing grapes or making wine." She turned to Bernard as she said those words.

Bernard, realizing that the man was ill at ease, said in a friendly voice, "It is a very large job. Look around you: are you sure that you want to take on such a chore?"

Gaspard looked at the man, sizing him up, then at Henri before he answered. "Twenty years ago we had hoped to make this a great winery. Enough time has passed that I'm willing to try it again. If you want me, I will work for you, but only as long as I have something to offer."

He had made his simple speech, and had no more to say, but in those few words Bernard recognized a man of integrity. He also suspected that Alix was right in her estimation of his abilities. And he needed someone right away to help him get started.

"Would you be willing to come again in the morning so that we can begin?" asked Bernard.

Gaspard shook his head gently. "No. I will not work on the Lord's day. But I will come early on Monday."

"Monday then." And Bernard offered his hand to Gaspard, who shook it to seal the bargain. He turned as if to go, but instead walked to a corner of the room, where one of the large beams joined the wall. He took a glove from his pocket, and after putting it on, reached high into the crevice above the beam. He seemed to search for a moment, then drawing back his hand he brought out a small shallow cup. Bringing it forward, Thérèse could see that must be silver, though now it was dark with tarnish.

Henri's eyes brightened immediately. "The tastevin! Look, Bernard." Henri reached eagerly to take it from the other man's hand and show it to his friend. "How did you know it was there?"

"I placed it there the last day I worked here. It was used by the old vigneron to taste the wines, and it would have passed to me one day. I was afraid of some sort of trouble, and didn't want anyone to find it. The family crest is engraved in it. You will see it when it's been cleaned. It will be up to you, boy, to decide who will use it now."

Having finished the business that he came for, Gaspard turned to leave. Alix caught his arm just as he reached the door, and he turned to face her.

"Thank you, Gaspard," she said simply.

His response was soft and almost inaudible to the others, but still they heard him say, "I failed him once, Alix. I won't fail him again." Then he was gone.

7

NOT LONG AFTER GASPARD LEFT, the group emerged from the vat house into the warm summer sunshine. They walked leisurely toward the back of the château, talking amongst themselves and seemingly content to enjoy the beautiful day. They stopped near the rear entrance, where the lawn sloped gently down toward the grapevines. Henri took particular pleasure in showing Thérèse how he had begun to clean out the little fountain that she loved so much.

"I don't know if it will ever work, but I will have someone look at the cistern and see what can be done," said Henri.

"But that," said Bernard pointedly, though with kindness in his voice, "will have to wait until the estate is again in working order. Even now your Aunt Catherine is in Paris gaily spending money on all the things that she thinks you must have, and though the vines and outbuildings should come first, I am afraid that we will have to concentrate on the château right away. You know how she and your cousin Camille love to shop, and it is worse now that your uncle seems to have given them the freedom to buy whatever they think you will need."

"I would be glad to help," remarked Thérèse, thinking that cleaning here somehow seemed more exciting than at their little cottage.

"We could not ask that of you, Mademoiselle." Bernard smiled as he spoke. Then he turned to Alix and added, "However, if you can suggest some people who are in need of work, we will require a cook and household staff right away, as well as workmen."

"There are never enough jobs in St. Vivant these days, Monsieur Montreaux. I can think of several women and girls who are excellent workers, and one marvelous cook in particular. Gaspard would be the best person to help you find the men for building and working the vines." Alix paused then observed cautiously, "I said nothing before because I was not sure if Henri would be able to afford a staff so soon."

"Monsieur Girond is fully committed to restoring the estate and building the winery into one of the best in this region. His winery in Bordeaux has more demand than he can handle, and he feels that his merchants in Paris will be able to sell all the wine we can produce, if it is of the right quality, of course. But wines from this region have such an excellent reputation; he is not worried. When I left him earlier this week he reminded me once again to press ahead with the work, and said that the funds would be readily available to meet all of our needs. I am taking him at his word."

"Well, then, I will begin to spread that news. May I tell them that you will be interviewing on Monday?"

"Why not?" agreed Henri eagerly. "The sooner that we get a staff working here, the sooner I can begin to search out the local records to prove that the estate is mine."

At those words, a troubled look came into Bernard's face, and he spoke with concern. "Henri, remember that your uncle said not to worry yourself too much with that. He is sure that his lawyers in Paris will be able to verify your claim. He said only to look when there was time."

"But Bernard, you know how important that proof is to me! I will not be satisfied until the records are in my hands."

"I understand, but remember that many papers were burned in the chaos of those days. I don't want you to feel such an urgency." Then with an earnestness in his voice he added, "Just do not make too much of this search. Trust your uncle. He has always known what was best."

"But someday I must begin to decide what is best for me."

Henri's eyes looked directly into Bernard's as he spoke these words in a low but firm voice, filled with intensity.

Thérèse and her mother had listened to the exchange, and were becoming uncomfortable with the turn that the conversation had taken. Henri's last words were followed by a silence, and the two women were searching for something to say when their attention was diverted by the sound of a bell from the far end of the château.

"Oh, how dear," exclaimed Thérèse. Around the corner came a large white cow with a bell tied around her neck. As she slowly grazed on the grass, she was followed by a tiny little calf. "Where did they come from, Henri?"

"Bernard brought them with him yesterday," he replied.

"I stopped at a farmhouse one night, and as we talked I told the farmer that I had never seen such a pure white cow before. He had several and indicated that he might be willing to sell the pair. They slowed us down considerably these last two days, but I was sure that we would need them soon. He called the breed a Charolais."

"Do you think that I could pet the calf?" asked an excited Thérèse.

"Why not? The cow seems to be very friendly." And Henri walked across the lawn with her, leaving Bernard and Alix alone.

"He is a nice young man," commented Alix as she watched the two petting the calf and talking. "Catherine Girond must be a very special person to raise such a well-centered young man."

"The two have a very special relationship, as you will learn when she arrives." Bernard smiled as watched the two young people walk away.

"You were lucky to be able to keep Henri out of the army," said Alix. "So many of our young men died in foreign battles."

"That was one very fortunate result of his Uncle Georges' negotiations to bring him back to St. Vivant. And, of course, his army connections." Bernard was silent for a moment before he continued. "He could say that Henri had to learn about the business before he could manage the estate. Now there is this wonderful opportunity for Henri to become his own man and secure his place for the future. I just hope it will come together as his uncle plans."

"For that we must wait and see," responded Alix, still watching the two young people. Then abruptly she turned to Bernard, saying, "Would you mind if I went to the chapel for a few moments? I found it distressing to have it get to such a dirty state, and so I have been cleaning it these past many years. I need to do a little dusting."

"Certainly, Madame Condé. I have seen for myself that someone has cared for it." And he accompanied her into the château.

The two walked straight through the château back to the front entrance where Alix had left her baskets. Excusing himself, Bernard went on to where the workmen had almost cleared a path large enough to allow the wagon to pass. Taking a clean cloth from the top of the basket, Alix made her way past the study to the little chapel. She crossed herself as she entered, then walked softly in the silence to the altar. There, on the floor in front of it, lay a bouquet of white wildflowers tied up with a ribbon. Alix looked down at them for a moment, then picked them up and placed them on the wide flat surface. She had learned to accept their presence, and not fear the spirit who left them. Smiling, she knelt to pray.

Outside, Thérèse and Henri had wandered down toward the edge of the lawn, to where the tangle of vines began. Henri looked past the gently sloping field at a small boat moving slowly around the curve of the river and out of sight. Thérèse stood beside him in silence, delighting in the splendid scene of the valley below, luscious and green in the full glory of summer.

They stood together for a long time, not feeling a need for words. Then Henri reached out and took Thérèse's hand, and turning to her said, "I have never felt so at home anywhere in my life. From the first moment that I stood here and looked out over this land, and really believed that it could all be mine, I have been at peace. I don't know what will happen, Thérèse. It all seems to be rushing along now as if something greater controls the events." He looked back over his valley again. "But I know that I really have come home."

And so the work started in earnest. True to her word, Alix began that very afternoon to contact people. On Sunday she hitched up her wagon and drove into town to see an old friend and her husband, who had at one time lived on a farm near hers. The husband had a spinster sister named Marie Judith, who had the reputation for being a cook of incredible talent. It was also common knowledge in the village that she and her sister-in-law had a difficult time sharing a kitchen. They all welcomed the news that there was the possibility of a job, and her brother readily agreed to drive her to the château on Monday.

On the return trip, Alix stopped for a moment at the cottage of Madame Gerricault and left behind the green fabric, the illustration, and Thérèse's measurements. The seamstress had recently agreed to make a new wardrobe for the wife of the mayor to take on her trip to Paris, but promised to begin the dress as soon as possible.

In a very short time the atmosphere at the château changed from that of a deserted building to one of a bustling, working estate. Marie Judith was hired immediately, and she agreed to act as housekeeper as well as cook until Henri's Aunt Catherine arrived. In no time she had several young girls busily scrubbing the kitchen from top to bottom and carefully cleaning the grime of years from the walls and floors of the château.

Gaspard had presented to Henri and Bernard a series of workmen whose skills had become apparent immediately. The old barn was torn down quickly and soon a large new barn was rising, big enough to accommodate both the animals and carriage until new stables could be added. Among the workmen were three older men who, Gaspard assured Bernard, were the best wine makers in the region. These men, under Gaspard and Bernard's directions, began carefully pruning the massive tangle of overgrown vines and restoring the vat house.

Alix and Thérèse visited often to see the work as it progressed. When a small kitchen garden was started, Alix hitched up the wagon and brought a large collection of plants from her own farm. She and Marie Judith spent the day planting them and making a list of additional plants that would be needed. Marie Judith had no interest in the garden of medicinal herbs, but Alix did show her one or two that were useful for cooking. Thérèse spent time one day helping one of the young maids as she cleaned the upper stories, and the two had a glorious time snooping through newly delivered boxes, giggling as young women are accustomed to doing.

When Thérèse arrived with a note from her mother for Henri one morning in mid-July, she paused at the edge of the forest, where she could see the estate laid out in the bright summer sun. The change was so dramatic. Now there were people busily moving across the grounds, and in and out of buildings. The sounds of voices and animals could be heard above the sounds of the saws and axes. The château had come alive. And as she stood and watched, Thérèse imagined that this must have been how it looked in the days before the Révolution.

She noticed a wagon coming up the avenue, now cleared and wide, and recognized the face of the dry goods merchant from town. The people of the village had accepted Henri as the comte de St. Vivant with very little resistance. Alix said that too many of them had known nothing but hard times for too long, so that they gladly welcomed someone who could provide jobs, and spend money in their shops.

There were still tales of noises in the night, and two of the workmen refused to stay after dark, fearing the two great owls, one white and one grey, that were seen often in the trees at the edge of the woods. And the maids still found the unexplained bunches of flowers in the house from time to time. But instead of fearing the appearance of the bouquets, they found them a romantic mystery from the past, and had placed a vase on the altar in the chapel to hold them.

Thérèse smiled to herself, finding comfort in the restoration of the great house. She knew that her papa would have approved of Henri and the work that he was doing here.

Remembering her mother's admonition to return quickly, Thérèse forced herself to stop watching the pleasant scene and hastily walked on to the château. A large wagon was in front of the grand entrance, and several workmen were swiftly unloading the contents. Thérèse could see where one of the workmen had been repairing the façade of the great doors, but had laid his tools to one side to help the others. Henri walked out with a sheaf of papers in his hand just as Thérèse was starting up the steps.

His greeting lacked its usual enthusiasm, and he was soon grumbling to her as they entered the château. "I can't believe that there is much else to buy in Paris. Aunt Catherine must be spending every waking hour shopping. And Uncle insists that I carefully check every list to make sure that the shopkeepers have not cheated us on an order. Yesterday I spent hours counting tools and equipment to make sure that we received every item that was listed." The exasperation in his voice was obvious.

"But your uncle is a businessman, Henri, and I'm sure that he just wants you to learn how important details are."

"Yes, but he does not do this. He has a clerk who keeps track of all the small details so that he can conduct the more enjoyable side of his work. Instead of counting spoons, I would rather be out in the fields with Gaspard pruning vines or helping Bernard clean out the vats. This paperwork is just awful," he complained.

Thérèse was about to offer her help when Henri shouted to some workers beginning to carry a chest up the stairs, "Wait! I must find that on the inventory before you take it." He hurried over to check the tag attached to the item, then, after finding it on his list and marking it off, threw the papers on a table near the bottom of the stairs, and declared, "It's time for a break. We have been going at this for two hours and you all need a rest." He directed the workers to go down to the kitchen to get something to eat, then sat at the bottom of the stairs with a forlorn look on his face.

Not sure just what to do, Thérèse decided to sit on a step near him as she tried to comfort him. "You knew that there would be a lot of work, Henri. Soon all of the things will have been delivered, and you won't have to do this anymore."

"But the paperwork doesn't stop here. Uncle wants me to write him constantly, answering his questions about the workers, reporting on whether I have checked the books on the wages that are being paid, providing him with new lists of things for everything from the kitchen pots to how many nails I will need." He looked down at his shoes, and sighed, "I never liked to do inside work, Thérèse. And I hated doing papers for the tutors. Bernard is getting all the fun."

Looking at his disgruntled face made Thérèse want to reach out and smooth his hair in a maternal fashion. But she also knew how just that simple touch would affect her. In the last few weeks she had begun to feel a welling of desire whenever she was with him, and she knew that any attempt to comfort him with a touch would be almost more than she could bear. Instead, she tried to encourage him: "But look at how much you have accomplished. Just look around at this room, and remember how it looked that first day."

Henri lifted his head and took just a moment to gaze around him. The grand entrance was slowly beginning to take on the magnificence that it had known in times past. The doors had been replaced and the floors scrubbed to a shining brightness. The great staircase had been repaired and the broken chandelier removed, waiting for a new one. Amidst the boxes were wonderful pieces of furniture waiting to be settled, and on one wall a huge gilt mirror had been hung. "I guess you are right. There has been so much to do that I haven't taken the time to look at how splendid it is becoming."

"And every day it is getting better, Henri. I know that soon you will be able to show your uncle a fabulous estate and know that your hard work made it happen."

"Yes, well, if things don't change soon, I shall write him and tell him that if he wants all this paperwork done that he can just come and do it himself."

"Come on, cheer up," teased Thérèse. "Tell me what wonderful things have you received since I was last here."

"Just more furniture for the rooms upstairs, some things for the kitchen. There are several big barrels of this china." He walked over to a barrel to hold up a plate bordered in royal blue and gold.

"Oh, Henri, it's magnificent!" Thérèse took the beautiful piece in her hands admiring the fine workmanship.

"Aunt Catherine wrote last week saying that she had found a woman who was so destitute that she was willing to sell off many precious things that had belonged to her family. That china is Sèvres, I believe."

Thérèse laid it carefully back in the barrel. "How sad for the woman, but how nice that she could find someone who was able to buy it."

"Oh, but that is not the best thing." Henri was getting back his old exuberance. "You must come up and see the chest that came in the shipment this morning." Grabbing her hand, Henri pulled her up the stairs to the second floor.

As they hurried toward Henri's bedroom, Thérèse could see everywhere more boxes and several new pieces of furniture. The empty old rooms were taking on a grandness that almost made her feel ill at ease as she compared it to her simple cottage home. For a brief moment, there was something akin to a feeling of sadness inside of her.

In the great bedroom, a large carved canopied bed had been delivered the week before, accompanied by three matching chairs and a low chest. But against one wall she saw the new piece, the most splendid one yet.

"Look at this, Thérèse. Isn't it beautiful! Aunt Catherine sent a note along with it saying that it is supposed to have come from Versailles and belonged to the queen herself. Come feel the fine texture of the wood."

As instructed, Thérèse walked forward and put her hand out to touch the smoothness of the regal cabinet. It was made of a deep red oak, and was as tall as Henri himself. At the bottom were three drawers and at the top a beautifully curved door on either side of an impressive centerpiece inlaid with diamonds of beautifully shaped blue and white Wedgwood. The center of each door had been carefully carved with bouquets of flowers tied by flowing ribbons. The top curved up to an arch capped by a carved crown.

"I'm sure that I've never seen anything so magnificent," murmured Thérèse.

"Oh, but you haven't seen the best part." Henri reached up to one of the Wedgwood pieces, and pushed in. Instantly, the one below it popped out, revealing a hidden drawer.

Thérèse drew closer to see the secret compartment. "But look, Henri, there is something in it."

Henri smiled as he took a small box from the drawer. "Aunt Catherine sent this as a special gift for only me. And I will not use it until I am really proven to be the comte de St. Vivant. But I had to share it with you." Opening the box, he showed Thérèse a matched pair of rings, each bearing the crest of St. Vivant. "There is one for me, and one for the woman who becomes my comtesse." Henri looked into her eyes, adding softly, "And I've only met one woman whom I could ever imagine living here with me."

Thérèse felt the heat rising in her body. Here in his bedroom, near the very bed where he slept, and standing so close to him, she was almost overpowered by desire. Henri turned to place the box back in the drawer. Then, when he turned back and took her in his arms, she could not have held back even if she had wanted to. His masculine scent assailed her senses. Gently he kissed her eyes, then her lips, and she pulled her arms up across his back, returning his caress. Once more he kissed her, passionately, and she was losing herself in his touch, when suddenly the sound of quick steps was heard in the hallway outside.

Quickly Thérèse pulled away from him. She opened one of the

doors of the new cabinet to hide her face. She did not even turn around when the maid came in to tell Henri that Bernard needed him in the vat house as soon as possible. Only after she heard the retreating footsteps did she look at Henri again.

Suddenly she was overcome by embarrassment at having been almost caught in such an embrace in his bedroom. Even as she looked into his face, and saw the eyes that she adored, the lips that she longed for, she knew that she must leave immediately. She could not let her feelings get so out of hand this early in their relationship. Though her body nearly trembled with love for him, she knew that she could not yield to her body's demands.

"Thérèse," Henri put his hand out to her, obviously wanting to take her in his arms again.

"No, Henri. I must go back now. Mama is waiting for me." Suddenly remembering the note that had been the reason for her visit, she pulled the paper from her pocket and gave it to him. "I came to bring you an invitation to dinner this evening. Mama said that you deserve a night off since you have worked so hard. She would like both you and Bernard to come."

Henri looked at her for a moment, and sensing that he must not press her, replied, "We would love an evening out and away from our work. And I will insist that Bernard come with me."

"Until this evening, then." Thérèse looked one last time into his eyes, then turned and hurried out.

WHEN HENRI AND BERNARD ARRIVED at the little cottage in the woods, a delightful scene met their eyes. Since the weather had been so warm, and days were now so long, Alix had decided to set a table outside under a big shade tree. Thérèse, setting a bowl of flowers in the middle of the table, was a picture herself, dressed in softest white with her shining red hair flowing about her shoulders. Alix followed carrying a tray of fruit and cheeses. She had dressed for the evening in a simple gown of yellow banded high at the waist in green and completed with a sheer white shawl crossed as a collar and tucked in at her waist.

Alix greeted her guests with a friendly wave, and showing them to some comfortable chairs, said, "After cooking over the fire it was too hot to stay inside. This shady spot seemed just the place." She poured them each a glass of wine from a pottery jug, then sitting in a chair at the end of the table continued, "Thérèse tells me that you have received even more wagonloads of supplies."

Henri groaned, and Bernard replied with laughter. "Another arrived just as we were leaving. I think that Henri's Aunt Catherine is spending every waking moment in the shops of Paris. Apparently, Monsieur Girond made some simple drawings of the house when he was here several years ago and gave them to his sister. She seems intent on filling every inch."

"But Thérèse tells me that she is sending some very beautiful things. She must be working very hard."

"I don't think that you can use the term 'work' when you are talking about Aunt Catherine and my cousin Camille on a shopping spree. Obsessed is a better description." Henri smiled wryly. "Still, I'd rather they do it than I."

Thérèse had returned with another tray and, after setting it down, commented, "I am surprised that they have found so many things to buy. We seem to get very few goods for sale here."

"Paris is a booming city, Mademoiselle," said Bernard. "There are military reviews and parades almost daily. The rich and fashionable people of society returned long ago. And those with enough money can find anything, or can pay someone to find it for them. Sadly, the provinces farther away have not shared in the country's prosperity."

"St. Vivant thinks that prosperity arrived when you came. The villagers have not felt so hopeful about life in many years." Alix lifted her glass to the men as she continued, "You cannot imagine how just thinking that good times are here will help our people. I thank you for that."

Bernard looked at Henri and said optimistically, "I think, then, that this may be a new beginning for us all."

The dinner that followed was a quiet, restful affair. The hearty meat pie and savory potatoes browned in butter tasted perfect to the hungry men. For dessert, there were fresh berries smothered in sweet cream, followed by coffee and brandy, more fruits and cheese. In the dwindling light they sat and talked of the surrounding farms, and of the people. Alix and Thérèse shared many of the stories about the past that made up the history of St. Vivant. Bernard talked of Bordeaux, and Henri about their life as he grew up. Inevitably, the talk turned back to the work at the château.

"The men that Gaspard brought are very good workers. I never dreamed that the buildings would be repaired so quickly or so well," commented Bernard.

"My husband taught several of those men how to work with wood. They just have not had many chances to use their talents." Alix smiled with pride as she spoke.

"Well, I can't believe how quickly the barn is being raised," added Henri. "And you were wrong about old Gaspard, Thérèse.

He's not crazy at all. A bit quiet, and stubborn about some things. But he seems to know his grapes. One time when I was out there with him among the vines, he started talking about how he trains the plants along wooden rods and I must say that I learned a lot."

"He still frightens me," insisted Thérèse.

"But you know that he is very fond of you, dear, and he was a good friend to Nicholas." Alix reached out her hand and patted Thérèse's as she spoke.

"I admit to being curious about his relationship with the last comte." said Bernard. "He won't say anything about the old days."

Alix considered her words carefully before she answered Bernard. "The past is very painful for Gaspard. He had a very bright future before the Révolution. He became a loyal worker," she paused, struggling for the right word, "almost a friend, to the young comte de St. Vivant, and was very close to another man named Paul who also worked with them. I can only assure you that Gaspard was not involved the night the château was ransacked and the master and mistress killed. Paul disappeared and has never been seen again. After that night, things seemed to get continually worse for poor Gaspard. The mobs who wandered through the countryside killed almost all of the game. The dovecote and pigeonnaire were destroyed. Whereas the old gamekeeper always kept some breeding stock, the mobs slaughtered the animals for spite, feasted on the land, then went on to another town. The crops in the field were tramped down or destroyed and there was no one to organize the planting next year. People had not needed to rely solely on their gardens since the young comte took over from his father, and now there was no one to help the hungry."

"We had some very bad years. And Gaspard seemed to have more trouble than others. He had a wife and two babies, and although he knew a great deal about cultivating the vines, his heart was never in farming. He never seemed to produce enough food to feed them. Then, one really harsh winter, we had a terrible snowstorm. In the middle of it, his wife, whom he adored, became deathly ill. He tried to come here for help, leaving his wife and two little girls behind. But the storm became so intense that he lost his way. When we found him, he was delirious. By the time someone could get back to his cottage, his wife and daughters had frozen to death." Alix paused for a moment, searching for the right words to continue.

"Gaspard thought that somehow he was cursed, with the people that he loved destined to die. And so, for a long time, he completely withdrew from people. Slowly, my Nicholas was able to pull him out of the darkness with which he had surrounded himself. By the time Nicholas died, Gaspard was beginning to understand that these tragedies are a part of life, and that we must go on. He had to find a great deal of strength inside himself to come and work at the château again. I hope that this challenge will draw him back into a fuller life."

"That would explain why he prefers work that takes him off by himself. I thought that he just didn't like people. But even at that I could tell that when he talked with someone about a job, he knew what he was saying. I shall try to draw him out more," said Bernard.

"Just be careful," warned Alix, "as you would be with a wounded bird."

"It appears to me that, except for poor Henri's paperwork, things are going much better than anyone could ever have dreamed," said Thérèse. "And I think that the household staff has done a wonderful job."

"Yes, Marie Judith is a wonderful cook and a vigorous worker, but she commands the poor maids as though she were a general," commented Bernard, laughing. "When her brother and his wife visited last week you would have thought she was the mistress herself."

"She has a strong personality," agreed Alix smiling, "but she also has a heart of gold, and as she begins to feel at home I think that she will become a bit more flexible."

"Well, she has agreed to cook our first dinner party," announced Henri. "Next Sunday. I realized when Thérèse brought the note that we had not had a chance to repay your many kindnesses. So after you left," he looked toward Thérèse as he continued, "I went down and begged her to prepare a luncheon for you on Sunday. She said she didn't have all the equipment for a big event yet, but a party of four shouldn't be a problem. And I told her to use the new china."

"Oh, Henri, you mustn't use it just for us. It is too precious," exclaimed Thérèse.

"No, I have made up my mind. There will never be two more important guests than you, and that is what the best china is for."

"You honor us too much, Henri." Alix smiled as she spoke in her most gracious tone. "But we will accept gladly."

"And now, Henri, we must help these ladies return the furniture inside and say goodnight. You have a wagon to unload first thing in the morning," Bernard added teasingly.

Henri groaned, and the others laughed as they began to place the dishes from the table on trays. Their voices filled the shadowy dusk as they moved across the lawn, and they did not notice the soft hooting of the great white owl as it left a nearby tree and flew through the forest back to its mate.

Before leaving, Henri and Thérèse went out to the barn so that he could return the tools that he had borrowed from them. It was obvious to Thérèse that they had been well cleaned, and Henri carefully placed each one back where it had gone on the wall, checking the positions with Thérèse if he was not sure.

When he finished he turned to look at her in the lamplight and softly laid his hand against her face. "I should not have been so bold today, Thérèse. You are so beautiful, and it seemed so right. But you are a dear friend as well, and I would do nothing to harm our friendship. Are we still friends?"

"Of course, Henri," and standing on tiptoe she gently kissed his cheek.

Through the cottage window, Alix had watched the two young people as they entered the barn, then turned to Bernard. "Henri seems to be growing into this job. I hope all will go well for him."

Bernard frowned as he spoke. "I just wish he would forget about trying to find proof of who he is. There is so much to do, and yet he keeps champing at the bit, saying he must find time to go through the old town records. His uncle should never have asked him to search."

Alix had walked over to the fireplace to place a pewter pitcher on the mantle. As she did so she asked, "And what if there are no records for him to find?"

Bernard looked at her inquisitively, wondering what she meant, what she knew. "I know that the chances are slim. Still, if we can keep him busy enough at the château, maybe his uncle will produce the documents that he needs." He paused for a moment thinking. "One of the maids found a bouquet in the middle of the courtyard this morning. She said it was the on spot where the comte and comtesse died. I will ask Henri to find out who is leaving them and why. Maybe that will do if he needs a mystery. Anyway, as things stand now, his aunt and uncle are keeping him so tied up in paperwork that he will keep busy until Christmastide."

"Do you really think that you will keep him satisfied for so long?" Alix turned to look into Bernard's face as she spoke.

"I guess I will have to try," replied Bernard evenly, looking directly into Alix's eyes. "Georges Girond is determined that he will be confirmed as heir. We are all committed to make it so."

However, it was soon apparent that Bernard's attempt to keep Henri's mind on the business of the château had failed. On Sunday when Thérèse and Alix arrived for luncheon, an excited Henri met them at the entrance. "Come in quickly! I have such good news to share with you!" He took both ladies by the arm to hurry them inside.

"What has happened, Henri?" exclaimed Thérèse.

"Just come in and sit down, and then I will tell you," he said as he guided them to the petit salon. The sound of their shoes could be heard as they walked across the polished floor and into the room.

"Oh, Henri, this room is lovely." Alix looked about at the beautiful furniture covered in a dusky rose damask. The chairs and couches had been grouped about small mahogany tables, creating intimate spots for conversation. On two large cabinets placed against opposite walls great bouquets of flowers had been arranged in porcelain vases. Even though the huge windows were still undraped, the effect was quite impressive.

"I told Marie Judith that I wanted all the crates and barrels piled up in the grand salon and that for today the entrance way, dining room and this salon should look as if people really lived here."

"Then you must compliment her on her work," instructed Alix, "because she has done a wonderful job."

Thérèse could stand this polite conversation no longer and demanded, "Now, tell us your news."

A huge smile came to Henri's face as he spoke. "Well, on Friday I had another miserable day checking off inventory lists. And then a rider came from Uncle Georges with a letter asking for a complete accounting of how far the renovation of the vat house had progressed. I tell you that I was absolutely at the end of my patience. I sent the rider and all of the workmen away, and sat down on the front steps trying to decide what I was going to do.”

“As I sat there I saw a stranger coming up the avenue. He seemed to be looking around the courtyard all the time as he walked closer, very interested in everything. When he finally came to the entrance, he asked me to direct him to the master. I must say that he looked quite astonished when I told him that it was I.”

The women could tell by the tone of Henri’s voice that he had rather enjoyed the man’s surprise.

“Go on.” demanded Thérèse impatiently.

“He introduced himself as Perrin Dubois and said that he was looking for a job. I could tell by his build and rather sallow complexion that he was not a strong person, and so I explained that we had hired as many workmen as we needed right now. But then,” Henri’s voice grew louder as his excitement built, “he explained that he wasn’t a laborer at all, but was looking for work as a secretary. The man is the answer to my prayers!” crowed Henri. “Someone to finally take all of this horrid paperwork off my hands.”

Thérèse clapped her hands with pleasure at her friend’s good luck, but Alix was a bit more skeptical. “Are you very sure that he is capable of doing that kind of work, Henri?”

“Believe me, Madame Condé, as hopeful as I was that he would truly be able to take this burden off of me, I questioned him very cautiously. He told me that he was born right here on the estate. His mother was the cook, a woman called Margaret, I believe.”

“I do remember such a cook,” said Alix. “She had a cottage near here on the estate.” She did not mention the scandalous rumors that she had heard about the woman.

“Apparently, after the Révolution, she fell in love with a soldier and moved to Paris,” said Henri. “Through this soldier, young Perrin came to know an army Captain who was far from home and missed his family. He took a liking to the boy and taught him to read and write. Perrin was quick to learn and soon took over the job of preparing dispatches and receiving equipment for the man as he was promoted to major and then colonel. For the last few years, he has been living in the Spanish provinces and working as the colonel’s personal secretary. But when the man died last year, Perrin decided to come home. At a cousin’s house in a nearby town he heard that someone was trying to get the winery going again and decided to learn if there was a position available."

"And so you hired him!" exclaimed Thérèse.

"First I made sure that he was telling the truth about his ability. I had him read the letter from Uncle Georges out loud, and then I had him go over some shipping documents that were available. Every task he performed with speed and ability."

Alix smiled to herself with approval at his caution, and then asked. "And what does Bernard say?"

"Well, Bernard does not like him. He said he looks like a rat with his black hair and little dark eyes. But even Bernard could not find fault with the answers to all of his questions, and so we hired him. I explained what we were doing at this point, and showed him the library where I have been doing the paperwork and keeping the records. He will use my desk until another arrives. I'm sure Aunt Catherine won't mind having to buy something else." A wry grin came to Henri's face, then he continued. "He went back to his cousin's house to get his things, and will return on Monday. I've told him that he can sleep in one of the little rooms in the attic."

"And so now you can get into the fields with Gaspard and Bernard and do the work that you love," said Alix.

"No, Madame. Now I can begin to ride to the towns and see if there is anyone who can help me find the records that I need."

Alix looked thoughtfully at young Henri. She knew that there was disappointment ahead for him, and was not sure how he would take it. Finding anything in the destruction that had been left behind by the mobs was difficult, and she knew that this task was impossible. But she also realized that he was determined to search, and that no one would turn him back.

The sound of dishes and hurrying feet could be heard from across the hall causing Thérèse to turn to Henri and ask, "And where is Bernard? Is he not going to join us?"

With a hoot of laughter, Henri was quick to answer her. "Oh, he should be along soon. I only sent someone up to wake him a short while ago. However, I'm afraid that he will not be feeling very well when he does join us."

Concerned, Alix asked, "Has he been ill?"

Henri laughed again and said, "Not at all." Then dropping his voice so that he could not be overheard he continued quickly. "I will try to tell you all before Bernard comes down. Yesterday there was a terrible row. In an attempt to befriend old Gaspard, Bernard decided to ask him for some advice about making what little wine we will have this year. It all began pleasantly enough, comparing things like different ways that vines are staked in Bordeaux and here, but soon both men were raising their voices in anger. It seems that there are more than a few differences in how the wines are made between the Bordeaux and Burgundy regions, and it turned into an argument over technique.

"When Gaspard began to explain how the stalks were left with the grapes when they were put into the press, Bernard said that it was just sloppy work and wouldn't be done that way now. Gaspard tried to explain that through the years the growers here had learned that it produced better wines, but Bernard said it sounded like laziness to him. Well, that angered old Gaspard and he shouted that they had been growing grapes here longer than in Bordeaux and ought to know what was best, that the land produced a grape without enough marc – something in the grape solids – so that the stems were needed. Bernard claimed that even if the fields of Bordeaux were not as old, at least they produced a grape with enough marc to do the work.

"Then Gaspard puffed up, with hands flying, to explain that the extra stalks produced a boisterous fermentation that created the rich taste of the Burgundian wine – that even though men then had to go into the vats twice a day to break up the cap, it was worth it in the end. Bernard laughed out loud and said that he proved his point. In Bordeaux the production could be done more leisurely because they were careful not to use anything but the finest grapes. Gaspard shouted that that may have been fine for the dandified wines of Bordeaux where they plant rose bushes alongside the vines, but here they produce a good solid wine that a man could drink. Then Bernard shouted back that he was here just for that reason, to produce a better wine that could be sold, and not something that is only fit for ignorant country louts.

"At that, Gaspard shouted that obviously his expertise was not needed and he quit. Bernard said that was fine with him because he obviously did not know how to make a decent wine. The next thing I knew, Gaspard was storming across the fields and Bernard went stomping down into the cellars."

Thérèse could not believe what she was hearing, and Alix shook her head, her eyes wide with horror as she murmured, "Oh, no."

"But wait," Henri hurried on, "That is not the end of the story. In the late afternoon Bernard began to feel terrible about the argument. He is really a fine person, and realized that his attempt at befriending old Gaspard had gone all wrong. So he asked one of the workmen, Guy, to show him where Gaspard lived. The two left on horses as evening fell and did not return until almost morning. I do not know what the two men said, but apparently all was forgiven and they sat in his cottage drinking until they were both in a stupor. Guy had waited outside until the singing and boasting died down, then had a terrible time getting Bernard on a horse to bring him home. Bernard practically had to be carried to his room, and so I have left him to sleep as long as possible. If I know Bernard he will feel very sheepish when he finally comes down."

Henri's prediction was correct, for a rather subdued Bernard entered the salon a few moments later. He walked carefully over to the two ladies to greet them, then slowly sat in a nearby chair. Alix and Thérèse felt very uncomfortable trying to make conversation, and were relieved when a giggle was heard from the doorway. One of the young maids stood there dressed in sedate black with a small white apron, but with her fluffy brown curls peeking out from her cap. Farther behind, Marie Judith could be seen sternly prompting her.

Finally the girl cleared her throat and in as grand a voice as possible said, "Monsieur, luncheon is served."

9

BY LATE JULY, life had settled into a comfortable routine for the residents of the Château de St. Vivant. Bernard and Gaspard had worked into an easygoing relationship, each concentrating on the area he knew best. Gaspard worked out in the fields that he knew so well, directing the workmen as they trimmed the vines, which had been strangled by years of unchecked growth. Bernard continued the restoration of the vat house and planned the new racks that would be needed in the cellars for the bottles of wine he hoped to produce. There were still times when their raised voices could be heard in heated debate on the merits of the different methods of wine production, but it did not seem to affect their new-found friendship.

Perrin's abilities had lived up to his promises, and he quickly took charge of the large shipments which continued to arrive almost daily. Recently, he had begun to work more closely with Bernard, filling out the long orders for equipment which were then sent to Paris. Although Bernard still did not like him, he came to respect Perrin's ability and appreciate his thoroughness. Thérèse was also uncertain about him. He always seemed to be very polite, never tried to overstep in any way. And yet there was something about his eyes that she didn't like. Henri said that she just was not used to the funny little glasses he wore. But she could not forget the morning when she had been looking for Marie Judith and had seen him come from Henri's rooms. She did not trust the look of uncomfortable surprise that she had seen on his face.

The château itself was becoming ever more grand. Marie Judith, taking great pride in the fact that she was in charge of one of the finest manors in the district, was making herself indispensable in the life of the estate. Her years of frustration at sharing a home with her sister-in-law seemed to be released in a great burst of energy that kept the young housemaids constantly on the run. And yet, Alix had been correct in her prediction. As the weeks wore on and Marie Judith became more comfortable with her authority, she also became kinder rather than stern; she learned to direct rather than demand.

And for Thérèse and Henri, the long summer days included golden hours of gentle conversations, strolls down through the fields to the river bank, picnics in the sun, and moments of companionship that were slowly growing into something greater. In the afternoons, when she had finished her tasks at home, Thérèse would come to the château and sit on the edge of the lawn, watching Henri as he worked beneath the blue and white of the broad Burgundian sky. Always Henri would join her, and with his arm around her shoulder, holding her close, he would watch the workers and share his dreams of the future. Though never mentioned, Thérèse's place in that future seemed to be understood. They were gentle, halcyon days, seeming as if they would never end.

The time would have been perfect if only Henri had been able to forget his need to substantiate his claim to his title. And here Alix's prediction had been correct again. The roving mobs those many years before had been complete in their destruction of anything that would restore the monarchy and the slavery that they felt it brought to their lives. It was not that they knew what to look for, but, because most could not read, they distrusted any paperwork, and had created great bonfires in many towns, simply destroying everything. On those days when Henri went searching for the records of his family or his birth, he was met with the same response; the clerk would love to help the young monsieur, but there was nothing left from those years.

Thérèse thought about this problem as she walked down the road near the entrance to the château one hot dusty day. She had been sent to find some plants in the forest that her mother needed to make a salve, and suddenly found herself in almost the very spot where she had first seen Henri on horseback. She paused to try and remember that first meeting, such a short time ago.

"He has made such a difference in our lives," she thought. It seemed as if he had been there forever, and yet they had only known him for a short time. The whole town had been enriched by the work at the manor. No one made a point any longer about who he really was. They were just so grateful for a chance to work and for his business at the shops that the residents had been more than happy to accept him as whomever he claimed to be. If there were still doubts, they were now spoken only in private.

"Why can't he realize how much good he is doing and just accept it?" In her frustration she had spoken out loud, and the noise had frightened a rabbit, who scampered quickly down the road. As she watched him running down the lane and into the woods, her eyes caught sight of a horse coming toward her, with its owner walking slowly beside it. Suddenly it was just like that first day, only this time she knew who the rider was. And this time there was no air of energy and enthusiasm to envelop her. She moved her basket from her hand to her elbow and folded her arms in front of her as she watched him walk toward her, discouraged and dispirited.

Henri gave a little smile when he saw her standing there, and when he came close enough, stopped and sighed. "Another wasted day, Thérèse."

Standing there in the hot sun, dust on his fine clothes and face, and looking so dejected, Thérèse did not know what to say to him. She put out her hand and touched his arm, saying softly, "Oh, Henri."

He ran his fingers through his hair, then wiping the sweat from his forehead, tried to laugh. "I'm sure I don't look much like the young master at the moment," but when his voice broke at the end, she realized how completely demoralized he was.

"Come," she said suddenly, "I know where you can find the coolest water in the valley." Taking his hand she led him into the woods to her secret place. She tried not to think of the horse's hooves as they crushed the ferns that carpeted the floor. She only thought that she would share her gentle glade with him, the place where she could find peace when everything else failed.

They soon came to the little clearing where she had been that first day before they met. She pointed to a spot on the ground near the little stream as she told him, "Just sit there and rest. I'll wet this cloth to wipe your face, and then you'll feel better." Her voice was almost motherly as she commanded him.

Henri left his horse to wander in the coolness, and looked up at the broad canopy of trees with the soft light of the sun filtering through the leaves. The song of a bird filled his ears, and the smell of the damp earth filled his nostrils. Slowly he felt his muscles begin to relax as he sat on the ground close to the stream, watching Thérèse. She took a cloth from the top of her basket and dipped it into the little brook. Then wringing it quickly, she brought it back to him. "This should make you feel a little better."

He took the cool cloth and wiped his face, then his neck. Looking down at his hands he tried to clean them too. Thérèse saw how dirty the cloth had become from the grime of the road, and taking it from his hands she went back to the water to rinse it out. Carefully choosing her words, she spoke. "You didn't have any luck."

"No. This was the final place. I had heard that a few records were moved from a nearby church to the town hall when the church's lands were confiscated, and I took a chance that there might be something, anything. I had hoped that maybe there had been a priest...." His words trailed off as he sighed, "But I was wrong."

Thérèse looked down at the water as it swirled by and tried to speak gently. "Henri, don't you think that it is time to forget about this search, and just work at making the château the best winery in the region? Bernard says that your uncle did not mean that you must find proof, just that you should send him whatever turned up. The people in the village have accepted you, and your uncle seems determined that you will stay. Can't you just leave it at that?"

Henri looked at her and shook his head. "If only I could, but there are others..." Thérèse could see his hand draw into a fist, and he hit the ground. "I just thought that if I could prove that I was someone...."

"But you are, Henri." She came back and sat close to him on the ground. "You are someone very special." She looked lovingly into his eyes.

He put his hand softly on her face. "Oh, Thérèse, you make me feel so important. I wish you had been there all of those summers when I was growing up."

"But Bernard said that your Aunt Catherine always thought you were the most perfect little boy who ever lived."

"Yes, and it would have been fine, except for the summers when Camille and Gerard came to stay." Henri looked down at the ground, and frowned. "I never told anyone, Thérèse. I just listened to his taunts and told myself that someday I would prove him wrong."

Thérèse ran her fingers softly through his hair and said quietly, "Why don't you tell me about it now, Henri?"

And so he did. He told her about the terrible holidays when Gerard would come to stay and demand that Henri treat him as master. Gerard repeatedly told him that he was a no one, an orphan off the streets, who would do Gerard's bidding when they were grown or be thrown out. And when Uncle Georges' wife, Aunt Louise, was there, it was worse. His uncle had been kind, but his aunt had treated him as if his very presence were an insult and insisted that he be kept out of her sight. That meant that he was not allowed to eat in the dining room with the family when she was there, or go on the outings planned to keep their two children happy over the long summer days.

"Of course, Aunt Louise didn't know that I preferred it that way. I could spend more time with Bernard when she was there and didn't have to see Gerard. And Aunt Catherine always tried to make it up when they were gone. She said that someday things would be different. But I can never forget the taunts of Gerard. 'No one, no name, bastard!'" He paused for a moment, trying to forget the worthless feelings that he had known in those days. "Sometimes Gerard would have friends there for a day. They would chase me like a fox, and tie me to a tree, yelling at me and throwing sticks at me."

He dug angrily at the ground. "That is why there must be proof, Thérèse. Not just a paper some official signs giving me the title. Gerard will then say that it is only mine because Uncle Georges bought it. I must have proof."

Quiet filled the glade. Only the sound of the little stream as it tumbled over the rocks broke the stillness. Now Thérèse understood.

This was more than just a need to find documents. Henri, not his uncle, needed to hold something in his hand and feel that he had a right to be called the comte de St. Vivant. Surely there was someone who could know the truth. Thérèse thought for a moment, then she remembered the scene in the church when her mother had begged Gaspard to go to the château. Her mother had hinted that he knew some secret. Surely Gaspard must know the answer to Henri's questions.

"Henri, do you remember the day that Gaspard came to the vat house for the first time?" Henri looked up and nodded. "He said something about 'not failing him again.' He must have been talking about you, Henri. I'm sure that if you could get old Gaspard to talk, he could tell you most of what you need to know."

"I've tried, Thérèse. He has refused."

"At the château, maybe. But what if you go to his cottage in the woods? Maybe if just the two of you are there you could get him to talk. Tell him why you need to know. Confide in him. He has known so much sadness that maybe he will understand. But be careful, Henri. I have seen him screaming and uncontrolled, and I know that he can be dangerous."

Henri was staring into the forest, his eyes fixed on the quiet greenness. Then a spark seemed to come back into them. "Maybe you're right. I've been trying to look too far from home, and not asking enough of the people who were here." He looked thoughtfully at Thérèse. "That's what I'll do. I'll look for the right moment and ask old Gaspard. I'll find what I need yet."

Thérèse smiled at the old boyish spirit that had returned and said teasingly, "Well then, let me wash that smudge from over your eye before you go, so you'll look like the master should."

She picked up the cloth and reached out to wipe his forehead. As she did so she looked into his eyes.

"My darling Thérèse, whatever would I do without you?" Gently he reached out to pull her to him, and softly he began to kiss her face. He held her close, not demanding, but gently caressing her body, slowly pulling her down beside him on the forest floor. He gently touched the soft white skin of her neck, following it down to the softness beneath the fabric of her blouse.

Thérèse returned his kisses, hesitantly at first. But then she yielded to the passion that raged through her body, demanding satisfaction. She reached out to hold him tightly to her. And there, sheltered by the warm greenness of summer, she learned about the beauty of love.

82

10

THE OLD ENTHUSIASTIC HENRI seemed to return over the next several weeks. And as each day passed, his relationship with Thérèse deepened. He only spoke once of that day in the forest. He held her gently in his arms, and after kissing her eyes, promised that he would not let his emotions get so out of control again until his future was settled and they could be man and wife.

He had a fresh new attitude toward the estate as well. As he spent more time with Gaspard out in the fields, it was almost as if a curtain that had begun to obscure the real person began to lift. He stopped disappearing for long days, instead throwing himself into learning as much as he could about wine production in Burgundy. Not that it was a difficult task; the two worked well together. Gaspard never tired of answering his questions about the fields, the plants, the river, and how the wine had been made in the old days. Many famous wines were produced in the region around St. Vivant. He shared with Henri the excitement that the workers felt as the grapes ripened, and how it had been the privilege of the master of the château to proclaim the Ban de Vendage, the right day to begin the harvest. He told him about the Morvandiaux, people of the Morvan district who used to travel from one estate to another from August through September to help with first the harvest and then the vintage.

Gaspard taught Henri about the times of the year that were so important to the formation of the grapes in Burgundy. He described how a frost in late spring, after the sap began to rise, could ruin the new crop. How heavy rains in early June could wash away the pollen needed to form perfect fruit. Or, if the heavy rains came in September, the fruit could rot on the vine. Equally bad were the times in August when a lack of rain would ruin the balance of acid and sugar in the grapes and create a wine with a hard taste. Henri was like a sponge, absorbing everything that he could learn from the old man.

Henri worked as hard out in the summer sun as Gaspard and the other men. And from the window of the study one day in early August, Perrin watched him as he helped load a wagon with the limbs and branches that had been trimmed from the trees along the edge of the vineyard. A sneer crossed his lips as he watched Henri wipe the sweat from his face. Perrin was determined that he himself would never again need to work that hard.

Turning back to the cool air of the library, which Henri used as an office, Perrin returned to sit at the huge kneehole desk where he had left the papers that he had been reading. However, instead of working, he sat back and smiled to himself. "Perrin, old boy, you've done well," he said softly.

He could not believe his incredible luck. To have walked right in and found a position that would give him the time and opportunities to accomplish his mission was more than he could have wished for in his wildest dreams. And young Henri was so trusting! He had accepted Perrin's story without question, not even checking out the few details that Perrin had offered.

Not that Perrin had lied. His mother had been the cook at the château long before that August night. But the whore had also been more than willing to share the bed of the old comte, or that of any other man who had a spare coin in his pocket. At least there had been the little cottage to live in when he was a child. When she had followed that disgusting soldier to Paris, Perrin had been forced to live in wretched slums while she and her lover drank away the early days of the Révolution.

It had only been by chance, after his mother had deserted him to follow another 'citizen leader' that Perrin had met the officer who would teach him to read. But he had paid a high price all these years for his education. Perrin slowly crushed a sheet of paper in his hands as he thought about the years of disgusting degradation with which he had purchased his knowledge. And when he finally could not take another day of doing 'mon colonel's' bidding, he had felt no remorse in poisoning the man. The officials declared it a death by natural causes and sent the corpse back to France. But Perrin felt it was best to leave Spain immediately, and he suddenly found himself without a job and nowhere to go.

One evening, after crossing the border back into France, while sitting at a table in a roadside tavern and wondering what he should do, his mind turned back to that night so long ago. He could still see the comte and comtesse standing there on the balcony as the day was ending; the mob approaching with the night. They had been softly talking, but he could hear them. And he had never forgotten what he had heard. There was something hidden in the château – probably treasure; maybe gold, and even jewels. What if it had never been found? Should not he, a child of the old comte, have a bit of inheritance?

And that was when he had made his decision. It was strange how simple it had been. He had gone straight to the town near St. Vivant where his mother's family had lived. When his cousin told him about the new young master and his plans to restore the winery, Perrin had thought that probably he had lost his chance. But Henri was so trusting, and so obviously in need of a secretary. He had invited Perrin to move into one of the rooms in the attic without a moment's hesitation. That had been perfect for Perrin, who was now able to use the bright moonlit nights to search the attic. Old Marie Judith snored so loudly that he did not even worry about making noises.

And during the day he had free movement about the house. He had only to say that he was checking on something from an inventory if someone asked, but they never did. He had learned his lesson that day when Thérèse had seen him coming from Henri's rooms. Now he always carried a sheaf of papers with him, and he was more cau tious about the times he chose to search through the rooms. But it had not taken him long to learn the routines of the staff, and he had begun methodically to search for the secret hiding place. He was sure that he would find it soon.

As for now, he had a clean place to sleep, the excellent food that Marie Judith cooked to eat, and a job where he was left to work at his own pace. It would actually be a good job to keep, he thought, if he did not have better plans. He looked at the bills from an exclusive store in Paris where a recent shipment of linens had been purchased. "Soon I shall be able to shop in stores like this as well," he smiled to himself, thinking of the beautiful districts of Paris where he would find a home. Perrin turned to look through the window one last time out at the field where Henri was now standing beside Gaspard as he drank from a skin of water. Then he turned back to the desk and his work.

The time spent in the fields with Gaspard was useful for Henri, but it did not garner the information that he most wanted. On the day when Henri finally went to Gaspard's cottage to ask him about the last days of the young comte's life, he was met with a sorrowful silence. And a look of such pain came into the old man's eyes, that rather than press him, Henri simply went home. In his disappointment he did he not see the gray and white owls following him through the forest.

Thérèse learned about the meeting the next morning. She was coming home from a nearby wood where she had been out early searching for mushrooms before the day became too hot. The beautiful summer had suddenly become unbearable, with the temperature quickly following the sun as it rose high in the sky. As she approached the doors of the barn, she heard her mother and Gaspard's voices coming from inside. She had not meant to eavesdrop, but when she heard Henri's name, she could not help but draw near. Setting her basket on a bench, she listened.

"This is too hard on him, Alix. He must know soon. If you had only seen his face as he pleaded with me to tell him anything."

"And what did you say?" asked Alix.

"I told him that I had nothing to help him. And then I just stared into the fire, trying not to see the scenes of those days again. But I could not help but remember, Alix. Phillipe wanted so much for us all. And we let him down so terribly."

Through the slit where the door met the building, Thérèse saw her mother reach out to place a comforting hand on his shoulder.

"The land means so much to him, Alix. It is not fair to let this go on."

"I know. I had been waiting for the right time, and it never seemed to come. At first I just wanted to see if he would even stay. Then, about the time I realized just what a good young man he is, I saw how well he and Thérèse were getting along. You know that she is not interested in any of the young men who live here, and they seem so right together. I kept waiting, just a little longer. Hoping."

"I understand, Alix. But there is no doubt that they love each other. It's so obvious when they are sitting on the lawn together, talking about the future. He may not know it yet, but I have no doubts."

"I don't know, Gaspard," Alix's voice was heavy with worry. "If only Nicholas were here."

"I know. He and I used to talk about what would happen when this day came. But now he is dead, and for Henri's sake you must do something soon."

Alix looked at Gaspard and shook her head. "He is such a proud boy. If only I believed that he could force his pride to allow an aristocrat to marry a peasant."

At those words, Thérèse stole away as quietly and as quickly as she could. She kept running until she was deep in the woods along the path that led to the château. Only then did she allow herself stop and sit on a fallen log.

She couldn't believe what she had heard. Her mother had known the truth all along. She held the secret to Henri's future and had kept silent. And for what? So that Henri would marry her daughter. She was afraid that when Henri found proof that he was really the heir his pride would keep him from marrying a carpenter's daughter.

"How can she do this to him?" Thérèse cried. A wave of nausea swept across her as she sat in the summer heat. Sitting still for a moment, waiting for the feeling to pass, she tried to gather her thoughts.

Thérèse did not know what to do. Should she go straight and tell Henri the truth? Or should she confront her mother? But she knew that she could do neither. She must not let Henri know that her mother had let him suffer for so long just so that he would be sure of marrying her daughter. And she knew that right now she was not capable of confronting her mother with what she had overheard.

Thérèse wiped the cold sweat from her brow, and continued to think. The heavy August heat seemed to assail her even deep in the forest. She should not have run so hard. Trying to hold her shoulders straight, she breathed deeply and slowly. And soon the feeling passed.

When her head became clearer she realized that she must go and see Henri right away. These last few weeks he had been so happy, sure that soon Gaspard would give him the pieces of the puzzle that he needed to complete the picture of the past. Now he would be devastated, and she must find a way to let him know that all would be well while somehow not telling him about what she had just heard. She must think it all out carefully before she saw him, but she knew that she had to go to him now.

Carefully she stood, and started down the path that she knew by heart. She went slowly, knowing that in this heat she must be more careful.

Henri was not in the usual places, out working in the fields or in the vat house with Bernard. Going into the house, she did not see Marie Judith, and so continued on to the library hoping to find him there. Instead she found Perrin, carefully unwrapping a candlestick that he had taken from the box in front of him. He looked up quickly when he heard her footfalls as she came through the door.

"Mademoiselle Thérèse! I am glad that you have come so early."

"Hello, Perrin. How are you today?"

"I am fine, but I am afraid that Monsieur le comte is not. He seems terribly depressed."

Thérèse sighed. She looked very pale and fragile in the morning light. "I feared as much. Can you tell me where he is?"

"His aunt sent a crucifix for the altar. He took that along with a letter from his Uncle Georges to the chapel."

Thérèse groaned inwardly. Letters from his uncle were always a chore for Henri, and for him to get one today was more than cruel. "Thank you, Perrin. I shall go to him."

Perrin smiled gratefully at her. "That would be just the thing, Mademoiselle. You always cheer him."

Henri was just folding the pages of his uncle's letter when Thérèse found him in the chapel. She could tell by the frown on his face that something had displeased him. And so she put on a cheerful smile. "Good morning, Henri," she said brightly.

Henri looked up from the letter with a grim smile, "I only wish it were a good morning." He laid the letter on the altar, and held his hand out to her.

Thérèse came to him quickly, snuggling into his arms and trying to give him as much comfort as his closeness gave her. Henri kissed her forehead, and then pressed her head to his shoulder.

"Perrin said that your aunt sent something for the chapel. Is this it?" she asked pointing to a heavy crucifix of silver and rosewood.

"Yes, she found it in some shop, covered in dust. The owner said that it came from a famous church and practically gave it to her. Of course she had already spent a fortune on some other furniture there. She found just the pieces that she wants in her bedroom and they arrived on a wagon yesterday. We only found the box with this in it today."

"Henri!" Thérèse looked up into his face. "That means that she will be coming to live here with you soon. I will finally be able to meet your wonderful Aunt Catherine."

Henri looked down into her face, lit by her bright smile. She was so precious to him. He did not want to ever hurt her, and yet he knew that if his uncle's plans were carried out, she would be wounded deeply.

"What is it, Henri? Is she not going to come here?"

Henri pulled away from her and, looking her squarely in the face, told her all. "Yes, she will be coming soon. But there may be someone else coming, Thérèse. My uncle writes to say that he has made some great plans for me. He has found an official in the land registry who says that he can take care of the deeds for me and assures my uncle that he will procure a title to the land that will stand up in the courts."

Thérèse listened to his words, knowing how he hated their very sound, but also knowing that he must not lose hope. "I know that it is not what you want, Henri, but if it will allow you to stay and live here, to keep the land, then maybe it is worth a try." Thérèse tried to make her voice as soothing as possible. "And there is still the chance that something will turn up here." she added.

A bitter laugh filled the little chapel. "I've stopped believing in miracles, Thérèse. I went to see Gaspard last night, and if he knows anything he's not going to tell anyone. Anyway, everything was probably destroyed just like all those people tried to tell me. I just didn't want to believe them. Still, I won't go on like a fool forever."

"At least your uncle plans to see to it that you can stay." she said softly.

Henri forced himself to stand away from her and face her directly as he spoke. He knew that if he continued to hold her close he would never be able to tell her the rest.

"But there's more, Thérèse. It seems that he has also tried to track down some of the St. Vivant money that might have been left in banks or trusted to someone. He said that since there doesn't appear to be any money left in the St. Vivant name, that he has taken steps to provide me with enough capital to make the winery successful. It seems that he has found a rich old Marquis with an unmarried daughter who is an only child and looking for a husband. You would love the way Uncle Georges puts it."

Henri reached out and picked the letter up off the altar and read to her. " 'She is greatly lacking in both appearance and temperament, but I am sure that when you learn the details you will agree that her dowry and inheritance will make up for any problems that could arise from the other.' Mon Dieu! As if I could ever be happy with anyone else but you!" he cried.

Thérèse felt the blood draining from her face as he read the words from the letter. His uncle had found someone for him to marry. What would happen to her? She put her hand to her stomach, and tried to force herself to be logical. She would just have to convince her mother to bring out whatever proof that she had right away. She didn't know how, but she would put a stop to his uncle's plans. The sooner the better.

"How soon will you know if she agrees to this marriage?" Thérèse forced herself to speak.

"He said that she is out of the city because of the heat and he does not expect her to come back until September. I guess that I will know then."

Thérèse sighed with relief when she heard that there was so much time. "Then all will be well, Henri. Trust me." She reached forward to put her arms around him.

But she found Henri unresponsive, and he pulled away. "I wish I had your faith, Thérèse, but I don't see how you can believe that this will work out. My uncle is determined that I will marry money. And short of giving all of this up, I don't know how to get around his wishes."

The tortured look on Henri's face told Thérèse that this was not the time to press him, so she said simply, "You must believe me, Henri. It will work out."

Henri put his hand gently on her face, then spoke softly. "I need to be alone to sort through all of this, Thérèse. Can you understand?"

Thérèse nodded, gave him a gentle kiss and a smile, then left him standing in the hazy light that filtered through the leaded windows into the chapel.

They had not known that Perrin was listening at the chapel door, and he had hurried back to the library by the time Thérèse walked swiftly down the hallway. Perrin put down the candlesticks that he had been carrying in case anyone saw him near the chapel. Then he walked swiftly to one of the windows to watch her leave.

So, Uncle Georges is going to have the papers forged to prove that Henri is the heir, thought Perrin. This must mean a lot to the old man. And what if Perrin were to find the real documents first? He wondered what price they might fetch in Paris, what reward from the uncle. As he looked from the window he was surprised to see Thérèse stop at the corner of the barn. She seemed to hold on to the building to steady herself, then she was violently sick. After a moment, she raised her head, and after gently touching her stomach, was able to continue.

She must be catching something, thought Perrin. But then suddenly he thought back to some of the camp followers who traveled with the army, and how they would unexpectedly become sick, in just the same way and often in the morning. Then they would visit an old gypsy woman, he remembered, and return to their business soon after.

A suspicion began to grow in his mind. No wonder she had seemed so distressed when Henri said that his uncle had marriage plans for the little man, thought Perrin. A pity that she was in love with the boy. He could use a beautiful country girl like her to keep his bed warm. Maybe she would be available to him if this fancy marriage came to pass. Perrin ran his tongue over his lips as he thought about her youthful body next to his. His years with the colonel had not diminished his desire for women, and she would do just fine.

That night, as Thérèse was brushing her hair, her mother came into her room and sat on her bed. This was their first chance to talk together since Thérèse overheard her conversation with Gaspard earlier in the day. When she returned from the château, Thérèse had found a note from her mother saying that she had gone to a nearby farm to care for some sick children. She had only returned a little while earlier, and had eaten the small meal that Thérèse had saved for her.

"Are the Larousse children going to be all right, Mama?"

"I don't know, Thérèse. I took some tonic to them, and steamed some herbs for them to breathe. But it does not look good. Several years ago there was a sickness that was similar. You remember, that is when the Rolin twins died, and several others. This looks to be the same, and I am frightened that it may only be just starting."

Thérèse put down her brush and turned to her mother. "Can you do anything to make it better?"

"Not really. Except to tell people to avoid anyone who is sick, and hope that it will not spread. I have told Michael Larousse not to let anyone in the farmhouse until I tell him otherwise."

Alix looked closely at her daughter and added, "You don't look very well yourself, Thérèse. Are you all right?"

"No, Mama," she answered quite frankly, "I am sick with worry about Henri." And with that she poured out the story of how his uncle was going to force him to marry someone else if he didn't find something to prove that the estate was his soon.

Alix listened quietly until Thérèse was finished, then asked softly, "And would he mind so much if that happened? You have not told me that he has committed himself to you."

"Of course he hasn't, Mama. He wanted to be the unquestioned owner before he spoke. But I know that he loves me. And Mama," Thérèse looked directly at her mother, "I know that I love him. I don't think that I could ever love anyone else in the same way."

"There was Gilbert." Alix hesitantly reminded her.

This brought a small sad smile to Thérèse's face. "It was not the same, Mama. We were both so young."

Gilbert had been the only young man in the village that Thérèse had been really attracted to. They had been good friends when they were young, and he had a beautiful singing voice. He had worked with Nicholas for a time, and began to feel like a member of the family. Sadly, he had been conscripted, and three years ago word had come that he had been killed in battle.

Alix stood and walked over to the window. She drew back the curtain and looked out into the night, bright with the light of a nearly full moon. No one could imagine how difficult these years had been for her, especially without the counsel of her dear husband. It was as if the weight of all that happened so long ago rested completely on her shoulders, causing her to sigh. But, now finally, the time had come. As soon as she could find a free moment she would have to get the shovel and begin to dig at the south side of the barn. "Nicholas, I need you," she thought. He had been the one to bury the packet, and now she would have to find it alone.

She turned back to her daughter, and then assured her, "If you truly love him, then you will just have to believe that everything will work out." She walked back to where Thérèse was standing and laid her hand against her face. "Just as I found my Nicholas, you must have faith that Henri will be yours." Alix kissed her, then said brightly, "Now you must get to bed. I promised Madame Gerricault that you would come tomorrow for a fitting for your new dress."

Alix waited while Thérèse climbed into bed, then blew out the candle. Before she could leave, however, Thérèse asked, "Mama, why weren't you there the night the young comtesse's baby was born? You have always attended at birthings for as long as I can remember. Didn't she want you there?"

Alix hesitated for a moment before she spoke. "I was pregnant with my own dear baby at the same time, Thérèse. And unlike the comtesse, whose pregnancy was easy, I had lost two children already and had to spend most of the time in bed to keep from bleeding. I was older than she was, you see. There was no way that I could have gone to the château to help her. I did send Nicholas, with a bag filled with herbs and salves to try to make the time go more easily for her."

"So, you did know her well, Mama?"

"Yes, Thérèse, I knew her very well."

"And did her baby die that night, as everyone believed?"

Alix's sigh could easily be heard in the quiet darkness. "No, Thérèse, her baby did not die."

Thérèse's whole body filled with joy. The baby had lived. Henri must be the one! Everything would be perfect, she had only to wait. There were a million questions that Thérèse wanted to ask her mother, but sensing that this was not the moment, she said simply. "Thank you, Mama."

"Good night, my dear," her mother answered.

"Good night, Mama."

Thérèse lay quietly in bed, a thousand thoughts swirling through her mind, her heart ready to explode with excitement. Her head was too full of thoughts to allow her to sleep. And she did not pay attention to the hooting of the small grey owl in the old tree outside her window.

11

SLEEP CAME LATE FOR THÉRÈSE THAT NIGHT. And Alix, suspecting that the girl had spent most of her night thinking about Henri, let her stay in bed as long as possible the next morning. When she finally called to Thérèse to get up, the sun was high in the sky, and the heat already beginning to rise.

Thankful that her mother was outside hitching the wagon, Thérèse sat up slowly, carefully eating a few bites of bread from the tray which her mother had left by her bed. Then she wrapped the rest in a napkin to nibble on later in the day. After she wiped her face and neck with a cool towel, she dressed. Thérèse was just walking out to join her mother when she saw a farmer ride up, speak briefly to Alix, and then ride away.

Alix strode swiftly to the cottage door, saying, "You will have to take the wagon to Madame Gerricault's alone. The sickness has spread to the Rolin farm, and I must go there immediately." She went to a cupboard and hastily began to fill a bag with the packets and jars. "When you get there, make very certain that Madame has not been ill before you go inside. Then you must come straight home. If this spreads I will need a larger supply of medicines than I have prepared."

Alix closed the satchel, and began to give Thérèse instructions on which herbs to gather, telling her exactly what to do with each one. Then with a quick kiss she added, "Thérèse, you must be very careful not to go near anyone who might be sick. I will return sometime this evening." She left without further delay, heading down one of the forest paths.

Left on her own, Thérèse went back inside the cottage to get her bonnet, then climbed into the wagon and headed the horse toward the road. The day was heavy with the heat and humidity of August. Above, the sky was a hazy blue. Looking at the clouds beginning to build in the west, Thérèse thought, 'There will probably be a terrible storm before night, but at least it will bring some cooling relief.'

Sitting alone, high on the wagon bench, she could not help but feel disappointed that her mother was not there. She had hoped to ask her a thousand questions about the poor comte and his wife, trying to learn something more that she could share with Henri. Still, she could not wait to tell him what she had learned last night. The baby had lived! He was truly the comte de St. Vivant.

Arriving at the Gerricault cottage, Thérèse went to the door and knocked, calling Madame's name loudly as she did so. A cheery little face framed by the white lace of her cap looked from a window above.

"Madame, it's Thérèse Condé. Mama could not come because of the sickness that is going around, and I have come alone."

"But if your mama is ill I cannot let you come inside either. I do not want to catch it."

Thérèse put her hand up to shield her eyes from the sun as she looked up at the little old lady. "No, Madame Gerricault, Mama is not sick. She is just too busy taking care of those who are to come with me today."

"That is different then. And you are sure that you have not been sick?" quizzed the woman.

"Yes, Madame."

"Well then, the door is open. Let yourself in." And with that the little face disappeared inside.

Thérèse opened the door and walked into the welcome coolness of the small stone cottage. It took a moment for her eyes to adjust to the dimmer light, and by that time Madame Gerricault was there, showing her to a chair.

"My, my. It has been such a long time since I have seen you, my dear, that I would not have recognized you at all. You have grown into quite a lovely young woman."

"Thank you, Madame," murmured Thérèse.

"No, I would never have known you for Alix Condé's daughter at all. You don't look anything like her, do you?"

"No, Madame. I think that I must look like my father's family."

"Well, your face does look familiar. Old Madame Condé, your grandmother, has been dead a long time. But I cannot say that you look much like her either." The plump little woman looked critically at Thérèse. "Maybe around the eyes a little. And you have your father's height." Then she shook her head and smiled. "But no matter. Come, my dear, I know that you must be dying to try on the dress," and she led Thérèse into a back room where she did her work.

The dress, which had been carefully pressed, hung on the dressmaker's form. It was just as she had dreamed. Thérèse reached out to touch the soft green cloth, to run her fingers down the line of the sleeve.

"It is so beautiful, Madame Gerricault."

"I must say that it is as lovely a piece a cloth as I have seen in a long time. And the style should be perfect for your figure." Madame shook her head, thinking how long it had been since she had possessed a figure slim enough for a dress like that. "Come along, dear, you need to try it on."

Thérèse stripped down to her cotton chemise, then the seamstress helped to lift the dress over her head. It had a low, square neckline, and long narrow sleeves. The skirt was fitted under the bosom, then fell softly to the floor. Thérèse looked into the long mirror at one side of the room and wondered at the woman who looked back at her.

"I am sorry that it is so warm today, but I will try to measure the hem quickly. And I just have to check the fit in a few places." She began to pull and tug here and there to check the seams. As she pulled the dress closed in the back, Thérèse heard a little gasp of exasperation. "This can't be," Madame Gerricault said to herself; then she pulled the dress closed again. The tightly fitted bodice would barely close. "My dear, your mother's measurements must have been wrong. I know that I checked them carefully, but still the bosom is too tight."

Thérèse looked at her reflection in the mirror and thought quickly. "Oh, Madame. It must be that time of the month when the breasts and stomach swell. I just did not think about it when Mama told me to come today."

"Humph," snorted the lady. "Maybe so. But I will try to make the bodice a bit larger anyway. Thank goodness the skirt does not fit so closely." She pinned and marked a bit longer, then knelt to mark the hem. When she had finished she sat back on her heels and looked up. "Yes, the color is perfect for you. Your mother knew what she was doing." She stood slowly then added. "I know that it is hot today, but you must try on the Spencer as well."

The short jacket with its high collar and military braiding for trim was perfect. After seeing herself in the mirror, Thérèse could not help but turn to the little woman and give her a hug. "Oh, Madame, you are wonderful!"

"Nonsense, my dear. Just doing my job." But she was obviously pleased at Thérèse's response. She worked a little longer, commenting, "I'll let this jacket out a little as well, just to make sure." Then she helped Thérèse to take the dress off.

As Madame Gerricault turned to put the dress back on the form, Thérèse sat carefully down in the little chair. She was glad that Madame was chatting away as she worked on the dress, so that she would not notice Thérèse's behavior. Standing so long in the tight fitting dress had begun to make her feel faint, and she could not have worn it one moment longer. After a moment, when she was feeling better, Thérèse began to put her old clothing back on.

"I have not made the chemisette yet because the material has not come. But you will love it, my dear. Alix let me order a truly lovely bit of cloth to use."

The two chatted for a little longer, discussing the things that were happening at the château, the sickness that had appeared in the village, and of course the weather. Then Thérèse explained that she needed to gather herbs for her mother's medicines, and left.

Madame Gerricault watched the wagon as it pulled away, then went back to her sewing room to work a little longer. What a nice girl, she thought. And so sweet to try and cover her mother's obvious mistake. Madame shook her head in frustration. She had tried to get Alix to bring the girl in from the very first so that she would be sure to have the right measurements.

She knelt down to finish pinning up the hem. It had been a long time since she had worked for a young woman with such a lovely figure. Not since the young comtesse, must be some twenty years before, she thought. Now there had been a beauty! She sat back on her heels, and looking up at the dress remembered back to the days when she had worked at the château, and saw again the face of the kind young woman. Suddenly she gasped.

"It cannot be!" she said out loud. "Mon Dieu, but it cannot be!" She got to her feet and moved to the little chair, sitting in stunned amazement and wondering if her old mind was playing tricks on her.

It took the rest of the afternoon for Thérèse to gather the various herbs that Alix needed. The heat was so oppressive that she had to stop often. At one point she went to the bench in the shade under the old tree to rest and think. She would have to speak with her mother soon. Enough time had passed that Thérèse had been suspicious, but the recent bouts of nausea had convinced her. She had not thought anyone would notice so soon, but the incident at Madame Gerricault's made her realize that she could not wait much longer. And maybe her mother would have a potion that would make the bouts of nausea and faintness go away.

And what of Henri? Thérèse thought back to that afternoon in the forest, and knew that he would be surprised. But she had no doubts about his love for her. Placing her hand on her stomach in a maternal way, she dreamed about the time next spring when they would be living in the château with their own little baby.

The unbearable heat continued to rise, but though the afternoon passed, the storm never broke. Sweat poured down her body as Thérèse worked at the table in the kitchen preparing the herbs just the way her mother had instructed. It was not until long after dark when Alix finally returned. A rider had come to the Rolin cottage with word of another farm where she was needed. She would be leaving at first light next morning.

The two women worked swiftly together. Thérèse fixed her mother a meal, while Alix mixed medicines and prepared her bag for another day. She was obviously exhausted, and went to bed soon after eating. Thérèse cleared away the dishes, then spent a restless night trying to sleep on quilts on the floor near the windows in the kitchen. She had decided that her bedroom upstairs was too much like an oven for her to spend the night there.

When Thérèse was awakened next morning by the rooster

reminding her that he was hungry, her mother was already gone. She found a note from Alix saying that she might not be home until the next day and again leaving a list of herbs that she would need.

Going out to care for the animals, she saw the sky filling with low gray clouds. She had just enough time to care for the animals in the barn, and gather a few ripe vegetables before the storm broke.

Thérèse ran to the cottage just as the first drops of rain began to fall. Minutes later the rain pounded on the roof and as the storm worsened, the rolling sound of thunder filled the sky. Thérèse stood at the door feeling the cooling air that came with the rain, and watching the awesome wonder of the storm clouds blowing by.

In the afternoon the rain lessened, and at times was gentle enough for her to go out and check on the animals. By evening, it had stopped. Thérèse was able to return to her bedroom on the upper floor that night. The rain had left a cooling breeze, and Thérèse lay in bed planning what she would do the next day.

But when she awoke the next morning the rain had begun again, this time a steady drenching downpour. After completing her house-keeping chores, Thérèse sat down near a window to do needlework and watch for her mother. Alix was often gone overnight when she was needed to care for the sick. Once she had been gone for three days when she was called to an exceptionally long birth. The poor baby had died, and Alix had been depressed for days afterward. Thérèse hoped that this illness would not be one that took many lives.

In the early afternoon, as she tried to read, she noticed a movement along the edge of the forest. She hopped up to look from the window more clearly, but was disappointed when she found that, instead of her mother, it was a rider on horseback slowly moving toward the cottage.

The horse pulled up and the man dismounted to walk to the door. Though he was covered in a coat and hat to keep the rain off, Thérèse recognized him as Albert Thierry, from a farm on the other side of the château.

Thérèse quickly opened the door to ask him in, but was cut short by his appearance. His face was deathly pale, and covered with sweat, his eyes had the exhausted look of a man using his last drops of energy. Thérèse was torn between her mother's words of warning and the realization that to heed them she would have to leave an obviously sick man standing in the rain.

After only a moment's hesitation she insisted that he come in and sit to rest. Too tired to remove his coat, his wet clothes dripped on the floor as he sat near the fire. She gave him a cup of warm sweet tea that she had brewed only a little while earlier, and the warmth seemed to give him a little more strength.

"Is your mother here, girl? I need her to come to my farm right away. My mother and son are deathly ill, and my wife said that only Alix knows what to do." His voice was weak and breathless as he spoke.

Thérèse explained that her mother was gone to another farm, and she did not know when she would return. "But I will tell her that you need her as soon as I can," added Thérèse. "And mother said to give anyone who came this mixture to brew up a tisane for the sick ones. Have them drink it until she can get there." Thérèse gave him two packets of an herbal mixture and explained how to prepare them.

The farmer got to his feet and thanked her, then headed toward the door, his shoulders drooping as he shuffled along. Before leaving, he turned to thank her again.

"Ride with care, Monsieur Thierry, and make sure that you drink some of that medicine yourself. Your family will need you." She watched him get slowly on the horse and ride away, then went back to the window to sew and watch for her mother.

The rain slowed as the day drew on, and finally stopped about four in the afternoon. Thérèse was outside caring for the animals when Alix returned. It was obvious to the daughter that her mother was exhausted, and so, without mentioning the earlier visit, Thérèse took the bag from her and insisted that she go inside immediately.

Water was put in a kettle to boil while Thérèse went to the cupboard to prepare some food. With a tired voice, Alix told her how the sickness seemed to be spreading, taking its worst toll on the old and the children. "Many of the adults have had the fever before and will not catch it now, or something in their bodies keeps them from getting it. But the young ones are not so lucky, and the old ones do not have the strength to fight it. I have always wondered why that is so, Thérèse." Her voice seemed to fade as she spoke, and she closed her eyes to rest them for a moment.

When the tea was ready, Thérèse gently shook Alix's shoulder, then placed the cup on the table in front of her. She added a plate of meat, cheese and bread, with a bowl of fruit nearby. While her mother ate, she told her of Albert Thierry's visit.

"You should not have let him inside, Thérèse! This is not a thing to trifle with." Alix's voice was stern. "I have already sent a note to Henri suggesting that he tell the workers to go home and not return until they are notified. Somehow this illness spreads, and the best thing is for people to not get close to others until it is over."

"But I could not leave him out in the rain, Mama. And he was only inside for a moment." Trying to reassure her mother, Thérèse decided that it was probably best not to tell Alix that she had also given him a cup of tea.

Alix sighed, then spoke. "Still, you did the right thing giving him the medicine. I want you to mix some up and drink it as well. Since I must wait to see what effect it will have on his family, I think that I will rest for a while." Her voice seemed to get fainter as she spoke, and she would have fallen asleep in the chair right then if Thérèse had not insisted that she go on to bed.

As she put away the food, Thérèse noticed that her mother had eaten very little. "Poor Mama," she said out loud. Alix had been so very busy these last few days. Thérèse had not dared to ask her any questions about Henri's family, and felt selfish even thinking about wanting her mother to herself. There would be time to talk later, to tell her Mama everything. But for now she felt frustrated by events. It was as if she had been given a taste of nectar, and promised more, but never allowed the time to drink.

Later that night, after she had prepared for bed, Thérèse blew out the candle, then leaned out of her open window. The moon could be seen clear and strong between the clouds blowing quickly by. Thérèse listened to the soothing call of an owl. For many years she had thought of them as her owls, and she looked out trying to see either the great white owl or the smaller grey one that had always been a part of her life. She listened for their soft "hoo, hoo," and hoped for a better day tomorrow.

THE CHEERFUL SOUND OF SINGING BIRDS awakened Thérèse the next morning. Even before she opened her eyes she could sense a fresh newness in the air. The brightness of the morning sun greeted her, and the cool air that had been left when the rain moved on filled her room. A soft breeze was blowing through the windows, rustling the white lace curtains. Thérèse stretched her arms high above her head, then ran her fingers luxuriously through her hair before sinking back down into her pillows.

It was amazing how the cleanness that came after a summer storm could make everything seem better, she thought. Despite the terrible sickness spreading through the countryside and the threat of an arranged marriage for Henri, a surge of optimism spread through her. Her spirits seemed buoyed on a high riding wave.

Henri! Thérèse counted the number of days that had passed since she had seen Henri, then decided immediately what she would do. As soon as she finished her morning tasks, she would take a basket of fresh vegetables and fruit and go to him. 'With so many of the workmen gone until the sickness passes, he should have plenty of time for me,' she thought contentedly.

A shadow passed over her thoughts as she made her plans. Alix would not want her going to the château right now. But deep inside, Thérèse was confident that Henri was not sick. And if he were, shouldn't she be there to care for him? "In fact," she said aloud, "I should take some of Mama's herbal drink to keep him well. And I shall take enough for Marie Judith and any one else who has stayed."

Seeing herself as an angel of mercy, she sat up and completed her plans. The plaintive call of the cow needing to be milked finally forced Thérèse out of her bed. She got up slowly and made her way down the stairs to put a kettle on to boil for tea.

Looking for some bread to nibble on, she found a note that Alix had left. Poor Mama, Thérèse thought, she will be sick herself if she is not careful. The note reminded Thérèse of some tasks that needed to be done and warned her not to expect Alix to return that night, and maybe not the next. Thérèse walked over and laid the letter on the table where her mother mixed her potions and medicines. At times, the help that Alix gave to the people on nearby farms was very demanding, but Thérèse knew that she would not have it any other way. Had she been a boy, Alix probably would have become a doctor like her father and brother.

The bellowing of the cow, more demanding this time, reminded Thérèse that she needed to get started. "I'm coming. I'm coming," she said as she went back up the stairs to dress.

All of her work was finished by ten, but it was another hour before Thérèse headed down the woodland path that led to the estate. A sweet smell from the flower water that she had splashed on after her bath surrounded her like a cloud. She had carefully chosen a soft dress in a light shade of blue, which she held up as she walked so that the hem would not get wet from the dampness left by the rain. Her auburn tresses were tied up with a ribbon, and she hummed to herself as she made her way through the forest.

At the edge of the fields, she stopped to appreciate the peaceful scene that lay before her. A soft blue sky framed the towering trees as they swayed in the breeze. Neatly trimmed clusters of grapevines, lush and green, gently sloped down toward the river where a barge was floating by. The château gleamed in the sun, washed clean of the dust that had begun to settle everywhere from the dry August days. Softly walking across the lawn to the entrance, Thérèse realized that she agreed with Henri about the estate. It felt like home.

There was no answer at the door, so Thérèse let herself in. She called out, first to Henri and then to Marie Judith. Receiving no answer, she walked partway up the staircase and called again. Her voice echoed against the high ceiling, but no one replied. Undaunted, she decided to check the library and the chapel before looking in the kitchen below. The house was eerily silent, her soft shoes on the polished floor the only audible sound.

As she walked down the hall leading past the study, she was relieved to hear a voice and something sliding across the floor. Thinking it was Henri, she hurried to the door and playfully knocked, calling out, "Hello, in there!"

Startled, Perrin looked up from a box filled with books with a surprised look on his face. "Mademoiselle, when did you get here?"

"Oh, Perrin. I'm sorry I startled you. I did not get an answer at the door, and came looking for someone."

"Well, I am afraid that I am the only 'someone' here at the moment," he said testily. Laying the books back in the box, he walked toward her. "Everyone left after your mother's note came. Even Marie Judith has gone to her brother's house, leaving me to cook for myself. There is only one old stable hand still here and that because he has no where else to go. At least I won't have to care for the animals as well."

"But where are Henri and Bernard?"

"A letter came from Monsieur Girond and the two of them left immediately for Paris, the night before the storm began, I think." Perrin snorted with disgust. "Of course, no one thought of poor Perrin being left here alone to care for the huge estate without any staff."

Trying not to show her worry in her voice Thérèse asked evenly, "Do you know why they had to go so suddenly?"

"I can only tell you that they said they must go right away."

"Then, did Henri leave me a note or something?"

Little fool, thought Perrin. And almost cruelly he told her, "No, he did not mention you at all before he left, Mademoiselle."

"Did he say when he would return?" She could feel her voice tightening with fear as she spoke.

"They should be gone at least a week, Mademoiselle," he replied evenly, but with a malicious note in his voice.

Determined that her distress would not show, Thérèse forced a smile as she held the basket toward him. "Then I'll give these to you. There are just a few tomatoes and pears, and some other things.

Maybe they will keep you from starving while the staff is gone." Remembering the other reason for her visit she added, "There is also an herbal mixture to brew in hot water to keep you from getting sick."

With a cynical look on his face Perrin thanked her, adding, "After being with the army for so long I've seen just about every sickness that exists. I don't tend to catch anything anymore."

When he finished speaking a silence filled the air. Suddenly feeling uncomfortable at the thought that she was alone in the great house with Perrin, Thérèse turned to leave. As she did she said brightly, "Well, I must get back to the cottage in case someone comes looking for Mama."

Perrin walked quickly passed her to the door and barred it with his arm. He smiled at her, enjoying her discomfort, and said silkily, "Are you sure you can't stay and keep me company for a while? I feel very lonely here all by myself. And we haven't had much of a chance to get to know each other."

"I..., I really can't stay, Perrin." Thérèse forced another smile. "But I'll try to come visit you again, and I'll bring you some real food when I do."

Perrin stared at her for a very long, uneasy moment, then lowered his arm so that she could leave. Raising his eyebrow, he said pointedly, "I'll be looking forward to your visit then, Mademoiselle."

Thérèse said a quick goodbye. Trying not to run, she hurried down the hall and left.

He watched her go, then sneered as he laughed to himself. "I'm sure that you will hurry back to see me as soon as you can. I have only to await your pleasure." Shaking his head, he frowned as he went back to his work.

There were several boxes of books on the floor near the desk. They had been delivered some time ago, but Perrin had been so busy writing lists of equipment to order for Bernard that he had not had time to inventory them and place them on the shelves. With the house empty it seemed like a good time to do the work. Perrin picked up another stack and took them to the desk. But instead of sitting down, he went to the window to look out over the fields and think.

Suddenly he slammed his fist against the wall near the window and screamed, "Why? Why can't I find it? Why?" He put his hands to his forehead and closed his eyes to think. There could not have been a better time for him to look. No one was here! He had been free to search the house from top to bottom until late in the night. But there was nothing. He had not been able to find any false panels. He had pushed or pulled every piece of decorative molding in the entire house. He had tried every loose floorboard, looked carefully through every storeroom, both in the attic and the basement.

He had even overcome his superstition and searched through the chapel. But the entire time that he had probed and prodded in there he had felt as if he were being watched. Once he even thought he heard the sound of breathing coming from near the Virgin's statue. But although he had only given it a cursory inspection, he had not run. And still there was nothing.

He was certain that something was here. He remembered her words: "the things you have hidden," she had said. Perrin raised his head and looked out over the fields. A grim look came to his face. "What if they are buried somewhere on the grounds?" he thought. That would be an impossible task. Only the person who had hidden the treasure would be able to find it outside. Or someone who had been told where it was. "And if it was old Gaspard, he has probably taken it and hidden it somewhere else," he said to himself.

At least he had a comfortable job for the present. And maybe if he kept looking someday he would find whatever the treasure was. Despondent, Perrin walked back to his desk and sat down to check the books off of the inventory lists that had come with the shipment.

But as he worked, his mind kept going back to the frustration that he felt. Angrily he picked up the books and walked over to the end shelf to put them away. His temper finally got the better of him. "Damn!" he shouted and he slammed the books against the wood at the end of the shelf.

And that was all it took. Not having worked for so many years, the secret latch had rusted a bit, and did not work smoothly. But the force of the books hitting the right panel had jarred it loose, and the wall next to it swung open. Perrin stood still, staring at the opening in complete amazement. Then a sound bubbled up from his throat, almost the sound of a demented laugh. His eyes lit up, and Perrin danced around the room, his hands held high.

"I found it, I found it, I found it," he sang in a high little voice.

Then he stopped his dance as abruptly as he began it, and realized that the space behind the wall could be empty. Quickly he lit a candle and, pulling the wall as wide as it would go, looked in.

The space was small, and seemed filled with paintings. Carefully he began to move them, one by one, out of the space while looking for the gold and treasures. He leaned them against the bookcases and went back for more. After moving the pictures he found some shelves that seemed to hold silver trays and flatware. There even seemed to be some old books, which he took out and opened carefully, thinking that they were hollow and might hold the treasure.

But there was no pouch of gold. No box of glittering jewelry. Only books, and old paintings and trays. Disgusted, Perrin came out of the little space, wiping his hands together to get some of the old dirt off of them. There was not even a packet of papers containing the old deeds. And the books had nothing to do with the family. They just looked to be fancy old tomes in Latin.

Disappointed, Perrin walked over to the desk to get a cloth that he used to wipe off items as they came from the packing crates. Slowly cleaning his hands, he leaned against the desk, and looked back at the section of wall hanging out into the room at an angle, and at the paintings up against the bookcase nearby.

"So there's not any gold, old man," he sighed to himself. "But it's not a complete disaster either." His mind, the mind of a survivor, began to go to work. The silver could be pawned. And maybe the paintings were by someone famous. If not, he might be able to sell them to Henri's uncle, so that the boy could have some ancestors on the wall. "I'll have a home in Paris yet," he said with confidence.

Taking the cloth, he walked back over to the paintings. There seemed to be about eight or ten of them. The first appeared to be some type of religious painting with two hinged sides closed over it. On opening it up to its full extent, he realized the work was in a very old style, and when he tried to wipe it he noticed that some of the paint was starting to flake away. "This won't fetch much," he said. "And there's not much of a demand for papist pictures."

Poor Perrin. He carelessly moved it to one side to look at the next painting, not realizing that there was a king's ransom in that picture alone. It was an altarpiece, and had been done by Rogier van der Weyden two years before he painted his famous polyptych of the Last Judgment in 1443. Perrin could have taken it to any country that was still strongly Catholic and sold it for a princely sum.

The next picture was a large landscape of the château when it had first been built. And the rest seemed to be portraits. One he recognized immediately as the old comte, who was supposed to be his father. He laughed in its face and sneered, "It's amazing what we all come to, isn't it, your grace." In his mind he relished the thought that maybe now the old bastard was burning in hell.

He spread the paintings out, leaning them against the wall so that he could look at the entire set. After all, he thought, they were his family too. There must have been four generations in all. One was a family grouping, reminiscent of the style of the Dutch paintings. He looked at their faces, almost pathetic in his search for some royal feature that he might have inherited.

Finally, he looked at the painting of the young comte and his wife together, as they had looked soon after their wedding. They had been a handsome couple, he thought, but foolish dreamers as well. As he stared at it something caught his eye, something that he recognized. He peered closer, then stood back to get the full view again. "It can't be," he said. Walking quickly over to the picture, he carefully wiped away whatever dust was there and then stood back again, thoughtful in his silence. Slowly, a knowing smile spread across his face.

The proof was here. There might not be any records, but in front of him was indisputable proof. It was incredible how similar the two faces were. The eyes, the chin, the hair. This was all he needed, and if he were clever, he would be able to profit handsomely from it.

Perrin looked carefully at the painting again, his calculating mind racing. Narrowing his eyes, he bit his lip as he considered what to do, then he began to quickly place everything back into the opening. It had been safe there for all these years; it would be safe for a few more days.

He closed the wall. Then, frightened that he might not be able to open it again, he pressed the panel on the bookshelf. Nothing happened. Perrin hit it a second time, harder, and this time the latch released. His treasure was safe. Certain now of the course that he would take, Perrin ran up to his room to change into traveling clothes. Then he went swiftly out to the barn and ordered the old man to saddle a horse.

The beauty of the day no longer held any attraction for Thérèse as she walked back through the forest to her cottage. She began to sob once, but then forced herself to calm down. Trying to control her thoughts, she lectured herself sternly. Be reasonable, she thought. This was the perfect time for them to go to Paris. There was little that they could do without the workmen. It was a slow time for the vineyard, and the new equipment had not arrived for the vat house. Henri probably decided that he would take the opportunity to go and see his Aunt Catherine, and maybe try to talk to his uncle.

But when she thought of his uncle, the terrible dread assailed her again. He had received a letter from his uncle and gone immediately. Why else would he be summoned to Paris like that except to discuss the marriage? And why hadn't he come to see her before he left, unless he couldn't face her with the truth?

A sob began to well up inside of her again. She put her hand to her mouth to force herself to stop, but she could not control the tears that sprang to her eyes. Hurrying home, she rushed into her cottage and fell into her chair, weeping uncontrollably.

Time passed slowly, the ticking of the old clock counting each minute for her. Finally, totally exhausted from the rampant charge of her emotions, Thérèse knew that she must think clearly about the problem. She didn't know if Henri had gone to Paris because of this marriage, but sitting alone and crying about it would not help. Forcing herself to get up, Thérèse began to mechanically take care of the household chores, all the time trying to make some kind of plan.

How she wished for someone to talk to! But her friend Marie's mother was pregnant, and she dared not take a chance on going there with this sickness spreading so fast. Anyway, Marie was younger, and could not really help her with this problem. No, the one thing that Thérèse knew was that right now she desperately needed to talk to her mother.

Late in the afternoon, as she cared for the animals, she stopped for a moment to caress the big soft head of the cow. She looked into its large brown eyes and found a little comfort from the touch of another living being. Looking up at the soft pastels of the western sky gathering for their brilliant sunset display, she thought about how the day had turned. She had begun it so full of hope, and now...

now she was not sure of anything.

A dull ache was beginning in her head, probably from the strain of all those tears, she thought. She gently placed her hand on her stomach, then said, "I must not allow myself to get so upset. We'll be fine."

Later, after dark had fallen, she heard the sound of hoofbeats pounding up the lane to the cottage. Relieved that her mother was finally coming home, Thérèse rushed to the door to open it. The night was clear, and the moon bright so that she could easily see to greet Alix. But instead of her mother, another rider was getting down from the horse. When he turned to face her, Thérèse saw that it was Perrin.

She backed into the doorway. Impulsively she reached out to close the door, but he moved too quickly, and before she could do anything he was standing in front of her.

"I must talk to you."

She shook her head slowly. "Perrin, it is much too late, and my head has been throbbing. Maybe tomorrow." She reached out again to close the door, but he stopped her.

"Mademoiselle, I have to talk to you right away." His voice was urgent. "I won't even try to come in. If you'll just let me talk to you, I'll stand right here." He took a step back so that he was no longer in the cottage. Then appealing to her once more, he pleaded, "Just listen for a moment."

Realizing that she had no choice – he could easily push his way in if he wanted to – Thérèse agreed.

"First, I must apologize to you for my unacceptable behavior this afternoon. But I hope that I can make you understand. Henri made me swear that I would not tell you, and I didn't know what to say when you asked about him. I tried to put you off, and I only frightened you. I'm sorry. This is all such a terribly tragic situation." He put his hands up hopelessly.

Thérèse's eyes were wide with apprehension. "What do you mean, Perrin?" she demanded.

"Henri received a letter from his uncle telling him to come to Paris and meet the daughter of some marquis. His uncle has arranged a marriage. And apparently the poor old thing was so excited at the thought of having a husband that she demanded that Henri come immediately and that the wedding take place at once. Monsieur Girond reminded him that she would come with a large fortune, and wrote that this was the only way that he would guarantee enough money to keep the estate." Perrin paused for a moment, then seeing how Thérèse was affected suggested, "Do you need to sit down, Mademoiselle?"

Thérèse nodded silently, and when the two were seated at the table, Perrin continued. "There was a terrible scene. Bernard told him that he must do as his uncle said, for all of their sakes. Bernard does not want to go back to Bordeaux, and is afraid that he will be forced to if Henri does not comply with his uncle's wishes. Henri said that he loved only you, and could never be happy with another. Bernard said that marriage was not always for happiness and Henri would have to decide what was more important, you or the estate.

"I did not hear everything that they said, Mademoiselle, but Bernard pressed him very hard. In the end, when he agreed to go, there was such a tragic look on his face that my heart ached for him. He came to me and told me that he was leaving right away. He said that he could not tell you, and made me promise to keep it a secret. He knew that if he saw you before he left that he would not be able to go."

Thérèse sat very still. She stared at the wall, numb with pain. Perrin saw her shake her head slightly, as if trying to deny what she had heard. But in her eyes he could see that she believed him.

He reached out his hand to touch hers as it lay on the table. "Mademoiselle," he said softly, "are you going to be all right?" His words broke into her thoughts and she stared at him as if he were a stranger. "I know how much you love Henri, and I know that you are the world to him. I have envied the two of you when you were together, you seemed like such friends. I... I have never known such friendship with anyone. You must believe me when I tell you that this is as hard on Henri as it is on you. I don't know what will happen when he returns with his new wife and sees you. I'm afraid that it will destroy him." Perrin shook his head sadly. "I wish I could do something, anything, to help."

Thérèse looked at him as if she had seen him for the first time. He truly seemed disturbed by the turn of events. She looked at his face and thought how wrong about him they had all been. Only

Henri had seen past his pointed looks and taken the time to find the real person. "Thank you, Perrin," she said softly. "I know it is late for you, and I appreciate your coming to tell me the truth."

"This terrible secret has kept me awake at night, and I could not go another minute without telling you." He rose to leave. "Please forgive me for being the bearer of such bad news."

Forcing a smile, she replied simply, "It is not your fault."

He walked to the door, but before he left he added, "If there is anything that I can do, you have only to call on me, Mademoiselle." Then he walked on out to his horse.

Two great owls, one large and white and a smaller grey one, slowly blinked their eyes as they watched him ride away into the night.

13

ONCE AGAIN the sound of the clock was the only noise in the room. Thérèse sat perfectly still for a long while, her only sign of life the occasional shake of her head. Finally, she got up silently and walked up the stairs to her room. Without thinking, she picked up a brush and began to stroke her hair. The room was dark, the moon providing the only light. She stood there feeling utterly helpless. There was nothing she could do. Henri was gone. She didn't even know where to find her mother. Thérèse had never felt so completely alone in her life.

The scene at the table kept playing through her mind. Perrin had never been kinder, and yet something inside of her did not want to believe him. But then she would remember the last time that she had seen Henri, in the chapel. He had practically told her that he would do his uncle's bidding. And knowing the affection and trust he had for Bernard, she was sure that the older man's words would have a great deal of influence on Henri.

Placing the brush back on the bureau, Thérèse slipped out of her clothes and into her nightgown. The ache in her head would not go away, and she hoped that sleep would help. But the night was long and restless. A thousand "ifs" kept swirling through her head. Toward morning she finally dozed, but shortly after dawn she awoke with a start realizing that she had cried out in a dream.

It had seemed so real. She had been at the barn door and heard her mother and Gaspard talking. But instead of sneaking away she had gone inside and begun to scream at her mother. "What do you know, Mama? What are you keeping secret from Henri? Don't you know that he will have to marry someone else if you don't do something right away? Why have you kept silent? Why, Mama?"

And it had been the sound of her own cry as she asked that last question that had startled her from her sleep.

Alix could have prevented all of this, she realized incredulously. Her mother obviously knew much more than Thérèse had ever suspected. Her father had even been there the night that Henri was born. "How could you, Mama?" As she said the words aloud, Thérèse's voice was filled with pain. Alix had cruelly let Henri spend the summer searching for information that she had known all along. It was all so unbelievable, but it was also true.

A slow anger began to build inside of Thérèse. Because of her mother, her life with Henri was ruined. How could she ever live here with him so close, and yet not a part of her existence? And what of the baby growing inside of her? Had she married Henri, there would have been no problem; many a village child was conceived early. But now the love they had shared was nothing more than common mating, and her child would be fatherless.

Thérèse put her hand to her forehead, the dull pain was still there. And the nausea seemed to be worse than ever this morning, causing her whole body to ache. She knew that she must get up and begin the day, and yet her tired body cried for rest. A wrenching sigh escaped from her and she stared at the ceiling. How did one go on when there was no joy left in the future? Was there any reason to even go on living?

But as soon as she thought that, she knew how foolish the idea was. A new life was depending on her. She would not have Henri, but there would be a little baby to love her. And she would never do anything to ruin the life of her precious child as her mother had ruined hers. There was definitely a reason to get up and go on with life.

She threw back the covers and got up despite the ache in her body. She quickly dressed, determined to ignore the nausea and dizziness that assailed her. A new resolve gave her the strength to get through the morning, although at times she was forced to sit and rest until the swirling in her head disappeared. And all the while the loss of Henri fed the anger that was building inside of her.

In the late morning as she sat at the table cleaning vegetables she noticed how terrible her fingernails looked with the dirt from the morning chores. Looking more closely at her hands, she thought how rough and hard they were, not at all the hands of a lady. That fancy ring would have looked out of place on her finger anyway, she thought. Sorrow filled her chest again as she remembered the day that Henri had shown her the set of rings from the secret drawer in the armoire. Everything had seemed so right back then. "He meant it to be mine," she murmured sorrowfully.

Incredibly, a small germ of hope seemed to grow inside of her. What if the rings were still there? Wouldn't that mean there was still a chance for her? "Don't be foolish," she lectured scornfully. But the desire to see for herself if the rings were still there became an overwhelming obsession. She had to know.

Trying to ignore the weakness that she had been feeling all morning, Thérèse wiped her face with a cool cloth, and then headed for the château. In spite of the still cool air, beads of sweat broke out on her forehead as she trudged through the forest. But she forced herself to keep going, stopping only once to rest. At the château she did not even knock, but opened the door and went straight up the staircase to his room. Only when she was finally there, in front of the beautiful chest, did she stop to think.

Thérèse backed up, then sat on the edge of his bed. What if the rings were gone? Did she really want to see the empty space? But if they were there then she could still hope, and right now she needed hope. Determined to know, she walked over to the chest, and without hesitation reached out her hand and pressed the blue and white panel.

The little drawer popped open.

It was empty.

Perrin stood at the door and sneered to himself as he watched her actions. He had not expected her to come to the château, but it would make his plan all the easier to carry out. Quickly changing his demeanor, he approached her. "Mademoiselle Thérèse?" he said softly.

Thérèse stood there for another moment staring at the empty

drawer. Then she closed it and turned to him. "I needed to find something," she said simply, "But it's not there."

Perrin watched her closely, knowing how very vulnerable she was. He had to choose his words carefully if all of his plans were to work. He decided to ignore what he had just seen and instead said, "You don't look well, Mademoiselle. I just made some tea. Why don't you have some as well? Come down and rest in a chair and let me pour some for you."

The two walked silently down to the petite salon where Perrin had left the tray. "I will put in some honey and brandy for you, to bring the color back into your face."

She accepted the cup and drank the warm sweet drink down. It did seem to help. She held out her cup, indicating that she would like more as she said, "Thank you, Perrin. I do feel better."

He poured another cup, then set the teapot down and took a chair across from her. "I have been worried about you, Mademoiselle. I know that this has been a terrible blow."

Thérèse sipped the drink more slowly this time, looking down as she did. Then she looked into his eyes and said, "It is just something that I must learn to live with." There was an audible catch in her throat at the very end.

Perrin rushed on. "I am also very worried about the young comte. This will destroy him. Knowing that you are so close, and that he must stay married to someone else to keep the estate running. And he is too honorable a young man to try to keep you both."

He was right. She had wondered fleetingly last night how it would be if she became his mistress. But she knew that Henri did not have it in him to lead a duplicitous life, and she would not spend her years waiting for crumbs of his time.

Shaking her head she replied, "But there is nothing that we can do about it now."

"I thought so, too; still, I spent a long time thinking about it last night. Master Henri was so kind to me when I came here. He accepted me right away without reservation, befriending me. I… I have never known anyone like him. I would do anything for him, Mademoiselle. Even give my life."

Thérèse did not answer, just smiled gently, knowing how true his words about Henri were. He always looked for the best side of people, and Perrin was the perfect example.

"I know how worried he will be about you. What if something were to happen to your mother and you were left all alone? And so I thought, if you were willing, that I could marry you...."

"No!" her response was immediate. "I could never marry anyone else."

"Mademoiselle Thérèse, hear me out. I don't expect you ever to feel for me the way you feel for him. Believe me, I understand how great your love for him is. It would be a marriage in name only. I would make no demands on you. This would simply be a way for me to pay back the kindness of the young comte, and assure him that you would be cared for."

Thérèse stared out of the window, seeing nothing, as she spoke. "You don't understand. There are other problems." She paused for a moment. "I'm going to have his child, Perrin." There, she had said it out loud to someone. She had hoped that when she finally said those words it would be to Henri and with joy. Now her words were simply a statement of fact.

The crafty little man feigned surprise, and then appeared to be thinking. "Then it is more important than ever that you marry at once. You cannot let his child be born a bastard." He put extra emphasis on the last word, noticing how the sound of it seemed to slap her.

Thérèse sat quietly, and Perrin realized with elation that she was actually considering his offer. "I don't know, Perrin. We are not suited to one another, not even friends. I know so little about you...." Her words trailed off.

"As I said, Mademoiselle, this would be a marriage in name only. My simple desire is to care for you and the young master's baby. It would be my honor to do something for him." Perrin forced himself to stop after that rush of words, realizing that in his desire to convince her he was beginning to say too much.

Once again she sat quietly. He saw her shake her head once, as if arguing with herself. "No, Perrin. I cannot marry you and stay here. My life will be too painful if I live near Henri and know that at any time I might see him. It would just be too much."

"Of course, of course. That would be unhealthy for you and for the baby as well." Perrin's voice was kind and understanding, but his mind raced along, wondering what to say next. "My mother's family came from a village not far from here. And my grandfather left me some land and a little cottage. It is not as large as the one that you are used to, but it could be made into a nice place to live."

It was a lie, but he would deal with that later. Once again she seemed to be considering his offer. The room filled with silence. Thérèse stared down at her hands, rubbing the finger where her wedding ring would go, again seeing the empty space in the secret drawer.

Perrin let her think for as long as he dared. She must feel the pressure, but not have time to consider the other options open to her. "I know that you would miss your mother, but she could...."

"My mother is not important to this decision." She cut him off, her voice filled with anger. Then suddenly she looked straight into his face, a hardened glint in her eye. "Yes. I will marry you. But remember, it is a marriage in name only."

Perrin was stunned. He was not quite sure what had just happened. He had not expected her to agree so suddenly. But, not daring to give her a chance to change her mind, he decided to move swiftly. "My cousin is a magistrate in that village I told you about. We could go there right now and have him perform the ceremony. Later, when there is a priest available, we could have it blessed if you like."

Knowing that her actions would cut her mother to the quick, Thérèse hardened herself. "The magistrate will be fine, Perrin, and I would prefer to do this as soon as possible. I will go as I am." Her words showed no emotion, only rigid resolution.

Amazed at his success, Perrin strode immediately out to the barn and ordered the old man to help him at once to hitch up the carriage. When he started to argue, Perrin cut him short. "Do as I say, man. I was left in charge here, and I give the orders. I am going to my wedding and must take my bride in style. So move quickly."

Inside the château, Thérèse poured herself another cup of tea and waited. The ache in her head and body would not go away. And she could not allow herself to think of Henri and what she was about to do, or she knew that she would lose her resolve. It was time to take charge of her own life, and quit depending on people like her mother or Henri. She must learn to depend on herself.

Marriage to Perrin offered her a way to leave St. Vivant and the memories that would assail her every waking hour. It was time to forget the simplicity of childhood and accept the harsh realities of the adult world.

Later, on the trip back to the château, Perrin could not believe how incredibly simple it had all been. Thérèse had been waiting on the steps in front of the château when he pulled up in the carriage. She sat back in the corner, never speaking for the entire way. Perrin had been tempted to try and make conversation, but then fearing that he might in some way offend her, that she might recant, decided that silence was best. He did notice at one point the she seemed terribly pale, and asked if she was all right. She nodded to him briefly, then turned her head to the side.

The ceremony was performed without delay. Perrin had visited his cousin the day before and told him that he had gotten some poor farm girl pregnant and wanted to do the honorable thing by her. The cousin was amazed that a woman so beautiful would have an affair with someone as disgusting as Perrin, but seeing how ill she was, decided that her pregnancy must be a very difficult one and went ahead with the short ceremony.

There had been one moment when Thérèse seemed to hesitate. When Perrin had gone to help her from the carriage she began to shake her head and say, "No, Perrin, I don't think that I can after all." Panic rose inside of him, but then he remembered her strange behavior earlier when he had mentioned her mother. Again he offered to wait until she spoke to Alix, but the mention of her mother's name seemed to bring back her determination. A dull, hard look came to her eyes, and she was soon his bride.

On the trip back to the estate, Perrin fought hard to keep the elation he felt from bubbling over. She was his wife. The official document was in his pocket. Now everything that she owned was his. He would proceed carefully and try to keep up the pretense as long as possible. But first he would send someone to Paris with a letter telling Henri that the sickness was worse and not to return until he was notified. That would give Perrin time to arrange all of the next events to put himself in as good a light as possible.

Thérèse had been surprised when she learned that they were going back to the estate instead of staying at Perrin's cottage. But he assured her that it was not ready to live in, and added that they both needed to get their clothes and other possessions. Reminding her that Henri would not be back for another week, she accepted his actions, and they traveled on in silence.

At one point he heard a soft moaning from where Thérèse sat. He reached out to touch her arm as he asked how she was, and found that she was burning up with fever. Realizing that she must have caught the sickness, a new series of thoughts began to run through his mind. If he took her back to the château and told no one about her illness for a couple of days, then in her condition she would probably die. And he would inherit everything that she owned.

Perrin looked back over at her, thinking about her beauty, her soft fair skin. Smiling inwardly, he thought of how fine her body would feel beneath his. But that would come later. He had time to decide what to do with his beautiful little bride.

14

S UNSET WAS BEGINNING TO TINGE THE SKY with pink and blue as Henri pressed his horse swiftly toward the château. He had wanted to arrive much earlier in the day, but Aunt Catherine's errands had kept him busier in Paris than he had planned. Now he would get there too late for a visit to the Condé cottage. Never mind, he thought, there was always tomorrow.

His trip to Paris had not been at all what he expected. The letter from Uncle Georges had required that he and Bernard come to Paris immediately to discuss matters that concerned the winery. Henri had been certain that one of the matters was his arranged marriage, and had ridden to Paris filled with dread.

However, a pleasant surprise awaited him. His Aunt Louise had become concerned when she heard that the sickness spreading through the countryside had been reported in the suburbs around Paris. She had demanded that her husband remove the entire family to the estate at Bordeaux at once. Uncle Georges was a man to be feared in the business world, but at home his wife ruled with an iron hand, and the family carriage had left the night before Henri and Bernard arrived.

Aunt Catherine had refused to go, deciding instead to wait for Henri and Bernard to take her back to St. Vivant. When they arrived, she was in a terrible state, having been left with only one servant to help her pack the innumerable personal treasures that she had purchased on her many visits to the fashionable Paris shops. She also had special orders that were waiting to be picked up, and gave Henri a long list of errands to accomplish before she could ever consider leaving. Henri had helped until his patience had run out, then pleading a need to prepare her rooms at the château, he had left the day before, leaving poor Bernard behind to pack the wagon and transport his aunt and her maid.

Henri had ridden as fast as his horse would allow, but darkness was beginning to fall by the time he rode through the gates and up to the château. Running inside, he called loudly to Perrin and was surprised when he did not receive a response. He ran up the stairs to the landing and called up to the attic rooms, but still there was no answer. Beginning to worry that perhaps his secretary had fallen ill, he ran on up to his room, only to find it empty. A strange apprehension began to trouble Henri. The château had not seemed so empty since that first day when he had arrived. Not even a candle had been lit against the approaching night.

Deciding that Perrin must be out on the estate somewhere, Henri ran back down to the entrance and out to where his horse was waiting. The sight of the stable hand standing there, holding the bridle in one hand and a lantern in the other filled him with relief.

"Claude," he called out, "I am glad to see you. I was worried when I could not find anyone about."

"Monsieur le comte, thank God you are here. I fear that something terrible is taking place." Obviously upset, the old man fidgeted as he held the reins.

"Is the sickness worse?" Henri's first thought was for Thérèse and her mother.

"Yes, but Monsieur, it is not that. It is Perrin." Then stumbling over his words, the old man told him how Perrin had left earlier in the day with Thérèse.

"Are you certain that he said that they were going to be married?" Henri's voice was tight as he questioned the stable hand.

"I know, sir, I could not believe it myself. But he was bragging about how his cousin was a magistrate and would perform the ceremony right away. And I saw him help Mademoiselle Thérèse into the carriage with my own eyes. I couldn't believe it. I may be an old man, but I could see how that young girl felt for you, sir. I can't imagine why she would leave with him."

Henri stood in the still night air, trying to make sense of what he was hearing. Why would Perrin say that he was marrying Thérèse? She had never even liked the little man; like Bernard, she had never really trusted him. There had to be some mistake. Henri asked Claude once again to tell him what had happened.

"I know that it sounds impossible, but I swear to you that is what he said." The old man's voice was pleading with Henri to believe him. "You must go and find her."

Reaching out to stroke the neck of his horse Henri thought quickly about what he must do. He hated to ride the animal any farther, but changing horses might take too long. The night had already fallen and he would have to ride carefully to keep his horse from stumbling. Making up his mind, Henri swung back up into the saddle, and asked the old man the name of the town where Perrin had gone. Claude gave him some quick instructions, and then Henri wheeled his horse around and headed into the night.

The carriage went more slowly as it neared the château. Perrin had hoped to return before nightfall, but he had been forced to stop twice when Thérèse began to feel sick. That she was getting worse was obvious to him. In spite of that, he hummed to himself as he carefully guided the horse along the road. Knowing that he had so smoothly accomplished this deception made him feel powerful. He had been good at manipulating people for years, but he had never been able to achieve anything as splendid as this. It was obviously meant to be.

Perrin slowed the horse as he came near a large rut crossing the road. If his reckoning were correct, he was almost at the avenue. Seeing the entrance ahead, he pulled on the rein to turn the horse, when from out of nowhere a rider came charging down the avenue. Perrin's horse reared, nearly turning the carriage over, and he had to fight to keep control. Finally settling the animal, Perrin stood up to yell at the careless horseman. And as he did so, he found himself face to face with Henri.

"What is going on here, Perrin?" Henri tried to keep his voice even, still hoping that old Claude had made a mistake.

"Monsieur, I did not expect you back from Paris so soon." Perrin stumbled for words, unprepared for this sudden confrontation.

"So it seems. Do you have Mademoiselle Thérèse in the carriage with you?"

Perrin could see the hardened look that had come into Henri's eyes, and knew that he would have to move carefully. From the corner of the carriage Thérèse moaned softly. "Yes, she is here. But she is ill. Let me get down from the carriage so that we can speak without disturbing her." He slowly stepped down, and walked away from the carriage. As he had hoped, Henri dismounted and followed. Once he was clear of the horses, Perrin turned back to face Henri. There was enough moonlight to allow Henri to see Perrin clearly, and to see the pistol that he held in his hand.

"What is this, Perrin?" demanded Henri.

"I am now Monsieur le comte to you. I have today taken for myself a royal bride."

"You have done what?"

"I have married the daughter, the *daughter*, of the late comte de St. Vivant. I am now master of this estate." Perrin's eyes glowed with triumph as he said those words.

"You have gone mad, Perrin." Henri took a step toward him.

"I should warn you that I learned to use this quite well in my years with the army." Perrin waved the pistol as he spoke. "And I also learned to never travel the roads at night without its company. I'm glad that you are a more trusting sort. Now I am able to protect my wife from robbers, or from jealous young men trying to molest her."

Beginning to understand that Perrin was quite willing to use his weapon, Henri tried to take a more conciliatory tone. "I still don't understand what you are doing with Thérèse."

"She is the child who was born that night, not you, Henri. I found proof in the library, irrefutable proof. I don't know who you are, but you are not Henri Phillipe de St. Vivant. Your uncle has lied to you. She is the heir, and now she is my wife."

Henri stared in stunned silence. 'Perrin must be lying,' he thought. But why else would he want to marry Thérèse? Could it be true? But his uncle had assured him.

Watching the young man's reaction to his words, Perrin felt contempt for him. 'Little fool,' he thought. Then he smiled cruelly as he continued. "It wasn't even very hard to get her to agree. I only had to tell her that you had gone to Paris to marry your little marquise, and she was more than willing...."

"That's a lie," Henri shouted.

Perrin laughed out loud. "Of course it's a lie. But she believed me. And now she is my wife. And I want you to leave my land." A deadly look came into Perrin's eyes and he raised the pistol, pointing it directly at Henri's head.

In the carriage, Thérèse had been lost in a fevered sleep. But the voices broke through the fog in her head, and she heard the men speaking. Listening to what Perrin was saying, she realized with horror what had happened. Raising herself from her half lying position, she could just make out the forms of the men in the dark. Then, as her eyes adjusted she recognized Henri and Perrin facing one another.

"Henri!" She tried to shout but there was not enough strength in her voice. "Henri, he told me that you had gone to get your bride. I only married him to get away because I could not bear to live near you and know that you would never be mine. What am I going to do?" Hysteria began to rise inside of her.

Despite the gun that was pointed at him, Henri rushed over to where she sat in the open carriage. Placing his arms around her, he could feel her fevered body, see the terror in her eyes. Fury at Perrin for deceiving her suddenly flowed through his body.

"You won't get away with this, Perrin. No one will recognize this marriage as legal. You can't think that you will hold her to a lie."

"But I shall, Henri. She went willingly, the magistrate will swear to that. In fact, I asked her if she wanted to wait and speak to her mother, and she insisted that the ceremony go on. Ask the witnesses – they can tell you. She is now my wife, and this is my estate. I will ask you once more to leave my land and allow me to take my sick wife home."

Realizing how she had been duped, Thérèse looked with terrified anguish into Henri's eyes. "Henri, he lied to me. He said that you had gone to Paris to marry and would bring a new wife home. I couldn't bear to live without you and, knowing that, he tricked me. Do something, Henri!" Thérèse grabbed his coat as she begged him for help.

Henri held her close, her body racked with sobs. He gently

stroked her head, trying to comfort her. "It will be all right, Thérèse. I won't let him harm you, my dearest."

"And how will you stop me, Henri? Anything that you do to separate a man and his wife will break the law and you will be a criminal. Try to take her now and I will kill you."

Henri looked back at Perrin, wondering what could be done. He was sure that his uncle's lawyers would be able to void the marriage, but what could he do now? Sudden desperation began to build inside of Henri as he realized that he was depending on the uncle who Perrin said had been lying all along. If Perrin could prove that she was the heir, then he and his uncle had no rights at all in this case. And if Perrin was right, who was he? The confidence that Henri had gained in the last few weeks began to slip away and the void it left began to fill with despair.

Sneering at the little tableaux before him, Perrin sensed Henri's confusion at the turn of events. This was not how he had hoped to resolve the problem that the lovesick puppy presented, but maybe now was the time to get rid of him once and for all. Perrin had worked with men like the uncle before, and knew that in the end they could strike a bargain. With the paintings for proof, and the marriage contract an indisputable fact, Perrin knew that he had won. He saw Henri's shoulders sag. One more prod should send him running off.

"My patience is running thin, Henri." Perrin's voice was strong with authority. "I will ask you one last time to leave the estate. It is getting late, and the day has been long for my wife." He looked at Henri, saw the despair in the young man. Perrin's spirit was filled with elation. And that was Perrin's fatal mistake, because in his confidence he could not resist one final jab. "I need to get home. I have a honeymoon before me."

"NO!" Thérèse screamed.

Filled with sudden rage at his uncle as well as Perrin, Henri rushed blindly toward the little man. Perrin raised his gun to shoot, taking careful aim.

Thérèse watched it all as if it were a dream in slow motion. Henri pulling away from her to charge toward Perrin. Perrin raising his gun toward Henri. Then from out of the blackness of the night a great white owl swooping down toward Perrin, his wings outspread, his claws extended out toward Perrin's face. Perrin looking up in terror just as he pulled the trigger, and the black powder exploding into the night. Thérèse saw Henri fall backward to the ground, and she put her hand to her mouth as she cried out in anguish.

The talons of the huge white owl grabbed for Perrin's face, but then it suddenly swept up into the air when, from out of nowhere, a burly figure suddenly appeared in the space between Henri and Perrin. In a hand stretched upward, Thérèse saw the glint of a knife, then watched as the hand plunged down toward Perrin, crashing into his chest. The big man pulled the knife up toward Perrin's heart to complete the job, then slowly pushed him backward. He stood for what seemed like a million years and stared at the figure on the ground, then slowly turned toward Henri.

In the sky, the great owl circled as if watching the scene below. He was joined by a smaller grey owl, flying close beside him. In the moment before they left, Thérèse almost believed that she saw them look toward her with understanding in their eyes. Then the birds slowly turned toward the forest, and disappeared into the night.

Time and space returned to normal, and Thérèse realized that the big man was bending over Henri, lifting him away from the ground. Ignoring the terrible ache throughout her body she climbed down from the carriage, moving as swiftly as she could toward Henri. The big man heard her behind him, and turned to face her. Thérèse gasped with surprise as she recognized Gaspard.

"Is he alive?" Her voice was weak and she pulled down close to speak to him.

Gaspard looked at her with a gentle smile. "Don't worry, Mademoiselle, it's only his shoulder. We need to stop the bleeding at once, then take him to the château. I will ride out to get your mother, but once she is here to care for him I think he will be all right." Gaspard pulled off the shirt that he was wearing, and began to make a bandage.

Thérèse bent to help him, but was filled with sudden dizziness, and stepped back. "I... I don't know if I should help you. I'm afraid that I have the sickness...."

"Then get back in the carriage at once." Gaspard commanded. "I think he will be fine if he gets proper care, but if he gets sick as well, I don't know if he can survive. You must stay away from him."

Hurt by his words and the tone of his voice, Thérèse turned to walk back to the carriage. But seeing the body of Perrin lying in an ever growing pool of blood, she turned back to Gaspard. Pointing toward the body she asked, "And will he live?"

Gaspard snorted with disgust and said simply, "When you kill a pig you learn to do it in one stroke."

Thérèse took him at his word. She walked shakily back to the carriage and with her last ounce of energy pulled herself up and crawled back into the corner. She never looked back again at the body of her husband.

As Gaspard was finishing the bandage, old Claude arrived. He had heard the sound of the gun, and when he saw Perrin's body he knew that the worst had occurred. Not wasting words, he asked Gaspard what he could do to help, and was told to take the carriage with Mademoiselle back to the château at once. Gaspard warned him that she was sick and needed to get to a bed, but then told him that if he feared the sickness, he could leave her in the carriage until Gaspard arrived. Claude nodded, and took the horse by the reins and led the carriage up the avenue as quickly as his old legs would allow.

At the château he reached in to help Thérèse, telling her that he was not strong enough to carry her, but that he would help her up the stairs as best he could. The two moved slowly, each step seeming to take forever. Finally she arrived at the top of the stairs, and Claude led her to a room where she collapsed on the bed.

15

GASPARD TOOK THE CARRIAGE that Perrin had used and drove it through the darkness as fast as he dared. All the while, he could not get the scene out of his mind. Guilt assailed him as he went over and over what had just happened. Strangely, the guilt did not extend to the death of Perrin. Stabbing him had been a reflex, something that needed to be done. It brought back the memory of the one other time that he had taken a life. That, too, had been a necessity.

But what had happened to Henri could have been avoided. If only he had told him the truth the night that he came to his cottage. Or if Alix had been convinced to speak to him sooner. But the truth had never even been spoken between Alix and Gaspard. It had been a secret for so long that they were no longer sure how to say the words. Once again, the sound of the shot and the sight of Henri as he fell to the ground overwhelmed his emotions. If it had not been for the owl, Henri would be dead now; of that Gaspard was sure.

Driving the horses more slowly, Gaspard pulled into the yard of the farmhouse where he had left Alix earlier in the day. She had told him that she was worried about Thérèse, and Gaspard had promised to go to the Condé cottage and tell Thérèse that her mother was fine. That was the only reason that he had come to the château at all, to look for Thérèse. If only he had arrived there sooner, if only he could have stopped it from happening. He had told Thérèse that Henri would be fine. He prayed to God that he was right.

At the sound of the carriage, the farmer had opened the door, and Gaspard went in. He chose his words carefully, not wanting to frighten Alix. He simply told her that Henri was hurt and Thérèse needed her and that she must come immediately. Alix did not question him once as she packed her bag. She quickly told the mother what to do for her sick child, and smiled to assure her that everything would be all right.

It was not until they were in the carriage and headed back to the château that Alix said, "Tell me now, Gaspard."

"I don't really know what happened. I went to the cottage but couldn't find Thérèse. So I walked on to the château, hoping that she would be there. I had only just arrived when I saw Henri riding off down the avenue. Claude came running to me, saying something about Perrin marrying Thérèse...."

"What!" The word exploded from Alix. "Thérèse would never marry Perrin."

"I'm only telling you what little I know, Alix. We heard horses, and raised voices, so I ran after Henri as fast as I could. I arrived in time to hear Thérèse's scream and see Perrin shoot Henri."

"Was Thérèse hurt?" Alix's voice was frantic.

"No, Alix," he assured her, "only Henri was harmed. He took a bullet through the shoulder. I think that it is a clean wound, although he seemed to pass in and out of consciousness from the pain. When his head was clear he babbled on about what Perrin had found, and how he married Thérèse for the estate."

"Mon Dieu," she moaned. "I should have known something like this would happen. I should have done something sooner."

"You did what you thought best, Alix. That's all you can ever do." He hesitated, then added, "I think that Thérèse has the sickness."

Laying her head in her hands, Alix began to weep. "I should never have left her for so long. For days I have been running to take care of everyone else, but not my own. I always think she is so strong, Gaspard."

Gaspard reached his arm around her shoulders to comfort her. "She will get well, Alix. You must have faith."

The carriage had come to the estate, and Gaspard turned the horse toward the avenue. Suddenly, Alix gasped and pointed to a form on the ground.

"It is Perrin," Gaspard said in a matter of fact tone. "I will deal with the body after we take care of Henri. Whatever happened between him and Thérèse is no longer important."

Claude was waiting at the door when the carriage pulled up a few moments later. Alix went first to the petit salon where Gaspard had left Henri lying on a couch. He tried to smile and not show his pain as she gently checked his wound, but the searing ache became too great. He gritted his teeth and looked away, trying not to cry out loud.

"Take him up to his room now," she instructed Gaspard and Claude. "I don't want him to be moved again after I bandage his shoulder." She also told Claude to find some clean sheets and asked Gaspard to get some water. Then, while they carefully tried to lift Henri, she ran swiftly up the stairs to Thérèse.

Claude had left a candle burning in the room. Alix could see her clearly and thought how small Thérèse looked lying in the big bed. She did not want to wake her yet, knowing that she had to deal with Henri's wound first, and so reached out gently to touch her daughter's face. Her skin was hot and dry, telling Alix what she feared. The next two days would be the worst. She knelt in the dim candlelight and prayed that Thérèse would survive.

Soon Gaspard came to the door to tell her that everything was ready. Alix sent Claude down to the kitchen to begin heating water to mix Thérèse's medicine. Then she and Gaspard carefully washed Henri's wound and rebound it with strips of cloth. Gaspard had been right, the wound was clean, the ball passing completely through the shoulder so that Alix did not have to dig to find it. Still, Henri's pain was great, and she was thankful when they were finally finished. She gave him a strong sleeping powder, and then left Gaspard to watch with instructions to call her if the bleeding started again. Confident that he would be safe in Gaspard's care, she went to Thérèse.

As Alix had feared, Thérèse became much worse by morning. Her body burned with the fever, and she passed in and out of consciousness. Alix worked to keep her temperature down with cooling baths and spoonfuls of the herbal drink. And always, she carefully searched Thérèse's skin for signs of the rash that came about twelve hours before a victim died.

She barely left her daughter's side, sitting for long hours by her bed, holding Thérèse's hand. At times she tried to rest on the couch that Gaspard had brought to the room, but would be awakened by the sound of Thérèse's voice as she babbled on about Henri and Perrin. At one point that first day, Thérèse's hands clutched down at her stomach, and she began moaning in pain. When Alix saw the blood spreading on her gown, she understood what had driven her daughter to desperation in the last few days. She worked quickly to staunch the flow of blood, then changed the bedding, putting the soiled things aside to be burned. All the while, she bitterly blamed herself for not having been there to help her precious child.

Gaspard stayed with Henri most of the first day, leaving for only a short time to care for the animals at his and Alix's farm. While he was gone, Claude looked in on Henri and kept Alix informed of his condition. Alix only went into Henri's room once to check on his bandage, fearing that she would spread the sickness to him. The drug that she gave him kept him mercifully asleep.

By midnight of the second day, Thérèse's fever finally broke. She began to sleep more naturally, and Alix knew that the worst was over. Henri's shoulder no longer bled when the dressing was changed, and after this night he would not need a sleeping potion. He would still be in pain, but if he stayed still, the wound should heal swiftly. Relief seemed to sweep over Alix's tired muscles and for the first time in days she actually allowed herself to relax.

The sound, restful sleep that Alix had fallen into was shattered early the next morning by the sound of something falling. Alix sat up with a jerk, but realized she must have been dreaming. She began to sit back, then heard the sound of a voice, and another thud. She quickly ran to Henri's room and found his bed empty. Running down the stairs, she searched through the rooms, finally realizing that the noise was coming from the library. Hurrying to the door, she found Henri, pounding on the wall and shouting, "Where are you?"

"Henri! What are you doing?" Alix rushed to his side, and saw the spreading stain of blood on his shoulder. "You will ruin all of my hard work if you are not careful. Sit down at once and tell me what you are doing," she commanded.

"Not until I find it," he roared. "Perrin said he found the proof in here and I will find it, too, even if I have to tear the walls down!"

Seeing that he was in a frantic state, Alix tried to be more soothing. "Sit down for a moment and tell me what you mean. Then I will help you look." She pushed him to one side of the leather couch near the desk, deftly tightening the bandage where it had worked loose. Then she sat down at the other end, where she could see his face, but also keep an eye on his shoulder as he spoke.

Henri told her about that night that he had been shot and his few moments with Perrin. "He said that he found the proof in here. I have to know the truth." He stopped speaking abruptly, then looked at Alix and said, slowly, "But you know the truth, don't you?"

Alix looked at Henri with sad eyes and answered. "Yes, I know the truth."

"And Perrin wasn't lying?"

A sigh escaped from Alix. "I don't know what he found; but, no, Henri, he wasn't lying."

"Then why didn't you tell me from the beginning, instead of letting me go on hunting for something that didn't exist? Was it some kind of game?"

The look of hurt and anger in Henri's eyes filled Alix with overwhelming sorrow. She didn't know where to start. "It hasn't been as easy as you might think, Henri. Those were very dangerous times. And the young comtesse," she paused. Tears came to her eyes and she bit her lips as she remembered the sweet young woman who had lived here. "She was my dearest friend. When she heard that there were mobs of rabble coming out to the countryside from Paris, it was almost as if she knew how it would end. Nicholas and the comte arranged to secrete the baby in our cottage for safekeeping until the worst passed."

Alix stopped again. The words had been hidden for so many years and yet, they were still painful to speak. Her voice wavered as she said, "And then they were dead. We raised Thérèse as if she were our own child, but all the time Nicholas made plans about what to do when the times got better. Then Nicholas died, and I was left to do it alone."

"And did your husband never tell you about a secret place here in the study?"

"If he knew about such a thing he never said anything. But then, he died so suddenly that there wasn't any time to say more than good-bye." Her voice became very soft at the end, and she looked down at her hand, touching the worn and scratched gold band that she had never taken off.

Henri stared at her, his anger beginning to subside as he watched her obvious pain. He knew that, finally, he was learning the truth.

"Alix?" Gaspard's voice from the doorway surprised them both. He strode over to where they were sitting and handed her a leather packet. "It was not hard to find."

Alix ran her hands over the cracked maroon leather. A band of gold leaf could still be seen along the edge. "This is what you were looking for. Nicholas buried it the night he brought Thérèse to our home. The old papers that established the estate are here, and a document attesting to the birth of Thérèse, signed the night she was born."

The room was quiet. Henri looked up at Gaspard, saying simply, "So you knew as well."

A pained expression came to he old man's face. He walked over to the desk, then turned back to Henri and nodded his head.

"Tell him, Gaspard. He must know it all." The look in Alix's eyes encouraged him.

Gaspard stood in silence for a moment, then walked around the desk and sat in the chair where Perrin had worked. He folded his hands in front of him, and then began to talk. "I didn't know about Thérèse for a long time. I believed that the child had died. I even made the tiny coffin and carried it down to the chapel for them." He stared out of the windows at the field of grapevines, searching for the right words. "The comte was... an incredible man. He treated me as a companion, not as a servant. We worked together to make the winery a successful business. And he planned to share his profits with the workers as things got better. There were not many like him in those days."

"But then the Révolution came. The peasants who had been mistreated for so many years finally fought back and destroyed the system that had oppressed them for centuries. Sadly, the few members of the nobility who were trying to make changes were swept away as well." He cleared his throat, and then began to talk about that night that had changed their lives forever.

"I had heard that the mob was coming. And I went into the town to talk with their leader. I thought that I could reason with him, explain that this estate was different. Lazare just laughed, and said that all aristocrats were the same. He also said that he wasn't here to hurt anyone, just make sure that the rights of the common people were respected. Then he warned me to keep out of his way." Gaspard paused, not sure that the pain was gone even now. "He had done his work well. He knew about the people here, and about their lives. He said that it would be a pity if the mob happened by my farm and found my pretty young wife alone. He said that he couldn't always control the people who were with him." His fist hit the desk, and he clenched his teeth. "I should have killed him right then."

"But instead, I went straight to my farm, and took my wife and daughter to a cousin in the next village. I was afraid for their safety as long as he was here. I rode as fast as I could back to the château, hoping to get here before the mob. I was too late. The crowd was large and angry. They were already in the château and out on the balcony. I could hear the comte trying to reason with them and I kept remembering that Lazare said that he was not going to hurt anyone. So I hid behind a tree." His eyes looked off in the distance, the memories of that night were still so vivid. The emotions from long ago that he had tried to block welled up inside of him.

"I failed him. I watched from behind a tree as they fell from the balcony. He had done so much for me, and I wasn't even near enough to break his fall." Gaspard closed his eyes, trying to wipe out the image of the broken bodies on the stones. "I watched as they looted the house, threw furniture from the windows, danced in the clothes of dead people. I watched as the rains broke, and the mob went to the vat house to break open the casks of wine. When no one was looking, I took the bodies to the edge of the forest and hid them under the leaves until everyone was gone."

A steely look came to Gaspard's face. "I followed the leaders back into the town the next morning, and waited for my chance. I saw Lazare go into the church, and when there was no one looking I followed. But again I was too late. The priest was on the steps of the altar, stabbed through the heart. I saw Lazarre come from the store room at the back with a bag in one hand, and gold candlesticks in another. When I confronted him, he just laughed. He said that I should grab some of the wealth around me while I could, so that I would be prepared for the new order. I knew what had to be done. I pretended to thank him, and walked up to shake his hand. Then I rid the world of his useless life."

Alix gasped. "So that was you! I always thought that Nicholas had killed him."

Henri looked at her in surprise. "You didn't know?"

"You still don't understand, Henri." Alix's voice was filled with intensity as she tried to explain. "You didn't trust anyone. There was a reason they called the time that followed The Terror. Someone could denounce you, and the mob would turn on you in a moment. We all stayed at our farms, afraid to even go into town. And Nicholas and I were especially afraid. We had been their friends. We had their child. I just accepted Lazare's death and didn't want to know the truth. I didn't want anything more that I needed to hide."

"I didn't know about Thérèse until years later," added Gaspard. "And after my family…. I kept to myself for a long time, bitter about my life. Then I saw her in the forest one day. I had been drinking, and at first I thought that I had seen a ghost, so I ran away. But later I went to the cottage and saw Thérèse. I knew immediately who she was. I spoke to Nicholas, only once, to tell him that I would do whatever was needed to make things right. I swore that I wouldn't fail my dead friend again." He looked into Henri's eyes, "Afterward, Nicholas and I would come here and talk about what would be needed to fix up the vathouse, to repair the château. But we never talked about Thérèse. I haven't said these words out loud since then."

Alix stood, then walked over to the desk, laying her hand gently on Gaspard's shoulder. "There were many who came those first years and claimed the land for themselves. Many came and stayed only long enough to try and find some treasure. Others wanted to make something of the winery, but too much had been destroyed." A playful smile came to her face. "Nicholas became very good at making the sounds of ghosts and frightening them away. The village people came to believe that it was haunted and stayed way. After a while fewer and fewer came."

"So you're the one who left the flowers?" Henri questioned, looking up at Alix as he tried to comprehend it all.

Alix shook her head, and Gaspard spoke up. "I did that. And it was never to scare people. The young comtesse loved flowers, and her husband was always bringing her some rare and beautiful plant just to surprise her. It was my way of remembering how special they were."

Henri's mouth was agape with surprise at the idea of the gruff old man doing something so sensitive. Alix laughed out loud at the look on his face. "It took me many years to figure that out as well." Then she added more seriously, "But it was something that we never spoke about. I think that we were afraid that if we talked about the reality of who Thérèse was, that we might somehow ruin the future, that the past might somehow be repeated."

"Then you came, Henri. You were so different from the others. You were like Phillipe in your love of the land. And you and Bernard had the knowledge and the connections needed to make the winery flourish again. I know now that I should have told you the truth sooner." Alix smiled and patted Gaspard's shoulder. "Gaspard even tried to get me to say something. But I kept waiting. Hoping that there would be some kind of sign that told me the time was right." She hesitated, then added softly, "And I hoped that you and Thérèse might find something of what Nicholas and I had."

Alix stopped speaking. Henri sat silently, thinking about what she had said, trying to understand how she had felt. He knew that he should say something to let her know that he was no longer angry, but the words did not come. He just sat and looked at the two people that he had grown so fond of, and waited.

When Henri did not say anything, Alix went on. "Then the sickness began. And even though Thérèse told me about the letter from your uncle, I was never able to get away long enough to dig the packet up and bring it to you. I thought that your uncle was the problem. I never guessed that Perrin...." Here she faltered, at a loss for words when it came to Perrin's actions.

Gaspard snorted in disgust. "I should have known that he was up to no good and watched him more closely. His mother was a mean, conniving woman, and he was just like her. The world is better off without him."

A sudden worried look came to Henri's face. "Perrin's family! What if they come looking for him?"

Gaspard looked up at Alix, who nodded, then back at Henri.

In spite of his lack of concern for Perrin's death, Gaspard was still an honest man, and did not like having to lie. So Alix spoke up, saying firmly, "If anyone asks we must say that he died of the sickness and you were hurt in a hunting accident. Claude has agreed, and we must depend on you as well, Henri."

"What about Bernard?" Henri could not imagine keeping the truth from his old friend.

"Of course, Bernard will have to know," Alix answered. "But he is an honorable man, and I know that we can trust him." She finished with an encouraging smile, then waited.

Henri looked out of the window at the treetops swaying gently in the morning breeze. A multitude of thoughts were swirling through his mind. When he came here he thought that at last he had found his position in life, the place where he belonged. Well, he had no claim at all on this land or its future. Where did all of this leave him? Henri's shoulders sagged with the sadness of acceptance. He thought about Perrin and knew that he couldn't blame him; he had just been a player in this drama. Whatever he had found had just been too much temptation for him.

"I will think about Bernard, and when I see him again I will know what to do." Henri spoke with a voice now completely void of the old boyish enthusiasm. Still, he paused, looking around the room. "But none of this has solved the other mystery. What could Perrin have found in here that made him decide to marry Thérèse?"

16

Alix and Gaspard looked at each other, and Gaspard shrugged his shoulders and shook his head. Alix turned back at Henri, saying, "That is one question that we cannot answer. As I told you, Nicholas never said anything about a secret place here in the château. It could be anywhere."

Henri pushed himself up to his feet. "Then I must get back to work. Because I do not intend to leave this room until I have discovered what Perrin found."

Alix looked at Gaspard with a concerned face, then went quickly back to Henri's side. She put her hand firmly on his arm. "Let us be logical about this, Henri. Sit back down and we will try to think where he could have found his 'proof.'" She gently pushed him back down on the couch, then turned to look at Gaspard, her eyes silently pleading for help.

Gaspard looked around the room, realizing that there could be a secret compartment almost anywhere. They didn't even know how big this "proof" was supposed to be. It could be as small as a paper hidden in a crack, or as big as a secret panel in the wall. And there was nothing to guarantee that Perrin had put whatever he had found back in the same place. Still, he realized that he had to do something.

Gaspard looked back at Henri, "Do you know what he had

been doing? Maybe he found it when he was working."

Henri shook his head. "He was doing some paperwork for Bernard before we left. But Bernard took all of that with him."

"What about these?" Alix pointed to a stack of books as she walked over to the desk. "Maybe he found something in one of these." She picked up the book on top of the stack and thumbed through it. Then she carefully looked at the binding to see if it had been tampered with. Finding nothing, she picked up the next book.

"I don't think that he could have found anything in there. They came on a wagon from Aunt Catherine several weeks ago. Perrin had not had time to unpack them."

Gaspard looked at the wall thoughtfully, "So, if he was working on the books, maybe he started to put them away, and found something then." Getting up, he walked over to the book shelves and began to carefully examine them.

First he ran his fingers around the moldings to look for some kind of latch. Then he kicked the walls just above the floor, thinking that he might release something. When that produced nothing, he began to methodically pound his fist on the walls surrounding the bookshelves, then he stomped on the floor in front of them. Nothing worked, and so he began to pull, then push on each shelf, first carefully, then with more force. It was only a matter of time before he began to work on the side panels of the bookshelves, and the fact that Perrin had opened it so recently made the catch work more easily. All at once the wall swung forward, again exposing the hidden treasures to those present.

Alix gasped, and Henri rushed over to the opening, trying to look inside. "It's too dark to see much, but there are things in here. Quick! Someone get a candle."

Gaspard lit the candle from the desk, then gave it to Henri, who carefully held it up high as he peered into the small space. Gaspard pulled on the wall to open it as fully as he could and provide as much light as possible.

"It looks like there are just some old paintings in here," Henri spoke as he leaned forward. "But wait, there are some little shelves at the back as well. I can't see what's on them." He winced in pain as he tried to move the paintings, then looked out at Gaspard. "You'll have to take everything out to see what's on the shelves."

Alix had been standing near, excitement growing inside of her. She had never imagined that Thérèse would ever have any treasures from the old days, and now the realization that maybe something from her past was hidden in there was almost more than she could stand. "Henri, you must move and let Gaspard lift those things out of there." She went to the desk and brought the chair back to where he was standing. "Sit here and you can see everything just as he brings it all out."

Henri leaned forward as each picture was brought from its hiding place. Alix stood beside him and watched with delight as she recognized the paintings that had once been on the walls of the château. "Gaspard, look, it's the old comte." She could barely contain her emotions as she walked forward to run her hands along the frame in an effort to convince herself that they were real. "And his wife, too!" she cried.

"Hhhh," she breathed in sharply as the oldest pictures were brought out. "Mon Dieu!" Alix quickly crossed herself, then turned to Henri with a radiant smile. "That is from the altar in the chapel. It is very old, and was very precious to the young comte and his wife. I thought that it had been destroyed."

Gaspard continued to bring out the other paintings, and Alix tried to explain what they were or where they had been hanging. When the last painting was brought out and placed against the wall, Alix gasped and put her hand to her mouth. "Oh, Gaspard, look!" She breathed in and bit her lips. Tears came to her eyes as she looked at Gaspard, then back to the painting. "They were so young to have to die."

Gaspard was nearly overcome with emotion. "That is the young comte and his wife," he explained. "Painted soon after they were married."

Alix looked closely at the painting. Through the years, watching her daughter grow, she had known that Thérèse had some of her mother's features, but mostly thought that she looked like herself. Now, gazing closely at the picture of the young woman, she was surprised to find how very similar they were, almost like twins. Especially in the eyes, and the magnificent red hair.

"That was all he needed, Gaspard. One look at that painting tells it all." Alix turned to Henri. "I never realized how much they look alike."

If there had ever been any doubts in Henri's mind that they were telling him the truth, one look at the young woman in the painting dispelled them. The dress and the jewels were grander than any of the simple clothes that Thérèse wore, but there was no denying the resemblance in the two faces. Henri looked at the man standing next to her, handsome and regal. There was even a look around the nose that reminded him of Thérèse. Despair welled up in Henri's chest as he looked at the proof that he was not the heir of St. Vivant.

Gaspard continued to bring the items from the closet. Alix recognized the trays as some old ones with the family crest. And when the books were laid on the desk, Alix touched them with affection. "This large one is an old Bible that was in the chapel." she explained. Then she picked up a smaller one, continuing, "This once belonged to the young comtesse's grandmother, and she kept on a table beside her bed. It was her prayer book."

Henri had become very quiet, and as she looked through the Bible, Alix sensed what he must be going through his mind. She had grown to love the young man, and felt keenly for him, knowing that his dreams were being shattered.

"I need to go back and check on Thérèse." Alix picked up the prayer book, and walked toward Henri. "This will be devastating for her, Henri. She always thought that Nicholas and I were her parents. She will need you to talk to and to help her as she sorts this out."

"I thought that maybe I would go to Paris and see Bernard for the present."

"No! You must not travel with your shoulder so bad." Alix was alarmed at his words. "Gaspard, you must convince him not to go."

"She's right, Henri. Just the little bit that you were doing today started your wound to bleeding. Wait a little longer. Bernard will be here soon enough."

Henri knew that they were right. It was useless to leave when he was not strong enough to ride even half of the day. As much as he needed to get away, for the moment he would have to stay. Henri nodded his agreement, and with resignation in his voice, said, "You are right. I'll stay for now."

"Thank you," Alix breathed a sigh of relief, then put her hand on Henri's arm. "And don't underestimate how much Thérèse will need you – will need your support."

Alix asked Gaspard to follow her with the painting of Thérèse's parents, and went down the hall to the foot of the stairs. Henri followed. But they had only gone a third of the way up the staircase when they heard the sound of horses hooves and a wagon on the stones outside.

"It must be Bernard!" cried Henri. Clasping his arm, he hurried back down the stairs and crossed to the door, only to find on opening it, not Bernard, but Marie Judith getting down from the seat, and her brother coming around the tail of the wagon carrying her bag. She walked up to the open door, but then stopped short in surprise.

"What has happened to you, my boy? I never should have left you on your own. Look at the terrible wound you have!" The concern in her voice continued as she said, "Hello, Alix, Gaspard. What has happened here?"

"Marie Judith, what are you doing back so soon? I thought you were going to wait until we sent word that it was safe to return?" The surprise in Alix's voice was obvious.

"I know, but I would rather die of the sickness than spend one more night in my sister-in-law's house. Louis offered to drive me back first thing this morning and I agreed immediately. I was sure that there would be something I could do, if only feeding the cows."

Alix sighed, imagining what life must have been like for poor Louis with his wife and Marie Judith under one roof again. "Well, you couldn't have come at a better time. We haven't had coffee, much less any breakfast this morning."

Marie Judith looked triumphantly at her brother. "See? I am needed. I hope that you will tell your wife that I was welcomed back with open arms." And with that she took her valise from Louis and went straight down to the kitchen.

Louis followed her with his eyes, then gave them all an impish shrug before taking leave. Alix and Gaspard spoke softly together as they went on up the stairs, and Henri watched them silently, his mind and body in torment. The early morning exertion had left a throbbing pain in his shoulder. He needed to lie down and find a quiet place to think. He went in his room and closed his door soundly.

The noise of the wagon had awakened Thérèse and she was sitting up in bed when Alix came into the room. Gaspard said good morning, then leaned the painting against the wall and left to see what Marie Judith might need. Alix went straight to Thérèse's side, and felt her forehead, relieved to find that her skin was still cool and dry. She bent down and kissed her cheek.

"You don't know how relieved I am that you are better. You have been very lucky, my dear."

From the soft white pillows Thérèse smiled sweetly at Alix. "It was my own fault, Mama. You told me not to let anyone in the cottage, and I did anyway. I'm sorry that you had to spend your time with me when there are so many others sick."

"Don't ever think that, Thérèse." She took Thérèse's hand in hers as she continued, regret filling her voice. "You are my first duty, and I failed you. So much could have been avoided if I had been with you more these last few days."

Thoughts of that terrible night came flooding back into Thérèse's memory. She knew, because she had asked in her waking moments, that Perrin was dead and Henri badly hurt. "How is Henri, Mama? Is he in a great deal of pain?"

"His wound is bad, but should heal very well if he will give it the time it needs. But most of his pain is from the inside right now."

Thérèse began to cry. "Poor Henri. This is all so terrible, Mama. Perrin lied to me, he told me that Henri had gone to marry that other woman. And I was so angry with you." She told Alix about the day that she had overheard the conversation with Gaspard in the barn. "I thought that you could have kept Henri from having to go to Paris and blamed you for his marriage. So I decided to take my future in my own hands. Then, when we got back, there was Henri, and I learned that Perrin had lied. He said that he had married me only to get the estate," Thérèse put her face in her hands and softly wept as she remembered that horrible gunshot.

Alix sat on the bed next to her and put her arms around Thérèse to comfort her. Tears were forming in her eyes as well. There had been so much pain, and Alix blamed much of it on herself.

"You were right, Thérèse, I could have kept it from happening." Alix stroked the soft red hair as she talked. "I kept putting it off, waiting for the time to be right. And of course it never was. And maybe I loved having you as my daughter so much that I didn't want to tell you the truth." Alix finally admitted.

Thérèse looked down at the blanket, and picked at a loose thread. "So what Perrin said was true?"

Alix moved from her side and sat on the bed so that she could face the beautiful young woman that she had raised as a daughter. "Yes, Thérèse. It may have been the only truth he told the whole time that he was here. You are really their child, born here in the château three nights before they died."

"So you knew them better than you have said."

Alix smiled softly. "We were friends, dearest friends. It might seem strange, but you would have had to know them. And especially Gabrielle, the comtesse. She came to the farm one day looking for herbs and asked me to teach her how to use them. Through the next couple of years we became as close as sisters. Then, when we were both pregnant at the same time, it just seemed perfect. We spent long hours sharing our dreams for our children and wondering what the world would be like if the terrible things happening in Paris didn't stop. Then the Révolution began to creep into even our little village."

"And you took me for safekeeping?"

"Actually Nicholas took you. I sent a large valise with him the night you were born. There were some herbs and salves in it. He emptied the case, and waited, supposedly there to go for a doctor if one was needed. But I felt that she would have an easy birth, and I was right. After you were born she fed you once to make sure that you would sleep, then Nicholas wrapped you up, put you in the valise and brought you straight to me."

"And what happened to your baby?"

"She was stillborn, like the others. But this time I had you. I began to believe that you had been sent to me to make up for the child I could never give Nicholas."

Thérèse looked at Alix, trying to understand how she must have felt. "But, Mama, why didn't you ever tell me?"

"After Nicholas died, I just couldn't deal with the problems that trying to prove your claim would have presented. And the truth had such import that there was still danger for you. Then, when Henri came, I began to get an idea of how things could work out. I was waiting for just the right time. But Perrin and Uncle Georges had their plans as well."

A stillness filled the room. Alix looked through the open

window at the blue sky and thought. She had never really believed that this day would come. It had been ever on her mind, but always as something that would happen someday. It was strange how events sometimes come to pass on their own time.

Thérèse lay back on the white pillows and closed her eyes. When she was a little girl, she had played in these rooms sometimes, pretending that she was a princess, imagining what it would be like to live here. And recently she had dreamed of living here as Henri's wife. Never had she imagined that it was really hers. And even now she could not imagine living here without Henri. A cold shudder ran thorough her body. What if Perrin had killed Henri and she had been forced to live here without him? Life would not have been worth living! Thank God that he had been spared.

A tapping interrupted the quiet and the cheerful face of Marie Judith appeared at the door. She held a tray filled with cups, tea pot, and even some bread and fruit. "I brought some fresh bread with me, just in case, and I'm glad that I did. What was left in the kitchen had dried out so that it was not fit to eat. I've told Gaspard to start a fire in the oven and I'll have things back in shape in no time." She put the tray on a small round table near the bed, then turned to Alix. "I made tea instead of coffee – I thought that it would be better for Thérèse after she's been so ill. Gaspard told me about the hunting accident, and how Thérèse came down with the sickness. Thank goodness you were able to bring her here and take care of them both at the same time." She took one last look at the tray, nodding to herself with satisfaction that she had not forgotten anything, and then headed back to the door. "I knocked at the young master's door but he did not answer, so I'll wait until later to bring him something."

"I'm going to look in on him in a moment, Marie Judith. Then I'll come down and let you know what he wants."

The woman gave Alix a quick nod, then left, closing the door behind her. Thérèse smiled at her mother, both of them realizing how obviously glad Marie Judith was to be back where she was in command. Alix stood to pour a cup of tea for Thérèse, then fixed one for herself and sat back down in the chair.

"How is Henri, Mama?" Thérèse asked tentatively.

Alix shook her head. "This will not be an easy time for him,

Thérèse. I am sure that you know more than I what being master here meant to him. It gave him an identity, someone to 'be.' Now he is unsure again. I am very worried that the next few days will be a difficult test for his spirit."

"But it does not really matter who owns this land. I will tell him that we can just go on the same as before." The attempt at bravado in her voice failed entirely.

"You know that it will not be that simple, Thérèse. He is a proud man, and you will have to work very hard to convince him that this does not make a difference." Alix stood and put her cup back on the tray. "But at this moment you can do nothing about Henri. And right now I have something to show you." Alix walked over to pick up the painting and brought it to the bed. She turned it around as she said with a catch of emotion in her voice, "These are your parents as they looked when they first were married."

Thérèse looked at the handsome young couple, searching their faces for some knowledge of their lives. Her face brightened as she recognized how much she looked like her mother. How happy they looked! "Oh, Mama! Tell me everything that you know about them."

The shadows had grown long in the quiet room. The stillness of the late afternoon was broken only by the sound of breathing. Thérèse slept, exhausted by the emotions that had been released in the long hours that she and Alix had talked. After showing Thérèse the painting and the book of prayers, Alix had gone to check on Henri and speak to Marie Judith and Gaspard. But then she had returned and stayed to answer every question that Thérèse asked. Finally she had gone, leaving Thérèse to rest as she looked at the people and mentally sorted through pieces of the incredible story that was, apparently, her life.

Thérèse's thoughts turned to dreams and she slipped into sleep as the light of day turned into evening. She did not wake when Henri entered the room. And now he sat in the same chair where Alix sat earlier, watching her and waiting. She looked so pale and soft against the whiteness of the sheets, and his arms longed to hold her close, as much to gain comfort from her closeness as to give comfort to her. He longed to know again the familiarity of her embrace, to savor the sweet scent of her hair. And yet he knew that all was different, what had been familiar was now strange. She was now the noble person and he was... what?

The shadows drew out, until they were no more. The sound of the cicadas slowly filled the air, and finally Thérèse turned her head and opened her eyes. It took a moment for her to see him sitting quietly in the twilight. Then she smiled. "I'm glad you're here," she said simply.

"I wanted to see for myself that you were all right."

"And I wondered about your shoulder. Are you in much pain?"

"Not as long as I don't use my arm. Your mother... or Alix, said that I should be much better in a few days."

An uncomfortable silence fell. There was so much to say, so many questions that he wanted to ask. But where did one begin?

Finally he blurted out, "Why, Thérèse? Why did you go away to... marry him?"

"He lied to me, Henri." She looked down at her hands as she spoke. "He told me that you were going to marry that woman with all of the money. I didn't know what else to do."

"But how could you believe that I would leave like that and not tell you? I would never do something like that. I thought you knew me better."

"I didn't want to believe him, Henri. I didn't think that you would just go away like that. But then I looked for the rings that Aunt Catherine sent, the one you said you would save for your comtesse. And they were gone." Thérèse looked at him with an agonizing expression. "I thought that you were gone from me as well."

"I took them to get them engraved with your initials. I had decided to tell my uncle that I could never marry anyone else. I thought that even if I had to give up the estate, I would still use the rings to marry you. I thought that I would still be..." he stopped and did not finish his sentence.

"I didn't know," she said softly. "I only knew that they were gone."

Henri sat silently for a moment, then said in a hardened tone, "I still don't understand how you could go with him. Not with Perrin. Couldn't you wait and trust me? Didn't the fact that I loved you mean anything?"

"It was because of that love, Henri." A look full of sorrow and pain covered her face. "I knew that you loved me, and I couldn't bear to stay here, loving you, too, and knowing that you would feel trapped."

"Couldn't you have trusted me just a little? Given me a little time to work things out with Uncle Georges?"

"I was pregnant, Henri," she cried. "I was going to have your baby, and couldn't stand the thought of what that would do to you, to us. I knew that I couldn't stay here and have your child, and at the same time watch you in pain in a marriage to someone else. Then the sickness came on and muddled my brain, and I didn't know what else to do." She was silent for a moment, then added, "As awful as he was, he offered me something at a time when I thought I didn't have any other choice."

Henri stared at her with a stunned look on his face. "You're going to have a baby?"

Shaking her head, Thérèse lowered her face and looked down. She bit her lips, then answered him with tears in her eyes. "I was, but not any more. Mama said that because of the fever, and the carriage ride, and... everything...." There was a catch in her throat, and she could not continue.

The light was almost gone now. In the gathering darkness the two sat silently, not knowing what to say. Finally Henri stood. "I guess it wasn't meant to be," he said softly. Then he left.

17

THÉRÈSE WAS DOWNSTAIRS SITTING IN THE PETIT SALON the next day when the sound of a carriage was heard pulling into the courtyard of the château. The isolation of the upstairs room had been too much for her and, against her mother's protest, she had insisted that she be allowed to dress and go down where she would at least be near the château's activity. What she did not tell her mother was that she could not stay in the room and be constantly reminded of her conversation the night before with Henri. Alix had agreed, but only if Gaspard carried her down the stairs, and Thérèse promised to remain quiet.

The couch had been moved near a window so that Thérèse could amuse herself with what few comings and goings there were outside. With the news that there were still some outbreaks of the sickness, workers were staying away. But Thérèse was content just to watch the birds overhead and look at the flowers blooming in the unkempt garden. Alix had Gaspard bring the rest of the paintings in and lean them against the walls, and she explained, to the best of her memory, who they were. And everyone in the house made an effort to come by to talk for a few moments throughout the morning. Everyone, that is, but Henri. She had only seen him once that morning, from the window in the distance.

So Thérèse was the first to hear the wheels of the carriage as they rolled up the avenue, and she called out excitedly to Alix when she recognized Bernard driving the team of matched grays. When she saw two women sitting in the seat behind she knew at once that this must finally be Aunt Catherine and her maid. She was so fascinated with the sight of the woman, that she did not even notice that a wagon loaded high with furniture was pulling up behind.

Alix and Marie Judith had been cleaning the library when they heard Thérèse's excited call. When Alix realized who had arrived, she sent the older woman out at once to find Henri and Gaspard. Thérèse watched as Henri walked from the vat house to greet his aunt and help her from the carriage. She could see the sense of apprehension in his face, but his excited Aunt only saw the sling over his arm. Her immediate concern was for the bandage on his shoulder, and Thérèse knew, as she saw him shake his head, that Henri was assuring her that he was not in pain.

The little group stood in the midday sun and talked for a moment, allowing Thérèse to get a good look at Henri's aunt. She was of medium height, very fashionably dressed, and wearing a hat that covered most of her brown hair. But when she turned toward the château, Thérèse was shocked to see that half of her face was badly deformed, with one eye slanting down sharply toward her chin, and very little cheekbone.

She was stunned! Neither Bernard nor Henri had ever mentioned it; in fact, the way they spoke of her, Thérèse had thought that she must be very handsome. Thankful that she had this time to get accustomed to the face before she met Aunt Catherine, Thérèse watched the little tableau.

Bernard was talking, pointing to the vathouse. Henri shook his head and spoke for a moment. Then Gaspard joined them and held out his hand toward the château so that Thérèse was sure he was suggesting they come inside. She sat up a little straighter and checked to see that her hair was as neatly tied at the nape of her neck as the curly tendrils that surrounded her face would allow.

It was like a breath of fresh air when Aunt Catherine swept into the room and over to the couch. "My dear Thérèse. I would know you anywhere. Henri would talk of nothing else when he was in Paris but of his beautiful Thérèse." She moved quickly over to the couch where Thérèse was sitting and gave her a gentle hug. Then

Thérèse saw the wonderful smile that seemed to light up the whole room, full of kindness and love. And she knew why Henri and Bernard thought her such a beautiful woman.

The woman turned to Alix and continued. "You must be Madame Condé. I cannot thank you enough for being so kind to my Henri when he came. Bernard has told me of your thoughtfulness, and now you have also taken care of Henri's wounded shoulder. I will not forget."

Alix assured her that she had done nothing out of the ordinary, but had been more than glad to help Henri. As she invited Catherine to sit on a nearby couch, she turned to Bernard and told him that she had ordered a tray of cheese and fruit, and some coffee. Then she asked them how their trip had been

"It was absolutely awful, but thank you for asking," said Bernard with a grimace on his face.

"Now, Bernard, it was not that bad." Catherine turned to the others to assure them. "We had some unfortunate occurrences, but the weather was delightful, and the countryside between here and Paris is magnificent. I'm sure we would have seen some very quaint towns, but we had to keep avoiding them because of the sickness. Still, that took us down some lovely country lanes, and the wild-flowers were exquisite. The nights were cool and we slept out under the stars and awoke to glorious sunrises. What more could you ask for?"

Thérèse noticed an amused look passing over Bernard's face as she talked. Then, when she finished, he spoke. "For those of you who do not know our dear Catherine, I will interpret. One of the wagon wheels broke, and since she would not leave her things behind for fear of thieves, I spent one full day trying to get it fixed and the wagon reloaded. We were afraid to go through the towns because of the sickness, and so got lost on those lovely country roads. The wagon got stuck in several ruts and the grays had to be unhitched to help pull it out. Because of the sickness, we were also afraid to stay at inns, but Catherine did not mind as long as we took two mattresses off the wagon each night, one for her and one for Paulette, her maid, because, of course, they could not be expected to share. Other than that, the trip took twice as long as it should have, but was fine."

"Well, Bernard, if you insist on stressing the unfortunate occurrences I suppose you could describe it that way, but I think that you are being very negative," and a pout came to Catherine's face.

"And you, Aunt Catherine, are nothing if not positive about everything, which is why Bernard and I love you and put up with you." Though he was obviously holding himself away from the group, Henri could not help but interject a comment into scene.

Thérèse noticed Paulette, the pretty little maid, sitting quietly on a chair near the wall, watching everything with a big grin on her face. If this kind of banter went on often between Catherine and others, as Thérèse suspected it did, the young girl must find her employment extremely enjoyable.

But Thérèse also watched the conversation taking place with the full realization that Henri's emotions were on guard. They all chatted on for a few more moments. Alix caught Bernard up on the state of the sickness and which of his worker's families she had attended to. Gaspard had already assured them before they came in that Thérèse could no longer spread the disease. And when Marie Judith arrived with a tray of refreshments, she was able to tell them how things appeared to be getting better in the village. Then the conversation turned, as it must, to Henri's wound.

Catherine broached the subject when she turned to Henri and said lovingly, "Now, my darling boy, you must tell me how this terrible accident came to happen."

No one spoke. Henri looked down at his boots. Thérèse looked away and out at the sky. Then Alix sent a message with her eyes and an almost imperceptible nod to Gaspard. He hesitated for a moment, then asked the little maid to leave, kindly showing her where her mistress's room could be found. When he returned, he told them in a low voice, the entire story, only leaving out certain things, like Thérèse's pregnancy, that did not need to be discussed. When he came to Perrin's part, Bernard swore under his breath that he should have expected as much all along.

But the most surprising reaction came from Catherine, who began to cry and dropped her head into her hands, sobbing, "All my fault, it was all my fault."

"Madame Girond, you could have done nothing to stop him. I am sure that Perrin came here for just this purpose, and we all were duped." Gaspard was visibly upset at the idea that she thought they had been negligent on Henri's behalf.

"No, no! You don't understand. Explain to them, Bernard," she said as she wept.

Bernard sat thoughtfully for a moment, then answered her. "No, Catherine. You must explain. It is only right."

She looked up at him with pitiful eyes, her deformed face covered in tears. "I cannot, Bernard."

"You must, Catherine. The time has come."

Later, when Thérèse thought back over that afternoon, she wondered how Henri had been able to sit there and listen to Catherine's story. He had taken blow after blow in only a few days, but this was undoubtedly the worst.

Catherine wiped her eyes with a lace handkerchief, then spoke, hesitantly at first. "Henri," there was a long pause. "Henri, I knew all along that you were not the comte de St. Vivant. But when Georges saw this estate still vacant, and suggested that he might be able to make it yours, I agreed. I thought that if you had your own winery, your own property, that finally I could begin to make things right for you."

"What things, Aunt Catherine?" Henri asked his question cooly, with no emotion. But Thérèse saw a wary look come into his eyes. Silently, she wondered when she would once again see that happy open face that she loved.

Catherine saw the look as well. She patted the sofa next to her as she appealed to him. "Come and sit beside me while I tell you. And promise that you will hear me out."

First there was a moment's hesitation, but Henri complied with her wishes. Then she took his hand and began. She looked over at Thérèse as she spoke. "Since this plan seems to have intruded so terribly in your lives as well, I suppose that all of you should know my story."

"I was blessed to have very special parents, and so," she paused, then sighed, "I learned long ago to live with this face that I was born with. Our father was a fairly prosperous shopkeeper in the town where Georges and I lived. And he and my mother decided very early to deal publicly with the deformity. They did not hide me, so I was not a shock to villagers except at the very first. We were wealthy enough that my family did not have to tolerate any teasing from the children of other families. Papa never allowed Georges to mistreat me.

He expected Georges, who is seven years older, to protect me. And at home we talked honestly about the problem and how it affected other people. As I said, I was very lucky.

"In fact, I was lucky enough to actually have a beau, and to fall in love. He was the son of a family we knew, a young soldier. And we planned to marry. I was nineteen at the time, and so much in love. Around that time Papa's health had been failing, and my mother was pleased that I was to be taken care of. Then the troubles in Paris began, and he was called away to defend the palace at Versailles. Our last few days were filled with promises of undying love… and indiscreet passion." Catherine stopped, not quite sure of what to say next.

"He never came back. We heard he was killed. But I was not left alone, because I was lucky enough to have his child. A lovely little boy. You, Henri." By that time Henri had begun to suspect what she was going to say. He pulled his hand from hers and listened quietly, staring out of the window, but seeing nothing.

"Georges had married Louise, the daughter of a wealthy merchant, and she was furious about what had happened. But my family was very close, and our love helped us to not condemn people for what others saw as personal failings. Louise could never understand that.

"But then she never knew about Aunt Cecile, either. She was my father's only sister. A magnificent beauty, with a wonderful sense of humor and a low, husky laugh. She was the mistress of a very important and very generous duke for most of her life. She loved life and people, and thought that too many of us get so caught up in everyday trials that we forget to appreciate what we have. She warned me about that the last time I saw her. Supposedly she came to see my baby, but in reality she came to leave her fortune with my father. She felt certain that her duke would soon be taken to prison in Paris and she was determined to go with him. She told Papa that if anything happened to her, Georges should have the money, but all of the jewels were to be mine. When we were together that last night, she warned me not to underestimate the value of the jewels. They were worth twice the gold coins she had left for Georges, but she wanted to make sure that my future and Henri's were secure."

The room had become as still, as if no one even breathed. They were all transfixed by the woman and the story she told. All but Henri, who only wanted to vanish from their midst. He steeled himself for more.

"Her duke was soon taken to Paris, and the story goes that she went along, pretending to be his wife's maid. Along the road, when they had left their own province, she and the wife exchanged clothes, wigs, and identities in the hopes that in Paris, the maid would be allowed to go free. That is what happened, and Aunt Cecile died on the guillotine with the man she loved. We heard that his wife was able to get to safety in England."

Catherine smiled apologetically at them, "But I'm getting off the story. I warn you that I get sidetracked easily. Anyway, the jewels were hidden away. Georges invested his money in banks in England to protect it during the troubled times. And I lived with my parents, all of us loving our wonderful little boy. Of course, Louise hated it all. Out of spite she said that having a fatherless nephew would be an embarrassment to Georges' family in their growing social position. For once my mother listened to what Louise was saying and convinced me that for Henri's future as well as my own, Henri should grow up thinking that I was his aunt, not his mother. I was not as sure that it was a good idea, but Georges asked me to do it as a favor to him. So I became Aunt Catherine.

"But life does not stay the same. Papa died, and, because of the new laws, left his business to Georges and me as equal partners with Mama. She died nine months later, but even with half of everything I did not feel as secure as I wanted to be. Times were exciting for people who knew where to invest, and very dangerous for fools. And so I made a pact with Georges. I would let him use all of the capital from Papa's business, and sell most of my jewels for more, but half of everything was to be mine. And I would be taken care of for as long as I needed to be. I even had a contract drawn up by a lawyer so that if anything happened to Georges, Louise could not claim everything as hers. When Georges saw the magnificent pieces that Aunt Cecile had left me, he was amazed. I kept a few things, mostly pieces that I knew were her favorites, but he took the rest to England where he sold them at a good price, and our business began to grow.

"One day he took me to see the estate in Bordeaux, and said that he thought he could get it for a reasonable price. I fell in love with it immediately, and told him I wanted to bring Henri there to live. Louise didn't like having me near them, and was thrilled. The only problem was that she also thought it a healthy place to send the children in the summer, and I was there. She didn't like Henri around; she said he reminded her of my sin. And rather than fight with her I let him eat in his room, and kept him out of her way. It was best for Henri, but Louise came to think that I did it out of fear of her, and she became unbearably haughty when she was there.

"Those visits were the bad times, but the rest were wonderful. Henri was free to run and grow like a wild colt. And from an early age he would come in and tell me what wonderful things he had learned from Bernard. I knew that Bernard was the manager of the estate, but I didn't have many reasons to speak with him. And he didn't come to the château very often. I learned later that he was afraid he would offend me by staring. But as I realized how kind he was to Henri, I began to seek him out to thank him. We slowly began to know each other, and the more I saw of him the more I saw to respect. Finally, realizing that as Henri grew he would need more contact with such a man as Bernard, I asked him if he would consider taking his evening meal with us. He agreed, and we became almost like a family. They were wonderful years." She paused to smile at Bernard, then continued.

"Then a few years ago Bernard and I realized that we wanted to be just that, a family. By then we had shared our loftiest dreams, and many of our secrets. He knew who Henri was, and loved him all the more. The next time that Georges and Louise came, I spoke with them and told them about our plans. Louise was livid. She said that it was bad enough that I would have a child out of wedlock, but that now I wanted to marry beneath my station and embarrass them all. She said a lot of other things, but I have tried to forget them. It was partly my fault. I think that if I had spoken to Georges alone things would have gone better. But, shrew though she is, he loves Louise and didn't want her upset.

"I was ready to go ahead and marry, but Bernard, always the voice of reason, said that maybe we should wait and see if a better time wouldn't present itself. Reluctantly, I agreed, but only on the understanding that Louise was never to return to the château at Bordeaux as long as I was there. If I couldn't have complete happiness I wasn't going to put up with her haughty snobbery either.

"And so we went on as before. But each day I prayed that something would happen to give us the chance to be free. When Georges came to Bordeaux and told me about St. Vivant I believed that my prayers had been answered. He had asked the villagers about the château and learned the whole story, haunted buildings and all. In Paris, he had learned that all of the comte's family had been executed, so he could make up the story about the comtesse's brother rescuing the baby. Then he had the records checked to find out just how much land could still be claimed as part of the estate. He suspected that he could buy it, but if we let Henri pretend to be the heir, we could probably get it for free. He thought that the local people would be so thankful for the new business and jobs that they would accept Henri's story without too much fuss. And Georges would use the winery to begin spreading his business to eastern France, then to Germany.

"I listened, thought, prayed, and discussed it all with Bernard. The next day I told Georges that I thought that it could work, but I wanted it as mine. Through the years I had never asked when he bought a town house in Paris, and a large country estate for Louise. Now I reminded him of our contract and told him that I wanted this for my own. And I wanted the money to re-establish the winery, and completely furnish the château in a style that the comte de St. Vivant would be proud of. Dear Georges. He agreed immediately. He said that he had been wondering when I would ask for some of my profits. And he offered to let Bernard come and get things going here. I think that he knew all along that we would get married as soon as we could get away. And with me in eastern France, and Louise in the west, maybe he could finally make us both happy."

Catherine paused for a moment, then looked sheepishly around. "So that is how it happened. We told Henri the story of how he had been spirited away in the night for his own safety. And now that he was coming of age we felt that he should begin to assume his position in life." She turned to Alix and said with a voice filled with sincerity and sorrow, "We never would have done any of this if we had dreamed that there was really an heir, or rather heiress, still alive."

Bernard, who had been so quiet, letting Catherine tell it all in her own words, finally spoke. "You must believe that, Madame Condé. Monsieur Girond was convinced that the estate had no owner, and we believed that we could make a difference here by giving the local people work. We would never try to take land that belonged to someone else."

Alix looked at them, amazed at the intricate story. She knew that Catherine had acted out of love, but she also knew that a shrewd business sense had been at the base of this plan. Still, Thérèse's future had to be at the forefront of her thoughts, and that future needed to include Henri, so she chose her words carefully. "It is normal to want the very best for the ones you love. I think that both Thérèse and I can understand that."

"Well I don't!" shouted Henri, and he bolted from the room.

18

"OH, BERNARD, BERNARD," CATHERINE CRIED, "What have I done? My poor boy," and she broke down into tears.

Bernard rushed to her side, trying to comfort her. "He had to know, Catherine. Once he learned that the château belonged to Thérèse, he knew that we had not told him the truth." Putting his arms around her, he continued in a soothing voice. "You could not have told the story in any better way, my dear. Now we just need to give him time to accept it all."

Raising her tear-swollen face to look at Bernard, Catherine put her hand gently on his cheek. "I should never have agreed to this. It was a deceit, a sin, and sins will always find you out in the end. I thought that finally our time had come, but I should have known that trying to buy happiness with a lie would never work." She laid her head on his shoulder and quietly heaved a sigh while the tears trickled down her face.

Thérèse watched the middle-aged lovers with amazement; handsome and graying Bernard comforting the deformed Catherine. Never would she have guessed that the day would take such a turn of events. Poor, dear Henri. To have his entire world so shattered within only a few days was more than she feared he could stand. She turned to Alix and in a worried voice whispered, "Mama?"

Almost as if reading her mind, Alix interrupted Bernard and Catherine, saying, "I think someone should go and find Henri. The boy's mind must be in a terrible state. I would go, or Gaspard," she looked quickly to Gaspard who nodded silently, "But I think that it should be one of you."

"He will not want to see me right now, of that I am sure," said Catherine sadly. "You must go to him, Bernard. You have been so close to him these last few weeks – maybe he will talk to you."

"Let me give him a few more minutes alone, my dear. Then I will see how he fares." Bernard sat beside her quietly and held her until her tears subsided.

When she was more composed, Catherine turned to Alix and Thérèse and in an apologetic voice said, "This was not at all the way I planned for our meeting to go. I hope you will forgive me. Maybe we can talk together later in the afternoon. But right now I am too worried about Henri to be pleasant company. He told me about the wonderful chapel that you have here. If you could show me where it is, I would like to go there to be alone. I think that we will need God's help to sort this out."

Without a moment's hesitation, Alix responded that she understood completely and stood to show Catherine the way. As she passed Bernard, she told him that she would tell Marie Judith to plan their dinner for early evening. Then she turned to Gaspard and insisted that he come to dinner, too. Having done that, she invited Catherine to accompany her and preceded her to the door.

Bernard left immediately afterward to find Henri, leaving Thérèse alone with Gaspard. They sat in silence for a moment; then she asked him, "Do you think Bernard will be able to reason with him?"

Gaspard walked over to one of the long windows, and looked out into the bright day. "I don't know. Sometimes when a man takes blow after blow, he finds that the only way to survive is to shut himself away from any situation that might hurt him. For some men, that is the rest of their lives. Other men get a new chance at some point and come back to life. I don't think Henri can shut himself away forever, but I don't know how long it will take him to realize that."

Shaking his head, he continued to look out of the window, then turned back to Thérèse. "I should go and help with the wagon."

Nodding his head toward her, he turned to leave.

Alone in the big, quiet room, Thérèse thought about the last few days. Never had she dreamed that her life would take such an amazing turn. This château was hers. In this very room her parents and grandparents, the people in the paintings leaning against the wall, had laughed and talked, and lived.

And yet it did not feel like home. Even now she longed to get back to the quiet little cottage, to sit under the big oak tree with the cat in her lap and think. She wanted to get away from all of the people here, and work with her mother in the big kitchen while they talked without being disturbed. As she sat on the beautifully upholstered couch in the grand room, Thérèse longed for her shabby, comfortable old chair, and realized that she was homesick.

The afternoon passed slowly. Catherine stayed in the chapel for a long time. Then she went to lie down on the bed in her room until nearly dinnertime. Paulette placed soothing cloths on her forehead and massaged her neck to relax the muscles that had grown taut from stress. While Marie Judith baked fresh bread and pastries, Alix went to her cottage in a wagon driven by Gaspard so that she could bring back fresh vegetables and fruit, as well as cheeses and meat to supplement the larder at the château. And Thérèse could only wonder what had happened between Bernard and Henri. Bernard did not say.

Thérèse was allowed to walk back up the staircase in the late afternoon to rest and change for dinner. Thankful that Alix had also brought back one of her dresses, Thérèse washed, then carefully brushed her hair and tied it up, hoping that she looked presentable, though without a mirror she could only guess.

When Thérèse entered the petit salon, Alix and Bernard were already there. Alix was showing him the old documents that Gaspard had dug up. Soon Catherine came sweeping into the room in a fashionable gown, and she was obviously determined to present a cheerful attitude. When she joined them, she also expressed an interest in seeing the old papers, and then wanted to know who the people in the paintings were. Thérèse listened closely, intent on gleaning any new item about her family each time she heard the story. As Alix was finishing, Gaspard joined them and added a little more information about where the paintings used to hang.

It was not long before Marie Judith came to announce that dinner was served. Alix looked first to Bernard, then to Catherine. "Should we wait for him?"

"I'm not sure what to do," answered Bernard. He looked toward Catherine for some kind of decision.

She was just about to open her mouth when Henri walked in, dressed for dinner, and nodded to them. In an effort not to allow an uncomfortable silence to come between them, Gaspard spoke up, his voice almost too cheerful. "You've arrived just in time. Shall we go in?" And in a very gallant gesture, most uncommon for Gaspard, he walked over and presented his arm to Catherine to accompany her to the dinning room.

Bernard escorted Alix, leaving Thérèse alone with Henri. She looked up into his eyes, and started to say his name, but he spoke first. "I'm sure Marie Judith has worked all afternoon on this dinner. We must not let it get cold." Then taking her arm, he led her through the door.

Dinner was a very uncomfortable affair. Talk centered around the sickness in the village, how the winery was progressing, what Uncle Georges would think, and how wonderful the house was. Henri said little, only replying when spoken to, so that soon the conversation was no longer directed his way. The candles burned low, as did the diners' enthusiasm. And by the time dinner was finished, the air was so heavy with unspoken words that it began to oppress them all. They only stayed long enough to complement Marie Judith for her delicious food, then each went his separate way in search of refreshing solitude.

Thérèse went to her room, which she was now sharing with her mother since the arrival of Catherine and her servant. Still weak from her illness, she sank down into a troubled sleep, her head filled with dreams of Henri running away from her, forever just out of her grasp. Then someone grabbed her arm, and tried to pull her away, and as she struggled she awoke to find her mother trying to rouse her.

"Thérèse, you must get up right away!"

"Mama, what's wrong? What time is it?"

"It's early morning, but you must get up quickly." Alix's voice was filled with urgency. "Henri is leaving."

"Leaving!" she cried.

"Yes. I heard voices and got up to see what the problem was. Catherine had gone in to Henri's room to check on him, and found him packing. She begged him to stay, but he insists that he must get away. He's gone down to the barn to saddle a horse. You're the only one who can convince him not to go."

"But if he won't stay for Catherine, what makes you think that he'll stay for me?" Thérèse cried. "Tonight he wouldn't even speak to me. What can I say to him, Mama, short of begging him to stay?"

"What's wrong with begging?" Alix looked at Thérèse sternly. "Don't you love him?"

"Of course I love him!"

"Then if you have to, beg." Tears came into her eyes, and Alix softened her voice. "Thérèse, if I thought that by begging I could spend one more precious minute with my Nicholas, I'd be down on my knees in a heartbeat. Don't let misplaced pride keep you away from the one you love. Henri is hurting right now in ways that we cannot imagine, and if the only way to get through the hurt is to beg him to stay, then that's what you must do."

In that minute, Thérèse began to understand what mature love was all about. She suddenly looked past the giddy, goosepimpled feeling that she had thought was true love and began to see how real love puts the needs of the other first.

"Hurry! There's no time! Just slip on those shoes, and put this shawl around your shoulders," said Alix. Bernard went down to light a lantern to follow him. You must hurry." Thérèse slipped into the soft shoes, not really fit for outside wear, and taking the shawl from her mother's hands, put it on as she hurried down the stairs. Bernard was waiting for her at the front entrance, and wordlessly led her into the night. When they got to the barn, she took the lantern and motioned him to stay outside.

In the pale light she watched as Henri tightened the straps on the saddle. Not sure where to start, but hoping that their love would show the way, Thérèse silently walked nearer to him, then softly said, "Henri, please don't go."

He stared at the saddle for a moment, then turned to her and in a tortured voice answered, "But how can I stay?"

"You just stay, Henri." Thérèse stepped closer, and gently placed her hand on his arm. "You know this is where you belong. You told me once yourself that you felt that you had finally come home."

"But that was before, when I thought that the land belonged to me, when I believed that I was someone special." Hurt and anger began to creep into his voice and she knew that he was remembering the taunts of his childhood. "But this is not my land, and I'm nothing more than a bastard. How can I stay, knowing that I am not fit to be even a stable hand?"

"That's not true!" Thérèse cried. "I don't care how you were born. What I know now is that you are the man I love, the man I need to teach me how to live on this grand estate. You were once quite happy to take a poor peasant girl and make her a comtesse. Well, that poor peasant girl needs you now. I've been through a lot these last few days, as I know you have. I need you to stay. We can help each other."

Gently placing his hand on her face, Henri looked sadly down at her. "I'm sorry for all the pain I've caused you. I just wanted to love you, not to hurt you."

"You would stay if there was still a baby, wouldn't you?" she said accusingly. The look on his face was answer enough. "So why won't you stay just for me?"

"I can't." Henri turned and swung up into the saddle, turning the horse so that he could look down at her one last time. "I wish that I could, but I just can't."

Thérèse grabbed the bridle to stop the horse and cried out, "Please, Henri. I'm begging you. I love you. Please, stay."

"And I love you," he said softly. Then wrenching the bridle back, he galloped out of the barn and into the darkness.

Thérèse ran out to follow him, tears streaming down her face. "Please come back," she called, then she collapsed into a sobbing heap on the ground.

From the limb of a tree that grew close by the barn, two owls, one great white one and one smaller grey one, watched as Bernard came to gently lift her up, and take her back into the house. Into the silence of the night the owls raised their voices – a soft hooting cry – to try and comfort her.

19

A FRESH AUTUMN BREEZE WAFTED GENTLY THROUGH THE WINDOW as Thérèse studied herself critically in the mirror. She was trying to duplicate a hair style that Paulette had shown her the week before, and she was rather pleased with the result. Some of her soft red hair had been pulled into a curly mass and secured at the crown of her head. The rest had been curled and left to frame her face and fall gently on the nape of her neck. Thérèse gave one curl a final pat, and stood back to judge her appearance.

The image reflected in the full length mirror that Alix had insisted on bringing up to Thérèse's room for this day was one of a beautiful, well-dressed young woman. Not a fancy Paris lady, but a young woman of grace – standing tall and straight in the soft green merino dress that she and Alix had planned in the heat of last summer. Thérèse was satisfied that she looked stylish but sensible, a person that the village could respect, yet continue to regard as a friend.

And how the village related to her was very important to Thérèse, because today she was finally going to move into the château and assume her position as the comtesse de St. Vivant.

That she would ever look forward to this moment would not have occurred to Thérèse that hot August night two months ago when Henri had ridden away. She had gone back to her room and collapsed in bed, weeping in Alix's arms. Then Thérèse had begged to be taken back to their cottage as soon as a horse could be hitched to the wagon.

Catherine had pleaded with her not to go, but Thérèse had insisted that she needed to be in her own home. Sensing her fragile emotional condition, Alix had supported her wishes, and by noon Thérèse was back in her own room upstairs in the little cottage, drinking a soothing tea that soon put her to sleep.

The next day, however, Alix insisted that Bernard, Catherine and Gaspard come to the Condé cottage, knowing that they had to make some type of arrangement concerning the estate and the winery. Soon the sickness that had swept through the district would begin to subside, and the workers would want to resume their jobs. There would be many uncomfortable questions to answer if they were sent away. Some type of accommodation would have to be reached.

After the subdued greetings, they all sat around the large farmhouse table. Alix had made tea and served her delicious gingerbread, but no one doubted that this was anything but a serious meeting.

Bernard cleared his throat. Then, with an encouraging nod from Catherine, he spoke. "Catherine and I were up late last night discussing the situation. Of course we hope Henri will come back and that eventually a marriage will take place between him and Thérèse.... or, I mean, la comtesse."

As he stumbled over his words, Thérèse turned pale and a sinking feeling began to invade the pit of her stomach. She moved as if to leave, but Alix put her hand firmly on her arm to keep her in her seat. "I think that we would all feel more comfortable if you just call her Thérèse." Alix smiled and nodded for Bernard to go on.

"As I said, we talked about this at great length last night, and what we would like to do is find some arrangement where we can stay here and carry out the work that we have started. I confess that I have found a great deal of satisfaction in rebuilding the winery, and I think that we could produce a very respectable wine in due time, one that would sell well in Paris and in other parts of the country."

No longer able to keep silent, Catherine broke in to add, "And I dearly love the château and grounds. I made Bernard spend the entire morning showing me the all over the estate, and Marie Judith was more than pleased to show me the château and all of the improvements that have begun. And the state of the gardens breaks my heart, so much there to be done. Henri," she hesitated a moment over his name, then in a faltering voice continued, "Henri wanted it to be a grand estate again. He was right. It should be."

Alix listened to them thoughtfully, then turned to Gaspard and asked, "And what do you think?"

Gaspard had been listening pensively. His words were few and to the point. "The people of the village have begun to think that the terrible hard times are ending. It would be a pity to have their hopes destroyed again."

Alix sighed. "That is just what I had been thinking. I remember the young comte saying what a heavy burden it was to have so many people depending on you. I'm beginning to understand what he meant." She tapped her fingers on the table before she continued, looking at Bernard and Catherine. "I must be honest with you. We do not have the money to pay back all of the work that you have done at the estate. I have a comfortable sum left from my father. And when Thérèse's father came to see her before he was murdered, he left a sum of gold. But Nicholas and I always knew that there was not enough to do everything. And so we have a half-finished winery, a half-renovated estate, and not enough money or knowledge of the business to finish it."

"And we have the money and the knowledge, but not the land or the buildings." Bernard took Catherine's hand in his as he spoke. "We have grown tired of waiting for the right time. Catherine and I want to begin to build a life of our own. And that is why we want to propose a partnership of some sort. If we can stay and finish what we have begun, we will find some way of dividing the eventual profits so that we can all benefit from the venture. However, you must understand, there probably won't be any profits for several years."

"And of course Catherine's investment must be paid back," interrupted Alix.

"I don't think that we should worry about that just now," commented Catherine. "Just a simple agreement is what we need today. Then we will see how the next few months go."

Thérèse knew that she was referring to Henri. Catherine was

still hoping that he would be back soon and that a marriage would remove the need to worry about her investment. But Thérèse remembered how much Henri had counted on being master of his own estate, and she was not sure that he would be able to come back to live at St. Vivant as anything less.

"I would want Gaspard to continue working there as Thérèse's representative, and also to make sure that the people of the village will continue to be the ones who are hired." Alix spoke pointedly at Bernard.

"Catherine understands how important this venture is to the economy of the village and to the residents. You will find that she feels much the same way you do about duty and obligation." Bernard's comments were reassuring.

Alix paused for a moment, trying to frame her next words carefully. "As a personal request, Catherine, I was wondering if you would consider teaching Thérèse what she will need to know to manage the château. I can teach her about some things, but not how to direct servants or to manage elegant affairs. I confess, even at my father's house in Dijon, I preferred to leave that work to someone else."

"But of course, I would love to." Catherine's face visibly brightened and her voice was full of enthusiasm. "We will begin just as soon as she is better. It will be such fun. We can go from the top of the house to the kitchen below. The mistress of a house must be familiar with every inch and corner. I will start right away to make lists of everything that she will need to know."

Bernard sat low in his chair and groaned. "We didn't tell them about your lists Catherine." He turned to the others and continued, with an indulgent look on his face. "Catherine learned the wonderful art of list-making a few years ago when she started forgetting things. Now she cannot do anything without great long lists that organize every moment. You will learn about her lists."

"Now Bernard," Catherine pouted. "You know that my lists have made things go much more smoothly. I don't see why you and Henri have to pretend that they make life so unbearable."

"She'll have you as organized as the emperor's army before you know it. In fact, Henri and I call her the little Napoleon at times."

"Bernard!" Catherine's voice was full of indignation. "I never knew that."

Thérèse and Alix exchanged glances. Alix was inwardly pleased to see a hint of a smile beginning to come back to Thérèse's lips. Finally interrupting Bernard and Catherine, who sat quarreling amiably, Alix said, "So we have an agreement. From this point on we are partners. We can formalize it with papers and specifics at a later date, if that is acceptable."

The arrangement was agreed on by everyone at the table, and after a short discussion about the state of the steadily ripening grapes, Catherine and Bernard went back to the château. Gaspard stayed a bit longer to help with some long neglected work in the barn and the garden.

While he was outside, Thérèse turned to Alix and asked softly. "Have we done the right thing, Mama?"

Alix sighed. "I hope that we have, Thérèse. I prayed about this a long time last night. I think that they are honest people. We have known Bernard these last two months and have no reason to doubt him. Sometimes you just have to do what seems right, and trust in God."

And from the progress made in the last two months their trust had been well placed. The men soon came back to work, and before long the harvest was well underway. Gaspard and Bernard continued to work well together, each doing what he knew best, and neither carrying a grudge away from their fairly regular arguments about techniques.

Catherine was in her element. Thankfully, she and Marie Judith worked well together too, and Catherine had a glorious time hiring additional maids, then organizing the staff in the château so that everything ran like clockwork. She also requisitioned some of the workmen and spent hours rearranging the furniture, then ordering more so that soon all of the rooms in the château were arranged to suit her standards of what she considered fashionable. She particularly loved the ballroom across the back, and made sure the maids kept the windows and the new mirrors sparkling clean. She also interviewed a string of workers until she found just the people that she wanted to begin restoring the gardens and avenue to their former glory. She and Alix spent time together in the herb garden at the château with Alix teaching her about the special attribute of each plant.

In all of this Thérèse was included. True to her word, Catherine dragged the young woman from the attic rooms to the cellars, teaching her everything that she knew about managing a large household. Soon, Thérèse's head was swimming with so much new information that she sometimes thought that she would never learn it all. But they also had fun, and Catherine was ever mindful of the fact that the château was Thérèse's home and made certain to ask her opinion on the various projects that were always in an ongoing state.

Before long Thérèse established a friendly rapport with the older woman, and with daily contact soon forgot, as had Henri and Bernard, about the disfigured face. Instead she learned to love the kind and generous woman as they talked at great length about plans for the estate.

Now the château was perfect. The small harvest had been gathered in, and the process of making wine had begun. This evening they would hold the first celebration that the estate had seen in twenty years. The staff had been working hard the last two days to prepare the mounds of food which would be needed to fill the plank tables that had been set up in the dining room and on the terrace above the river. A great new chandelier was filled with candles waiting to illuminate the grand entrance and the magnificently restored staircase. The salons were spotless and the ballroom filled with fall flowers blazing in glorious yellows and reds.

Everything was in readiness. And it was only fitting that the first guests were to be the workers of St. Vivant and their families. They had been invited to come that evening and celebrate the harvest, and the future.

Thérèse looked at herself again in the mirror. Her dress was perfect. She wanted to look elegant, but not grand. It was very important to her that the villagers she had known all of her life continue to accept her as one of them. And so, while she would love to have had a fancy dress like the ones she had seen in Paulette's style books, like the one her Aunt Marguerite had wanted to send to her, she was beginning to understand that duty to others often dictated that one make decisions based on the needs of one's guests. Tonight she wanted her guests to feel at home.

However, for the small, intimate luncheon that Catherine had planned for the afternoon, Thérèse would allow herself one item of luxury; she would wear one piece of extravagant finery. She reached over to the top of her dresser and took a small velvet pouch. Gently she untied the satin string, opened it, and from the softness of its interior took a magnificent ruby and diamond necklace.

The fire of the jewels never ceased to delight her. She could not believe that it was really hers. She sat on the edge of her bed and looked down at the gems sparkling in her hands. To have even touched something so magnificent would have been a wonderful experience. To know that it was hers, and that it had belonged to her mother as well, was almost too much for Thérèse to comprehend. It had been the answer to a prayer.

Thérèse thought back to that day. It had been a week after Henri had gone. Her health was back to normal, all effects of the sickness were gone. And yet everything was wrong. A tension was building inside of Thérèse that she didn't understand.

She was the same person, but she wasn't. The trauma from the night Perrin had been killed would not leave. The new identity seemed to haunt her. Alix was kind and understanding, and yet every time Thérèse spoke to her, something was wrong. She hesitated at the word "Mama" as if not sure what to call her.

Alix knew that something was amiss, but was not sure of just how to approach Thérèse. She could not lose the guilt that she had been feeling ever since Thérèse's illness. And so, in trying hard to make up for her perceived negligence, she was working too hard to be everything, and as a result the gulf between them was growing wider.

And so, that Sunday afternoon, after they had all gathered in the little chapel at the château for prayers, Thérèse had gone to the old cemetery at the edge of the woods, just on the outer perimeter of the estate lands. She had been there many times before, to decorate Nicholas's grave, and this time she thought that maybe by talking to Nicholas, all alone, she could begin to understand what was wrong with her.

The afternoon was hot, the summer sun burning high above. The animals had all retreated to the coolness of the forest depths to find some relief. Only the soft buzzing of insects in the tall grass could be heard. And high above, hidden by leaves, two great owls, who appeared to be asleep, rested and watched Thérèse as she wandered among the graves.

She went first to the spot where Nicholas lay, but somehow that did not provide the solace that she needed. So she began to wander among the other graves, looking at names, wondering about their lives. She carefully avoided one far corner where the fresh dirt of a newly dug grave, marked only by a cross, was easily visible.

But as she carefully stepped between the headstones, she began to notice how many of the graves were marked only by some sort of cross, with no name or identity to be found. And she began to wonder if somewhere in this hallowed ground the bodies of her own mother and father had been laid to rest. It was not something that she had ever thought to ask Gaspard. She knew the story of that terrible night, but this was the first time that she wondered where he had buried them. Maybe if she could find their graves, she could go there and gain the comfort that she needed.

The need to know became a compulsion for Thérèse. And so she went quickly through the woods to her cottage. Gaspard, who had also attended prayers at the château, had planned to walk there with Alix to borrow a certain tool from the barn. If she hurried, Thérèse hoped that she would still find him there.

Rushing into the cottage, Thérèse surprised Alix and Gaspard as they sat enjoying a cool drink. Alix, fearing trouble, quickly asked, "Is there something wrong?"

Not knowing what to say, Thérèse blurted out, "What did you do with my parent's bodies?"

Alix and Gaspard stared at her, stunned.

"What do you mean, Thérèse?" asked Alix.

Realizing that her question had sounded more like an accusation, Thérèse explained to them about the unmarked graves. "I just wanted to know which ones belonged to my parents."

"They are not buried there," answered Gaspard.

A surprised look came to Alix's face, and she turned to him. "Then where were they buried?"

"There is a vault beneath the chapel," Gaspard explained. "All of the direct heirs were buried there. I hid the bodies until I could build some coffins, then, in the middle of the night, I took them down and placed them side by side on the large stone slab in the middle of the vault."

"But how did you know where it was?" questioned Alix.

"It was never really a secret. It was just something that no one talked about. Comte Phillipe had asked me to help his father's valet carry the coffin of the old comte down there after he died. They would leave the coffin in the chapel for three days, then late in the night after the third day, quietly take the coffin down and leave it on the stone slab until the next person died. Then that coffin was moved to one of the spaces carved into the wall when a new coffin was brought down. The old Comte was so hated, that they wanted to move the coffin quickly. They told people he was sent to Paris to be buried there. We started to refer to it laughingly as Paris. After that awful night, when I thought it was safe, I took their coffins down to the crypt to place them where they belonged."

Thérèse, who had been standing there quietly listening to the exchange, asked, "How do you get down there?"

"There are steps underneath the altar."

"Will you take me there now?"

Gaspard looked at Alix, but she only nodded her head and shrugged her shoulders, unsure of what to do. "Are you sure that you want to go right now?" he asked.

"I don't really know," she answered, "But I need something, and so I think that I must."

They left immediately and returned to the château. Bernard was working in the library when they found him and explained their mission. He sent a servant up to Catherine's room, where she was resting, and then went with them to the little chapel.

Gaspard went to the statue of the virgin and pressed down on a small dog that lay at her feet. "That pushes down the catches on each side of the altar so that it can be moved," he explained. Then, with Bernard's help, he pushed the altar back, revealing a flight of stairs that descended into darkness.

Catherine arrived just as Bernard was lighting a torch, and Alix quietly explained why they were there. Gaspard led the small group down the stairs, and soon they were all standing around the massive stone slab.

In the coolness of the large underground chamber, Thérèse stood and looked at the two coffins lying side by side. Hesitantly, she reached out to touch one, hoping to gain some comfort by her touch. But it was only wood, and she realized that she had learned nothing new by coming here. A sadness welled up inside of her, a longing for some contact with her past. Yes, she had the paintings and the deeds, even the old prayer book. But none of those things spoke only to her.

She sighed, stepped back and looked around the room. It was then that she realized there was in fact a third coffin lying on the slab at the foot of the two coffins. It was very small, and made of rough hewn lumber. And with fearful insight, Thérèse suddenly realized that it must have been made for her.

The others had been standing there silently, not wanting to disturb her. Catherine had crossed herself, and stood with her eyes closed, silently praying. Alix had also been watching, not sure of what to do. But when Gaspard saw her look at the third coffin, he hastily explained, "The comte asked me to build that after he told me the baby was dead. He wanted it done quickly, so I went to the barn and used whatever wood I could find. Then I brought it to him just before morning broke. I wondered why he was in such a hurry, but decided that he was probably worried about the mob that was supposed to be on the way and wanted the poor little thing laid to rest before they got here."

"And you never guessed that it was empty," commented Bernard.

A quizzical look came to Gaspard's face. "But it wasn't empty. I knew what it felt like empty – I had made it. There was definitely something in there."

No one spoke. Alix watched Thérèse carefully. She could see that something was bothering her, and yet she felt the same inability to satisfy her needs that she had been feeling all week. There was a chasm between them, and she did not know how to bridge it. Feeling as though she needed to fill the silence, she said softly, "I'm sure they just wrapped something heavy to fill it, Thérèse. You know that no one is in there."

"But what did they put in there?" Thérèse asked. A desperate fire seemed to be burning inside of her now. "Maybe there's something that we are supposed to find. What if they hoped that someday we would come here and open it?"

She was speaking with heated intensity, as if she were driven. Alix did not know what to say, and the others just stared. Finally Bernard spoke uncomfortably, "I suppose that we could open it if you think that is what you really want."

"Mon Dieu," exclaimed Catherine. "That would be a sacrilege, Bernard."

"But it wouldn't really be, if the coffin were empty," suggested Gaspard, in a faltering manner.

It was obvious that everyone was extremely uncomfortable with the turn of events. Everyone, that is, but Thérèse.

"I think that it is supposed to be opened," she said firmly. And even she was surprised at her resolve. Some strange emotion was driving her, insisting that the coffin had to be opened. They all stood in silence, unsure of what to do, until finally Bernard stepped forward and moved the little coffin to the edge of the stone slab. He looked to Alix for approval, then began to pry the top loose. The small nails in the dry wood gave easily, and the top fell back.

Thérèse stepped forward to look inside, and cried out. "I knew it, there is something inside."

Becoming quite concerned about Thérèse's mental state, Alix moved to her side and said cautiously, "Remember, darling, it may be nothing but a bundle placed there for weight. Don't get your hopes up."

Thérèse turned to her with a glowing face. "I just know that something is there." Then turning back to the little coffin, she reached in and took out the bundle. It was wrapped and tied in a cashmere shawl. As she slowly unwound it, she found first one candlestick, then another that matched it. Continuing, she soon found several little pouches, and then a piece of paper. Her hands were beginning to shake as she unfolded it. Then she looked up at Alix with tears streaming down her smiling face. At the top of the page were written the words, "My precious Thérèse."

20

THÉRÈSE REACHED FOR THE PRAYER BOOK on the little round table next to her bed. She opened it and took out the letter, to read it again. Not that she needed the paper to know what it said. She had memorized the words in the dozens of times that she had read it since the day the letter was found. But right now she felt a desire to see the words again. On today of all days, she needed to be as close to Gabrielle as possible. The neat and flowing words beneath the crest at the top of the page streamed into her heart.

My precious Thérèse,

I can only hope that you will never see this. But if you do, then at least it will mean that you have survived these terrible times. My darling daughter, I wish you could know the joy that I have felt these last nine months as I planned for your life. You have made Phillipe's and my love complete, and I hope that some-day you will experience the joy and passion that only real love can bring. I am placing my most treasured items with this letter, my present to you from the past. The ruby and diamond necklace was given to me on my wedding day, as it was given to Phillipe's mother before me. The pearls were his gift on our first wedding anniversary. Phillipe gave me the diamond earrings when he found out that you were coming into our life, and the matching brooch tonight when you were born. Lastly, I am putting in my wedding ring. When you hold it, you will know that it has touched the hands of your parents this night, as we both bid you adieu. Remember always that our spirits are with you and we love you.

It was signed, '*your mother, Gabrielle, comtesse de St. Vivant.*'

Thérèse took her finger and traced the name. It was strange how just that small communication from her mother had been the balm that was needed to heal her spirit. The same night that the letter had been found, she and Alix had sat here on her bed and talked and cried until early morning, each finally releasing the burden of painful emotions that had been building between them.

Thérèse refolded the letter and placed it back inside the prayer book for safekeeping. Then she absentmindedly felt at her neck for the thin gold chain that she would never again take off. The chain had belonged to Alix for many years, and it now held Gabrielle's wedding ring close to Thérèse's heart. It had seemed a perfect union of the two women, a way to remind her always that she had been luckier that most. She had been given two mothers who loved her.

Realizing that time was quickly passing and she was not ready, Thérèse walked back to stand before the mirror. She held the sparkling necklace in her hands and placed it around her neck. It was the final touch. Her grandmother had worn it on her wedding day, as had her mother, and now Thérèse would wear it as she became Henri's wife a short time from now.

A huge smile came to her face as she thought about Henri. Dear, precious, darling Henri. He had been back for four weeks and all of her dreams had been fulfilled. Goosebumps covered her arms as she thought about finally lying in his arms tonight and again experiencing the ecstasy of his love.

She had not been sure that she would ever again know that love. In the weeks that followed his departure there had been absolutely nothing from Henri, no word at all telling them where he had gone. Catherine had been in a terrible state, constantly worried that something had happened to him. Alix had been particularly concerned about his wound, praying that it had not reopened and left him somewhere suffering from loss of blood or infection. They all prayed that he had not caught the sickness and died alone.

Finally, on the last day of September, he had returned. Alix had awakened early to the sounds of the birds singing. Unable to go back to sleep, she had gone down to the cottage kitchen to set a pot of coffee to boil. When it was ready she had taken a cup outside to sit in the early morning sunlight. However, her seat on the bench near the door was taken by a sleeping Henri. She stood there looking at him for a moment, then she went back inside to get another cup. When she returned she gently shook his shoulder.

Henri opened his eyes, and looked up at her with a smile. "I hoped that I would find you here."

"Why wouldn't I be here, Henri? This is my home."

"I thought maybe... I mean it would have only been natural for you to move to the château with Thérèse."

Looking down at him, his clothes rumpled, his hair tousled, and his eyes swollen from sleep, Alix smiled and shook her head. "I will never live anywhere else but here. All of my happiest memories are in this cottage, and as one gets older memories seem to mean more and more." She went back inside to get a chair, then came back and sat beside him.

Henri quietly sipped the warm rich coffee, then laid his head back against the house and closed his eyes. Unlike the old Henri, he said absolutely nothing; he seemed perfectly content to just sit there and rest.

Finally Alix could no longer hold her questions, and inquired, "Where have you been, Henri? We've all been worried about you, especially Catherine and Thérèse."

"I just wandered the first week or so. I didn't want to ride too hard and make my shoulder worse. I had a little money and could buy some food from farms as I went along, although it wasn't very easy. Everyone was so afraid they would catch the sickness that they wouldn't let me get very near. Finally, I decided to go to the house in Paris. Even if all of the staff were gone, I was sure that I would have a place to sleep and some food. As it turned out, one old couple had stayed there and they were glad when I arrived. There had been some problems with wandering bands breaking into the empty houses and they thought that I would protect them."

"And so you've been there alone with them all this time?"

Alix asked.

"Not alone. About a week later Uncle Georges returned, without his family. He was surprised to find me there. He was even more surprised when I started roaring that it was all his fault that I was there without a family and definitely without an estate. He was so taken aback that he let me go on for quite a while, not usually his style. Finally, he began to understand some of what I was telling him; what he did next completely stunned me. He apologized! He apologized to me for all of the deceit. He said he never would have dreamed that there was a real heir somewhere, and had just thought this an easy way to get a good piece of land to add to the company. He had made up the whole story about knowing the comtesse's brother."

Henri paused for a moment to watch some squirrels chasing each other up a tree. Then he continued. "Uncle Georges said that he never would have forced me to marry that marquise knowing that I was in love with someone else. That had been Aunt Louise's idea to begin with. She thought it was a great way to add another royal connection to the family. And so Uncle Georges went along with it to humor her."

Henri looked at Alix. "You know, I had never really talked to Uncle Georges very much. I was always a little afraid of him, and I had Bernard for a friend. But because we were the only ones in the house in Paris, and it still wasn't safe to go out to conduct business, we spent a long time talking and listening to one another. He is a very good man. He wanted to know about everything that happened here and about how I felt about it. He really cared about my having a place to call my home. He even knew how badly Gerrard had treated me when we were children and hoped that my having a title would take some of the wind out of his sails."

He stopped speaking again. Alix sat quietly, waiting for him to find his next words. "Uncle Georges also told me a lot about when he and Aunt Catherine were young. It wasn't quite as easy as she lets on. Sometimes people were very cruel to her. But the young soldier that she planned to marry really loved her. He was a dear friend of Uncle Georges, and uncle said that, even today, he could not think of anyone as fine as he was. He told me that I would have been proud to have known him as my father." Henri looked down at his hands, not wanting to look into Alix's face. "He also reminded me that I was condemning my mother for the same kind of passion that I felt for Thérèse."

The sun was rising higher in the sky. A light breeze was beginning to dry the dew. Alix and Henri sat still in the early morning quiet. "Did you come to any decisions after these talks with your uncle?"

"No," Henri answered. "I made him promise not to let anyone know where I was, but he knew that I would have to come back here. Oh, he did not make me return today. But he said that I would never be able to find real happiness until I faced this problem. After a while I realized that he was right. I can't let my life wait for years while I wonder what to do. I had to come back, look at it all again, and try to figure out where I belong."

A long silence came between them. Some birds fluttered among the leaves of the tall trees, then the sound of cooing doves was heard. Alix watched the trees, trying to find where the sound came from as she thought. Then she spoke. "Henri, you once told me that Catherine was a woman of great faith. Well I have my faith, too. And I believe, as surely as the sun will rise tomorrow, that you were meant to come here. All of this was meant to happen so that we could finally give up our secrets and begin to live in the light again. Gaspard has not been so alive in years. Catherine and Bernard are finally planning to marry. They are going to stay and put the winery back into production, giving the villagers back their dreams for the future."

"Without you this would not have happened. For years I had known that I was not capable of doing much for Thérèse. Why else do you think that I had continued to keep the story a secret? What could we, without any knowledge of running an estate, much less a business, do about it?"

Alix's voice grew intense as she talked, trying to find the right words to convince him. "Don't you see? You were needed to bring it all together. Catherine's money, Bernard and Gaspard's experience, and Thérèse's land. But now you think, since you don't have a title or the land, that you have nothing to give." Her next words were filled with emotion. "I left the luxury of my father's house to marry a poor farmer, and I did not regret it one single day, because it was his love that gave me life. Before I met Nicholas, I did things that were expected. I went from day to day, but that is not living,

Henri. It's existing. I only learned how joyful life could be after I married Nicholas."

He started to interrupt but she held up her hand, "Let me finish. I know for your mother the same is true. Only she was lucky enough to find that kind of love twice. When Gaspard lost that joy, he lost his desire to participate in life. And for Thérèse, it is the same. When you came here and brought your fresh, excited view of life, she suddenly discovered how wonderful the world can be. Certainly, she can move into the château, and go around doing the expected things every day, but that is not living."

"All of the parts were needed, and you brought them together, Henri. But the puzzle is not complete without you. You cannot deny your love for Thérèse. I've seen it in your eyes when you look at her, I've heard it in your voice when you speak to her, I've seen it in the way you are when you are together. The puzzle will be made perfect, the full picture revealed only when you admit that you need each other to make your life complete. Don't let misplaced pride keep you from a lifetime of happiness, Henri. Don't worry about how it looks to the world. Old age can be very lonely without someone you love."

Henri stared out into the forest. He knew that Alix was right. Maybe he had been thinking too much about how he felt, about what others might say about Thérèse marrying a nobody, and not enough about how they felt as a couple. He had worked very hard these last few weeks not to let himself think about the two of them together, because it left a huge aching hole in his heart.

Knowing that he needed time to think, Alix rose to go inside. "Let me get you some more coffee, Henri. And see what there is for breakfast."

She left him sitting in the gentle morning sun. Henri put his head back and closed his eyes again, listening and remembering. He heard the creak of the half door and opened his eyes. But instead of finding Alix, Thérèse was standing there holding a fresh cup of coffee. "Mama asked me to bring this out to you and then go collect some eggs," she said simply.

He studied her for a moment, not moving. Her soft red hair hung in curls around her shoulders, held away from her face by a white ribbon. She was dressed in a white cotton nightgown, with a shawl thrown over her shoulders, just as she had been that last night when he had left.

"I didn't expect you to be here. I thought that you might have moved into the château, since it is really your home."

"I could never live there without you, Henri. You had all of the dreams and the ideas, not me. It would only be right with you. But I told you all of that once. I won't beg you again."

"I think that this time it is my turn to beg," he said with a half smile. "May I walk with you while you collect the eggs?"

Alix watched from the window as they headed toward the barn, walking side by side, not touching, but their heads moving and nodding as they talked. "I think that it will be all right, Nicholas," she said softly as she touched the ring on her finger.

In the trees high above, two owls – one large and white, one small and grey – nodded sleepily in the morning light.

Thérèse looked into the mirror and smiled. Since that September morning, things had each day become more perfect. She did not know what had been said between Henri and his mother. Maybe some day he would want to share that with her. But whatever they said, it had been the necessary words to put their relationship back together. And for now it was enough to know that she would be his bride.

Footsteps were heard outside the door, and Thérèse turned to smile at Alix as she stood in the doorway.

"My dear, you are beautiful," she declared. "How I wish Nicholas could be here on this day. But I'm sure he sees you, and I know that your mother and father are near, and are as proud of you as I am. Here," she said as she walked into the room, "I collected these flowers for you. The colors are perfect for your dress."

Thérèse took the bouquet of deep red chrysanthemums tied with green and gold ribbons. She could not help but smile as she watched Alix tie a simple wreath of the same flowers in her hair, leaving gold and green ribbons hanging at her neck. Finally, not able to hold her excitement in any longer, she cried, "Mama, I look so beautiful!" And the two turned to embrace one last time before they went down the stairs.

Waiting in front of the Condé cottage was an elegant carriage. When Uncle Roland and Aunt Marguerite had heard of the wedding, they immediately made plans to attend. For this special day, Bernard had offered to send a carriage from the château, but Uncle Roland had insisted that a man of Thérèse's family should have the honor of escorting her on her wedding day. Now, broadly smiling, Uncle Roland held out his hand to help Alix and Thérèse get into the carriage, where an excited Marguerite was waiting. He gave the driver a signal, then joined the others, and soon they were all quickly moving down the little lane under the brilliant autumn sun.

Later, as Thérèse stood in the soft pink light of the chapel, a wave of contentment swept over her. At the altar knelt Catherine and Bernard, receiving the final blessings of a priest. It had not taken Catherine long to pester the archbishop in Paris into assigning someone to the parish of St. Vivant. He was young, and not entirely sure of himself, but Thérèse felt that Father Joseph had the compassion needed to bring the lost flock of the village back to the fold.

As the priest made the sign of the cross, Thérèse turned and grinned at Henri. He was undoubtedly the most handsome man in all of Burgundy. And now it was their turn. He reached out for her hand, and they walked toward the front of the little chapel together. Just the way that they would face the rest of their lives.

21

THE NIGHT WAS BRIGHT WITH THE LIGHT OF A THOUSAND CANDLES shining from the windows of the château. The strains of music played by a quintet could be heard from the ballroom, and laughing, happy voices filled the air. As Henri and Thérèse walked arm in arm out to the terrace, they greeted their guests – the people of the village who were also learning to be their friends. Thérèse put her head on Henri's shoulder as they stopped to watch the moon shimmering across the river below. She sighed with contentment, and said softly, "This night is perfect. There is nothing else in the world that I need."

"Nothing?" asked Henri teasingly. "Are you telling me that I will never have to do another thing and that you will always be this happy?"

"You know that is not what I meant." She stepped away from him and looked at his face as she spoke. "It's just that I cannot imagine anything else that could add to my joy tonight. I am really your wife, do you realize that? We are married for ever and ever. What more could I want?"

She thought back over this extraordinary day. First there had been their beautiful wedding, with a priest to bless them. Then there had been a delightful luncheon with several courses of delectable cuisine prepared by Marie Judith. The mayor and his wife had joined them, and he signed the civil forms with a flourish, making both marriages legal. There had been many rounds of toasts with wonderful sweet champagne sent by the Widow Clicquot, a friend of Uncle Georges. Thérèse had especially loved the eloquent words said by Uncle Roland, as Aunt Marguerite wiped tears from her eyes.

She looked into Henri's eyes, and said again, but this time more softly, "What more could I want?"

"Well then, I will just have to save the surprise that I had planned for another time when you are not so happy."

"What surprise? Is there something else for me?" His hands were behind his back, and she reached out greedily to pull his arms forward so she could look in his hands. "Where are you hiding it?"

Henri laughed and fought off her hands. "It's not in my hands so you might as well stop that. People are looking and wondering what you are doing. They'll think that the young bride is too eager."

A blush covered Thérèse's face, and she looked around at the others standing on the terrace to see if they were indeed watching her. "No one is watching, Henri. So now, tell me what the surprise is."

"But I want everyone to know it." And he called out to one of the workers standing near the door, asking him to find Bernard and tell him it was time. Soon the terrace filled with people streaming out of the château, and lastly came Bernard with Catherine on his arm, followed by Gaspard, looking unusually handsome in a new coat, and finally Alix. They gathered together in the center of the terrace, Thérèse reaching out to take her Mama's hand as she drew near.

Then Henri took a torch from one of the poles that had been erected around the lawn to light the evening, and began to wave it back and forth. Soon another light could be seen at the top of the nearby hill. Henri put the torch back, and quickly walked back to Thérèse's side.

"Now you will see," he said, and he pointed to the fountain in the center of the terrace. It had been carefully cleaned and repaired, and filled with flowers floating in the water. But to Thérèse's joy and amazement, suddenly streams of water began flowing from the frogs' mouths, and like little diamonds shining in the moonlight, the water glistened as it arced into the air and flowed down on the column in the center where lizards and snails crawled among the grapevines.

The crowd cheered and Thérèse whirled around joyfully to face

Henri. "How ever did you get it to work?"

"It was not easy, especially with Bernard complaining about the workers taking off the time. But Gaspard helped to find all of the lines, and we repaired the cistern on the hill. And there it is. Just for you, my darling."

Thérèse turned around to look at the little fountain again, clasping her hands in front of her like a child. "It is more beautiful than I thought it would be, Henri. It is magnificent!"

Henri drew close behind her, putting his arms around her. Thérèse pulled them tight around her waist as they watched the little fountain. "Now everything really is perfect," she murmured and laid her head back on his chest.

Henri put his mouth on the side of her neck and softly kissed her. "It's not quite perfect yet," he whispered. "But I promise you that it will be before morning."

In the sky above the château, two owls soared high into the air, and as they flew across the moon, their wingtips reached out to gently touch.